MURDER BY NUMBERS

MURDER BY NUMBERS

KAYE MORGAN

WHEELER
CHIVERS

This Large Print edition is published by Wheeler Publishing, Waterville, Maine, USA and by BBC Audiobooks Ltd, Bath, England.

Wheeler Publishing, a part of Gale, Cengage Learning.

Copyright © 2008 by The Berkley Publishing Group.

The moral right of the author has been asserted.

Sudoku puzzles on pg 346 copyright © 2008 by Mark Danburg-Wyld, http://sudokuplace.com.

A Suduko Mystery.

The text of this Large Print edition is unabridged.

Other aspects of the book may vary from the original edition.

Set in 16 pt. Plantin.

Printed on permanent paper.

LIBRARY OF CONGRESS CATALOGING-IN-PUBLICATION DATA

Morgan, Kaye.
    Murder by numbers / by Kaye Morgan.
        p. cm. — (A suduko mystery) (Wheeler Publishing large print cozy mystery)
    ISBN-13: 978-1-59722-759-9 (pbk. : alk. paper)
    ISBN-10: 1-59722-759-5 (pbk. : alk. paper)
    1. Women public relations personnel — Fiction. 2. Motion picture producers and directors — Crimes against — Fiction. 3. Motion pictures — Production and direction — Fiction. 4. Oregon — Fiction. 5. Large type books. I. Title.
PS3613.O7454M87 2008
813'.6—dc22
                                        2008006088

BRITISH LIBRARY CATALOGUING-IN-PUBLICATION DATA AVAILABLE

Published in 2008 in the U.S. by arrangement with The Berkley Publishing Group, a member of Penguin Group (USA) Inc.
Published in 2008 in the U.K. by arrangement with The Berkley Publishing Group, division of Penguin Group (USA) Inc.

U.K. Hardcover: 978 1 408 41177 3 (Chivers Large Print)
U.K. Softcover: 978 1 408 41178 0 (Camden Large Print)

Printed in the United States of America
1 2 3 4 5 6 7 12 11 10 09 08

To my editor at Berkley, Michelle Vega, who took this book on in midstream, and with her energy, understanding, and talent helped the writing of it immensely.

■ ■ ■ ■

PART ONE:
IT'S A MYSTERY
TO ME

■ ■ ■ ■

I'm always amazed to see the number of folks in the sudoku nation who seek out puzzles rated "Insanely difficult — guaranteed to vaporize your brain." Yet this segment of the population is also responsible for the cutting edge of sudoku research. These are the people who try to find the sudoku with the fewest clues (17 clues, according to the most recent findings), the most (77 out of 81 to generate a single discrete solution), and who figure the number of valid sudoku (5,472,730,538 according to one mathematical estimate — a sum just a little shy of the number of humans on the planet).

While sudoku requires no arithmetic, it does involve some high-order math concepts. Still, when I hear terms like "nondeterministic-polynomial problems" and "constraint programming," I wonder about the fun factor. (Although that second one sounds kind of kinky, doesn't it?)

It's like reading a mystery novel. Sure, people look for psychological insights or an interesting prose style, but what keeps the pages turning is the puzzle aspect — "Whodunit?"

With sudoku, it's more a case of "How'd they do that?" And, of course, nobody has to die . . .

— Excerpt from *Sudo-cues* by Liza K

1

Liza Kelly got out of her car, glad she'd managed to snag a parking space on Main Street. Not that downtown Maiden's Bay was usually a parking nightmare. But just lately it had risen to the level of a constant challenge.

The town was enjoying an onshore breeze, but Liza couldn't catch any smells of the sea. Whether she was suffering from some sort of allergy or the hotsy-coldsy weather that had afflicted the Oregon coast this autumn, Liza had a touch of something that rasped her throat and made her feel a bit like she'd stuck her head in an aquarium. Sounds echoed strangely, the world felt as if she were separated from it by a sheet of glass, and her sense of smell was long gone.

Worse, it seemed, was to come.

Liza sneezed, rattling display windows all through the town's shopping district. Things had changed since she'd come here as a kid jingling her pocket money. The army-navy store where 90 percent of the male towns-folk bought their clothes was still in place, as was Naomi's Dress Shop, where Liza's mom occasionally used to get an outfit. But Mort's Menswear was long gone — who bought suits anymore?

The old hotel building had lost its top floor to a fire. Though repairs had been made, the resulting two-story structure had a curiously moth-eaten appearance. Nowadays it housed the Marine Bar. The fortress-like home of the local savings and loan had been knocked down years ago and was now replaced with retail space and a glass-and-steel storefront bank branch that looked about as secure as Ma's Café across the street. The bookstore where Liza had spent a lot of time and much of her allowance had transformed itself into a New Age crystal-and-candle emporium for the Californians who'd transplanted themselves into expensive developments on the outskirts of town.

Liza crossed Main Street, heading for the anchor — no, *the* bedrock — of downtown Maiden's Bay. Schilling's Pharmacy was now going into its fourth generation. In his youth, Liza's dad had swept out the store with Matt Schilling, the grandson of the founding pharmacist. Liza remembered old

Mr. Schilling, the third-generation pharmacist and an imposing presence behind the counter, very well. He'd medicated her colds and bumps and bruises, occasionally deigning to give her a lollipop when she behaved.

Her reminiscent sigh turned into a disgusting snuffling noise. He would have come in handy now, in fact.

When she'd come home on breaks during college, she'd visited the pharmacy to see not only old Mr. Schilling but also a tall, gangly kid pushing a broom — the fourth-generation Schilling, young Gary.

Schilling's still retained that old-time pharmacy look. The display window dated back to the 1920s, when old Gustav Schilling had opened the place. Mysterious glass flasks — red, green, and blue — dominated the space, contrasting brightly with the displays of modern nostrums and announcements of weekly sales.

The interior of the store was a mixture of old and new. Vintage glass-fronted counters stood round the perimeter while tightly packed shelving units filled what had originally been more open space. The intriguingly naked but sexless plaster dummy that had stood by the door demonstrating an old-fashioned truss had disappeared, now

11

replaced with a display of crutches, canes, and walkers.

Guess anybody in the market for one of those wouldn't be likely to grab one and make a run for it. The irreverent thought hit Liza as she entered. *Good place to put it — shoplifting prevention at its finest. Come to think of it, truss customers would have the same problem, too. Maybe some things don't change.*

She threaded her way to the rear counter where Nora Schilling presided over the cash register. It had been a bit of a shock when Liza returned home a few months ago to find that old Mr. Schilling had passed away. But she'd been dealing with a lot of shocks right then. Her husband had separated from her, and Liza had been trying to assess whether she wanted to return to the Hollywood rat race where she'd enjoyed considerable success as a publicist, or whether her old hometown was a better fit for her these days. A lot more had happened — she'd encountered her old high school boyfriend, who was now running a nearby upscale inn. And she'd experimented with a new career, doing a newspaper column devoted to sudoku puzzles and about how to solve them.

In the end, she'd been looking for peace,

and she'd decided in favor of Maiden's Bay.

I just hope that puzzle-solving streak keeps working, Liza thought. The peace she'd sought here wasn't materializing. Lately, her life was more like a juggling act, balancing her soon-to-be-ex-husband, Michael, and her old boyfriend, Kevin the innkeeper, her publicity job, *and* the sudoku column. She was happy, but running on empty to keep up with the demands on her time. In the next few hours she had a conference call where her publicist side had to take center stage, without any . . .

Another thunderous sneeze interrupted her thoughts.

Time to figure out where this place kept the cold meds.

Nora Schilling looked up, her professional smile turning more genuine as she recognized Liza. Mrs. Schilling was a handsome woman who must have been beautiful once, though that had been before Liza's day. All she could remember was a woman who looked like an imposing old-maid schoolteacher, in spite of standing behind the counter with her husband.

At first glance, the years had been kind to Nora. She looked much as Liza remembered her from her college years, in spite of the decade she'd spent caring for an ailing husband, keeping the business going despite the vagaries of small-town life, retail fluctuations, and competing chain stores. After Matt died, she struggled on with hired hands doing the prescription work until her son Gary had graduated from pharmacy school.

On second glance, Liza found herself thinking of beach glass, how millions of sand grains inflicting tiny scratches wore away sharp edges and turned transparent glass milky. Nora's light brown hair hadn't gone silver, but rather gray. Her skin hadn't aged so much as grown paler and strangely translucent. Her blue eyes seemed somehow faded as she listened to Liza's symptoms and then deferred to the young figure she beckoned forward.

Gary Schilling had gotten past the string-bean stage, filling out till he was in danger of having his mother's cooking create a potbelly. His face was still a little too round and youthful, something he clearly tried to counteract with a scraggly mustache. Or maybe that mustache was to make up for the way his hairline was already retreating at the temples.

He might be heading toward geekhood, but he knew his stuff. Gary listened attentively to her symptoms and then recommended an over-the-counter nasal spray and some lozenges.

"No pills?" Liza asked, a little surprised.

"You don't want to overmedicate. The spray will get at the basic problem more directly," Gary assured her, "and the aromatic lozenges will soothe your throat and help with any postnasal drip. You'll feel better, your symptoms will recede, and you won't be struggling with drowsiness like you would with an antihistamine."

Nora could undoubtedly have made the same recommendations, but was content to watch as her son went into lecture mode. "Under Oregon law, the most effective antihistamine is no longer available over the counter, but is a Class II restricted substance. You'd need a doctor's prescription to buy it." He shrugged. "It can really wind up your blood pressure. Besides, I guess the folks in Portland felt they had to do something. People cook up the pills to make crystal meth, you know."

"Even in Maiden's Bay?" Liza said.

"Not that I know of," Gary admitted. "But meth labs have turned up in stranger places."

Liza thanked the young pharmacist and his mother, paid for her purchases, and headed outside. *My head feels like it's under-*

water, she thought. *I wonder if it's too gross to take a quick snort of this nasal spray right now . . .* She stopped between two parked cars to look inside the small paper bag. As she did, a heavy truck rumbled right past her on Main Street.

I almost stepped right in front of that, Liza thought. *I'm not thinking right. This stuff had* better *clear my head.*

She watched as the truck joined several others parked near the town piers. So which was it this time — the boardwalk extension or the film shoot?

For the past year, the new mayor in town had done everything imaginable to get enough funding to extend the block-long boardwalk on the waterfront. The idea had been to make Maiden's Bay a little more tourist-friendly. Even now, the project had only gotten to the pile-driving point. Construction work had been spotty, since the piers were an integral part of the filming going on in town.

Liza supported the movie project her friend Derrick Robbins had been putting together for his niece Jenny before he was murdered. And after the dramatic rescue that took place right in this area, it had seemed a brilliant idea to do location shooting for the film in Maiden's Bay. At least, that's the way Liza had seen it at first.

It had certainly made her life easier. She could live up to her commitment to act as publicist for Jenny while still doing her puzzle gig for the *Oregon Daily.*

The townsfolk thought the idea was pretty cool, too, especially the money being offered for using their homes and businesses as locations for the shoot — and themselves as extras.

Liza had never envisioned a career in front of the camera for herself. With her height and hourglass figure, the movie camera lens would make her look like a football halfback — a pretty curvy one, but a halfback nonetheless. Still, when she first came to Hollywood after her postcollege sabbatical in Japan, she'd scored a couple days of work as a film extra to earn some cash.

It had just put a big, red underline to Alfred Hitchcock's famous line about actors being cattle. Hitchcock had tried to defend himself by saying that he merely intended that actors be *treated* like cattle. In those days, he could get away with it, she supposed. Somehow, Liza couldn't imagine Glenn Close putting up with that now. The extras in films, however, definitely still got the livestock treatment. Liza had noted that the film crews even called the production assistants in charge of extras "wranglers."

A couple of days on set back then had been enough to put Liza off acting forever. But the extra gig was going like gangbusters in Maiden's Bay. For most of the good folks in town, every nice day for the past few weeks had involved time in front of the cameras.

"Excuse me, dear."

Liza stepped back as the sprightly figure of her next-door neighbor darted across the street to stand beside her.

"What's the occasion, Mrs. H.?" Liza asked. Instead of the old denims and the disreputable relic of a straw sombrero she wore while gardening, Mrs. Halvorsen wore a new creation from Naomi's with a fine broad-brimmed straw confection on her gray curls.

"I just thought I'd go by where the movie people are," Mrs. H. said airily.

Liza hid a smile. It didn't matter how old a person might be, or where they were — the dream of being Discovered with a capital *D* lived on.

"I've worked quite a few days as an extra," Mrs. H. went on. "That's why I decided to splurge on a new outfit, even though the check hasn't come yet."

Mrs. H. was always very animated when

she spoke. But this time as she smiled and nodded, the oversized straw brim of her hat fluttered in time, as if it were a flimsy pair of wings laboring to lift the older woman's head up, up, and away.

Liza managed to restrain her giggles until after her neighbor had wished her a nice day and set off down Main Street for the knot of the usual suspects gathered in front of the trailers brought in by the production company. She could have spotted Deke Jannsky's disreputable orange hunting hat from a mile off — and she was a lot closer than that.

She shook her head. That had been a mistake on the part of the extra wranglers. Sure, at first glance he looked perfect, a photogenic example of a grizzled small-town salt-of-the-earth type. But Liza knew all too well that Deke was trouble. The only earth that hung out around him was just plain dirt of the lowest order. Deke hadn't held a real job in years. He'd been living off the taxpayers, the result of some sort of dubious disability claim. Oddly, it interfered horribly with anything Deke didn't want to do, but never troubled him a bit when he was doing something he enjoyed, and that included such strenuous activities as hunting, fishing, and brawling in bars. Taking

19

that man on was just asking for trouble.

A closer look revealed to Liza that trouble had already found the little knot of people.

A truckload of workmen was swinging into action. A tarp on the shed they'd been shooting yesterday went down, revealing large letters spray-painted in glittery pink — PISS OFF.

Well, there's a headache for the continuity people, Liza thought. *Bet that wasn't there the last time they wrapped filming.*

She grinned at the thought that perhaps some of the locals seemed to be coming round to her opinion about location shooting and extra work.

Then she frowned. On the other hand, that bit of graffiti meant a very expensive clock was ticking as the production crew went to work trying to remove the shiny pink mess. Something this simple could throw off the whole shooting schedule. And if it messed with the shooting schedule, it also goofed up the town's major public work again. It wasn't even solely the boardwalk at risk. The new mayor, Ray Massini, hadn't just planned an extension to the wooden decking fronting the harbor. The mayor's plans, at least according to the *Oregon Daily,* called for upscale shops and a trendy snack bar to replace several disreputable sheds and marine businesses now facing the water. The first step to completing all that, however, was getting sturdy pilings to support the boardwalk driven into the silty beachfront. There was a reason that references to pile drivers cropped up in any comparison of humongous noise levels. That sort of banging couldn't go on while the movie cameras were running on the docks. So the graffiti was actually holding up two kinds of work.

Neither the director nor the mayor is going to be happy today. On the other hand, a suspicious little voice in the back of her head cheerfully pointed out, *it leads to another day of extra work for some lowlife like Deke Jannsky.*

Hmmm . . . Would he be stupid enough to risk everybody's paychecks in the hopes of fattening his own? She looked down again at her little bag of meds. If she was this easily distracted *before* she started taking the drugs, it didn't bode well for her day's work at the computer.

Liza's attention went back to the dock as she heard angry voices in the air. Had Deke somehow been identified as the rude sign painter?

No, he'd been busted for a lesser crime. Liza could hear him profanely denying that he'd taken food from the craft table — stuff meant for the film crew and lead actors, not the lowly extras. However, he was still holding the evidence — a huge chocolate-covered donut — in his hand. This was apparently the last straw for the aggravated film people. One of the wranglers told him to turn in his papers and leave the set.

Deke smugly played his ace in the hole, pointing to the distinctive hat he wore. He must have been annoying the filmmakers for a while, because one of the PAs produced a hand-aged replica of the cap and gave it to one of the other extras.

Deke's profanity and sound level rose considerably. "You think you can get away with pulling this kind of crap?" He demanded in one of his more printable tirades. "I'm gonna mess you up — I'm gonna mess this *whole freaking film* up — but good!"

"We don't need any amateurs doing that," Liza muttered to herself as she crossed to her car. The film shoot hadn't been the smoothest she'd ever seen in her years in the film-publicity business. "Not when we've got a bunch of highly paid professionals already on the job."

2

Liza decided to wait till she was in the relative privacy of her car before dosing herself with the cold nostrums. *At least the box on the nasal spray doesn't say anything about not operating heavy machinery,* she thought as she pulled out onto Main Street and hurried home. *Maybe I won't get as flattened by it as I usually do by cold meds.*

She braked at the end of the gravel driveway leading up to the old family homestead on Hackleberry Avenue, got out, and went to open the kitchen door. Rusty greeted her with a few loud barks and some vigorous tail wagging. Translated from his mixed-breed Irish setter dialect, this meant, "See how alert and careful I am, guarding the house?

Any treats for this good dog?"

Like the mutt had to ask.

Liza gave him a dog biscuit and popped another throat lozenge for herself. Rusty's gung-ho attitude made her glance guiltily at the computer set up in a corner of the living room. Her cushion — the backlog of unpublished columns over at the *Oregon Daily* — was getting pretty darn flat.

She frowned at the puzzle already up on the screen. It had come out even simpler than her usual standard for low-difficulty puzzles:

	8						1	
9			4		6			2
4			5					7
	1		2				8	
6			3					9
5			7		9			4
	2						3	

I could wrap another "Introductory Sudoku" column around it, Liza thought, unwilling to abandon her creation. The problem was finding more time to develop sudoku. She might have to cheat, maybe use a computer program to devise a few run-of-the-mill puzzles. *It's not cheating — exactly,* Liza told herself. *I'm working with the programmers on that Solv-a-doku project.*

Most sudoku creation and solution programs used the computer's mechanical strength — the uncomplaining ability to undertake repetitive tasks that would drive humans up a wall — and harnessed it for a brute-force approach to filling the eighty-one spaces of a sudoku puzzle. The rules were simple — fill each of the nine rows and columns with the numbers one through nine, no omissions or repetitions. The grid was also broken into nine boxes of nine spaces each, which also had to be filled with the magic digits between one and nine.

For a creator, this meant presenting a partially filled grid (usually with twenty-odd clues) that had one single solution. For solvers, it meant taking this sudoku and filling it in. No adding, subtracting, logarithms, or other math was required. The whole thing worked on strict logic.

In the computer world, this logic rested on an enormous number of yes/no questions, answered at tremendous speed. "Will these numbers fit together?" "Will this number work in here?" If not, another candidate would be shoved into place until the grid was created or completed.

Humans would find such an approach

time-wasting and crazy-making. But then, humans could see relationships within the puzzle that would require complicated programming for a computer. The guys at Solv-a-doku were attempting that programming, based on Liza's hierarchy of twelve proven sudoku-solving techniques. Well, eleven, to be honest. Number twelve involved taking a peek at the printed solution in the back of the book or magazine.

Some of the more esoteric techniques turned out to be programming problems, which didn't necessarily surprise Liza. But she did find it strange that the technique most humans picked up first in solving sudoku seemed to be a computer programming challenge.

She reached out a hand to the computer, only to jerk it back as the phone began ringing. Liza looked at the clock. Five minutes before Michelle Markson was supposed to call. That probably meant it *was* Michelle, who had risen to become the warrior queen of Hollywood publicists thanks to the vast arsenal of head games she deployed against actors, directors, studio execs, and, yes, her own partner. Maybe *especially* against her own partner — Michelle liked to remind Liza who was the boss.

Liza picked up the phone to hear Ysabel

Fuentes's voice on the other end. Ysabel was probably the highest-paid receptionist in Hollywood, someone who knew where all the lost files were at Markson Associates — and where most of the bodies were buried in the film business. About once a month, Ysabel and Michelle locked horns and Ysabel would quit. Part of Liza's job was to get the irreplaceable Latina back on the payroll every time she gave notice.

"Hi, Liza," Ysabel said. "I'll hook you up now."

A moment later, Michelle's brusque voice came on. "So you're having problems up in the boondocks."

Liza could just imagine Michelle's expression — the queen of the pixies dealing with an incursion by some blundering humans.

"You said it. Things have gone downhill quickly for *Counterfeit* since Terence Hamblyn's car accident." Liza paused. "Is he doing all right at Cedars of Lebanon?"

Terence had been Derrick Robbins's handpicked choice to direct the picture, and he'd nurtured Jenny's talent every bit as carefully as Derrick had hoped. But just when he was almost ready to wrap the filming, he'd gotten into a serious car accident on a fogbound roadway and had ended up being airlifted to L.A. It was hard to direct a feature film in a full body cast.

"He's all right." Michelle's voice was disparaging — she found Hamblyn too much of a nice guy. She preferred, not surprisingly, a go-for-the-jugular approach to filmmaking. "Jenny is having problems with the new director?"

"Frankly, I was surprised when they brought in Lloyd Olbrich," Liza admitted. "He is a name in the business. I thought the people at Mirage Productions would try to rush through the job with a bunch of schlockmeisters —"

She stopped talking when she heard an embarrassed cough, though it was a toss-up over who should be more embarrassed. Liza recognized that cough. She'd heard it from her estranged husband often enough.

"I guess they didn't tell you this was a conference call," Michael Langley said. He had a certain rep for being a schlockmeister himself, doctoring scripts for films destined to go direct to video. "I got in touch with Michelle after the people from Mirage Productions sounded me out on doing some script revisions."

"Revisions? Why? What's the matter with Mal Whelan's script?" Liza was really confused now. Malcolm Whelan had done a remarkable job of mixing comedy and suspenseful plot twists in *Counterfeit.* Jenny was playing a young woman whose father dies — or was he her father? The entire life she knew turns out to be a fiction created by a master con artist — who now has a pack of unsavory associates turning up expecting a cut from their latest job. Jenny's character needed a crash course in scamology just to survive.

"Well, right now, Malcolm is threatening to take the Alan Smithee option if the studio goes ahead with the changes they're talking about," Michael said.

Alan Smithee is the pseudonym members of the Writers Guild use to take their names off scripts when their work is completely trashed.

"Can they do this?" Liza demanded.

"Of course they can." Michelle's voice was flat. "Mirage Productions bought out Derrick's company lock, stock, and barrel. They need a successful film, because they haven't had one since Oliver Chissel took over."

Liza knew Chissel's name from the *Oregon Daily* — but not from the entertainment section. "I thought he was more of a businessman than a movie guy."

Michelle snorted. "He started out more like a con man, if the stories are true. Then he got into all sorts of shady trading. Lately he'd been buying companies and stripping the assets and pulling greenmail scams — scooping up pieces of companies on the cheap and extorting much higher prices from people to buy him out."

She snorted again, this time louder. "But he was the one who got taken in this last deal, winding up as president and CEO of Mirage Productions. Damned appropriate name, Mirage, when it comes to the company's assets. He didn't help himself by trying to go the blockbuster route."

Liza knew that story — paying forty million dollars to produce a film in the hopes of making two hundred million on the other end. The resultant film had flopped, bigtime. Mirage had tried that recipe again, making two sequels and a remake next — all to disappointing box office results. Derrick had been working on the other end of the scale, trying to assemble about ten million in funding for *Counterfeit* — but given the quality of the production, the script, Jenny's performance, and the built-in publicity, the film had a real chance of making ten times that.

"Given his background, I was surprised to see Ollie the Chiseler so hot to trot over *Counterfeit.* But he needs a quick, cheap success."

"If it's that important to him, why isn't he out here?"

"Don't invoke the name of the devil unless you want to have dinner with him — long spoon included," Michelle said. "The farther away Ollie stays, the better the film will be."

"Okay, then why is he screwing with the film via long distance? Doesn't he trust his director?" Liza wanted to know.

"He doesn't trust anybody. Furthermore, he's got the critical taste of a commodities trader. He probably thinks he's opening the flick up to a wider audience," Michael said.

"A nice way to say going for the lowest common denominator," Liza growled. "Or just plain dumbing a good movie down." She sighed. "Where exactly is this assortment of geniuses thinking of going?"

"The people from Mirage who talked to me thought Malcolm and Terence were keeping the film too light," Michael said. "They want it darker, more dangerous for the heroine."

"How? By adding a stalker in a hockey mask?"

"That's probably not too far off from their intentions." Michael took a deep breath. "There's a reason they came to me."

"You were involved in the news stories

about rescuing Jenny," Liza said. "Duh — publicist, remember?"

"More than that kind of publicity," Michael told her. "The new plot points in the script — they want to mirror some of the stuff that happened to Jenny after Derrick's murder."

Now it was Liza's turn to suck in a deep breath. "Jenny took a long time getting over that."

"And the new director — Olbrich," Michelle put in. "Like you said, he's got a reputation for wringing more out of a script, getting memorable performances. But he does it by messing with his actors' heads. I've heard rumors about one promising young guy who wound up in a rubber room after Olbrich got done with him."

"What can we do?" Liza asked.

"Nothing much. When Chissel and Mirage moved in to buy Derrick's production company — and save his deal — they got the whole ball of wax. Jenny doesn't have much leverage."

Liza nodded. "All she can do is pull out. And if she does that, Jenny gets the rep of being 'difficult' before she even gets a film on the screen." She paused. "You don't have anything on Chissel that you can use to leverage him into doing what we want?"

"With a nickname like Ollie the Chiseler, he's used to bad publicity," Michelle said. "And Olbrich is busy building himself a demon director reputation. I don't think we'll get much traction there."

She sounded as if she were grinding glass between her teeth as she went on. "All I can say right now is that Jenny will have to suck it up until or unless we get something going for her."

"And since I'm the one on-site, I'll have to give her the heads-up," Liza said.

"We're not going to take this lying down," Michelle said. "I don't want to get a reputation for being soft."

"Don't worry. That's not a problem," Michael said. "It won't cross the mind of anyone who knows you."

It was a bit of a surprise to hear her ex-husband lining up on Michelle's side. Part of the problem in their marriage had been Michelle's not-so-subtle suggestions that Liza should dump him and trade up.

"I'm putting Buck Foreman on this," her partner went on. Well, if Michelle wanted her pet Hollywood detective on the case, she was definitely looking for some sort of results.

"All right," Liza sighed. "No use putting things off. I'll get over to the set and give

33

Jenny a heads-up."

"Good luck," Michael said. "We're behind you."

"Yeah," Michelle sounded a little annoyed that the ex-husband had spoken first.

Liza hung up the phone and rubbed her hands on her thighs. They weren't exactly sweaty, but they probably would be by the time she got to Jenny.

The phone rang again.

"Hello?" She wondered who was calling.

Had Michelle done something unprecedented — like forgetting to bring up a point on a phone conference? Had Buck Foreman already dug up some dirt on Oliver Chissel and Mirage Productions? Was Michael calling back to offer something a little more than backup? Things had gotten warmer between them lately —

"Liza, it's Kevin Shepard."

Hearing from the other man in her life right after speaking to — and thinking about — Michael left Liza momentarily speechless.

"I'm calling because I need a favor for someone." Kevin sounded a little embarrassed. "Ray Massini."

"As in Mayor Massini?" Liza said. What could the mayor of Maiden's Bay want from her?

"That's right," Kevin replied. "Ray is an old army buddy, and he could really use someone with Hollywood savvy. When I look over my acquaintances, that's pretty much you."

"And what does he need me for?" Liza wanted to know.

"Ray's got a movie bigwig coming to town," Kevin told her. "His name is Oliver Chissel, and his plane is going to be landing soon."

3

Liza couldn't quite believe what she was hearing. "Oliver Chissel is coming to Maiden's Bay? What for?"

"That's what Ray would like to know," Kevin said. "He'd been dealing with a — what did he call him? — a line producer and the director, that Hamblyn guy. Then there was this new guy, Peter Hake, and Hamblyn was in the hospital, replaced by Lloyd Olbrich. Now all of a sudden, Chissel is aboard a corporate jet due to land in Manzanita about an hour from now. Could you get to City Hall and talk to Ray before that happens?"

"I'll get down there as soon as I can," Liza promised. "After I make a couple of calls to L.A."

I expect Chissel is coming up here to talk to the troops rather than to Ray Massini, she thought.

Kevin hung up and Liza hit the speed-dial

number for Markson Associates. Ysabel put her right through to Michelle, who listened in silence as Liza detailed the latest.

"I hadn't heard that Chissel was going out of town," she muttered darkly. "Does he think he's going to mess with one of my clients? And you say that Peter Hake is up there?"

"You know him?" Liza asked.

"If Mirage Productions had an honest organization chart, which it doesn't, Hake would be vice president in charge of dirty tricks. He's Chissel's enforcer and facilitator. On his old scamming businesses as well as his new career in films. He makes Tony Soprano's crew look like choirboys. Do you know how long he's been up in Maiden's Bay? I wouldn't put it past him to arrange the accident that took Terence Hamblyn out of the picture."

"You're kidding!" When she didn't hear an answer, Liza added, "Aren't you?"

"I don't know. Maybe not. Liza, you know that The Business is all about ego." When Michelle referred to "The Business," she meant the film business. "It's all about getting your way. Most big shots out here use money to throw their weight around. In the old days, they used to do more. When money didn't work, the old studios had fixers. They didn't care which side of the law they were playing on. They simply did what they had to do to get their way. Fixers were people like Peter Hake. I'm surprised you haven't heard of him. He's been making quite a name for himself. Oh wait . . . he's a new name for you because he came into Mirage while you were busy soul searching up in Oregon. If you'd kept your nose to the grindstone, you'd be up on all the gossip."

"Sorry," Liza said, not really meaning it. But it paid to throw in the odd symbolic grovel for her boss.

"Hake's worked as Chissel's 'special assistant' for the past few months, but he's been into nastier stuff than most Hollywood arm-twisters. Hake is nothing more than a thug with a three-hundred-dollar haircut — a *stupid* three-hundred-dollar haircut," Michelle added angrily. "He was Chissel's thug long before Ollie got stuck with Mirage."

"But Chissel is running the show now," Liza said.

"The question may be for how long," Michelle replied. "One of the things Buck is looking into is Chissel's financials."

"I have a hard time seeing him do that." With his size, handsome but heavy features, and perpetual sunglasses, Buck Foreman's appearance spelled C-O-P with a capital "intimidating." If you wanted brains and muscle, Buck was your guy. But, in Liza's mind, anyway, forensic accounting didn't look like it would be one of his specialties.

"When Buck investigates someone, he *investigates,*" Michelle replied. "That includes bringing in any necessary professionals."

"But you didn't hear anything about Chissel coming up here — or why," Liza pressed on.

"No," Michelle said in a "heads will roll" tone of voice. Her Hollywood intelligence system could probably rival the KGB's in its prime. Certainly, she used it as ruthlessly. "You can bet he's not heading out to bestow good news on the crew, though." She paused for a moment, and Liza heard the tickety-tack sound of computer keys in the background. She could just visualize Michelle leaning over the keyboard, calling up her calendar with one hand.

"Ysabel can cancel tomorrow's meetings — I'm going up there."

"Me, too," Michael's voice chimed in. "It'll be just like the good old days."

That's what I'm afraid of, Liza thought.

"Sure — the more the merrier," Liza said. They all said their good-byes and Liza hung up.

No sense running into hostile territory without proper war paint, she thought, and went to change for the big meeting. Oregon was probably ground zero for business casual. Even CEOs around here showed up for board meetings in khakis and polo shirts. But Liza's current baggy sweats and a baseball cap would definitely be pushing it.

An hour later, in a more sedate outfit of blazer and slacks, her makeup carefully applied, Liza stood in the mayor's office. Maiden's Bay's seat of power was a cramped, nondescript space in the rear of City Hall. The little coastal town was too small for a full-time mayor. Even the town clerk and the sheriff's deputies had busier — and larger — offices.

A large, elaborately carved wooden desk, at least a century old, took up most of the space in the room. It contrasted strangely with the rest of the décor, especially the mid-fifties furnishings dating from the building's last renovation. The desk was set at an angle because that was the only way it fit in the room. Despite its small size, the rest of the office looked pretty much like generic business space taken over by small-town politics.

Photos of former mayors with the political

movers and shakers of years gone by covered the walls. Then there was an "I Love Me" section that featured photos of Ray. Liza spotted one shot of a younger Ray Massini in desert camouflage and sergeant's stripes off to one side.

Ray had already graduated by the time Liza and Kevin reached high school, but his image had been one they knew from framed squad pictures of several successful football teams featured prominently in the field house. After serving several hitches in the army, Ray had come through Operation Desert Storm as an honest-to-Pete war hero. He'd returned to Maiden's Bay to put his G.I. benefits to good use. And he had, ending up with a successful insurance agency and a string of community good works. He'd run for the mayoralty of Maiden's Bay a few years back and won it easily.

Liza had seen Ray around town since she'd returned to Oregon. He had a strikingly handsome face, with the sharp, regular features of someone on an ancient Roman coin — except that he wore his graying hair cut short and brushed straight back.

He looked the part of a successful former noncommissioned officer.

Liza figured the Hollywood types would want him screen-tested the instant they laid eyes on him.

Right now, he rested one buttock on the corner of the old desk in a conscious attempt to look relaxed. Liza could just imagine Sergeant Massini engaging in the same sort of watchful waiting before leading his company out to attack.

In this case, the troops he was leading weren't evident. And the enemy he was facing at the moment came down to Liza. Massini looked as if he'd far rather deal with bullets from the Republican Guard than face time with some big film bozo from La-la Land.

Or maybe she was one of his troops. Hard to say.

Liza didn't know how much support she could offer him. She'd tried to warn the mayor that truthfulness was not something to expect from Hollywood — aka the Land of Make-believe. It was commonly said that the easiest way to tell if a bigwig in The Business was lying was to see if he was breathing.

"What am I facing here?" Ray asked.

Liza wondered how much of the truth to give him.

Whatever Chissel was coming up here about, he was looking for some sort of edge for his company and for *Counterfeit.* "Treat him like a large, important insurance client," Liza advised the mayor, "coming in with a dodgy claim. Or a tame tiger. He's flashy. But if things don't make him happy, he might just try to take a chunk out of you. Probably from your dead and bleeding carcass."

"Gee, thanks," Ray said, though not like he meant it.

The buzzer on the intercom went off, and Massini rose to his feet.

Showtime, Liza thought.

The office door opened, and in walked a large, soft-looking man who extended a hand. "Oliver Chissel," he said. "And this is Peter Hake."

"My name's Ray Massini," the mayor responded, "and this is Liza Kelly."

Oliver Chissel shot her a glance but said nothing. Apparently, judging by the look in his eyes, he knew who she was. Or at the very least he had met Michelle.

But he didn't look like he planned to play it light here. In fact, he looked like he planned to throw his considerable weight around. And Hake looked positively dangerous — though not in an attractive way.

In fact, neither of them were what she expected to see, which was surprising in an appearance-oriented business like Hollywood.

Liza had seen a couple of unflattering photos of Chissel in the newspaper — heavy on the double chins. In person, Chissel had a round, bland, undistinguished face. He looked more as if he should be dispensing medicine from behind the counter at Schilling's Pharmacy, or maybe selling insurance for Ray Massini, than like a wannabe movie mogul. In fact, he had the look of an old-time tent evangelist. He looked too well fed, too eager to meet them.

Yeah, Liza thought, *that would be a very successful face for telling people where to put their money — right until he left town with it.*

Chissel's well-practiced benevolent smile went well with his clean-shaven features. The only odd thing was that he wore his faded ginger hair unfashionably long for a businessman. Maybe it was an attempt to compensate for his pink, bald dome.

Well, it's better than Donald Trump's tease and combover, Liza thought. *And it's probably cheaper, even at Hollywood prices.*

Peter Hake had an expensive haircut as well, but Michelle was right. It did look stupid. Hake's dishwater brown hair was cut short on the back and sides but rose in gelled spikes from the crown of his head. It was like tying a ridiculous little silk tassel to the hilt of a sharp knife.

She looked at Hake's slightly pointed features, impassive as he stood a step behind and to the right of his boss.

Sharp knife — and definitely deadly, Liza thought. She could well imagine him messing with Terence Hamblyn's car if Chissel needed that done.

The Mirage mogul got right down to business. "Mr. Mayor," Chissel said, "we need to extend our location shooting."

Massini frowned. "Liza told me that sometimes films run over time and budget. But she also said this didn't seem to be that kind of project. We've got a construction project we're trying to get under way in the harbor. Mr. Hamblyn and your line producer assured me that you folks would be done by now. I've got a pile driver sitting idle — that's costing the town money."

"As you know, we've had a change of directors," Chissel said. "And Lloyd Olbrich has suggested a new direction for the film." He brought up a couple of his chins. "Perhaps if Terence Hamblyn hadn't gotten injured on one of your roads . . ."

"Mr. Hamblyn crashed on the coastal highway — a state road," Massini said evenly, "while he was driving up from the

45

Killamook Inn. It might not have happened if you'd lodged your people here in town instead of halfway round the bay."

"I understand the accommodations were better at —" Chissel glanced at Hake.

"The Killamook Inn," his assistant put in.

"But accommodations and services were all part of the pitch when your people first came to us," Massini said. "A boost for local businesses. A luxury place like Killamook Inn, I guess we'd have to expect that the stars and big shots would stay over there. But you've got the rest of your crew in less expensive motels around Killamook, too. And you're feeding them with a catering service that trucks everything down from Portland. Except for the occasional cup of coffee and bottle of iced tea, our local merchants haven't exactly benefited from your shoot."

Chissel shrugged. "I can't speak to that directly. But we have professional staff that evaluates local facilities and whether they can accommodate us. Apparently that wasn't the case here in Maiden's Bay."

Liza had a momentary vision of Ma's Café trying to deal with a crowd three times the size of the normal morning rush. Not to mention trying to come up with food to please delicate Hollywood palates. Whether she liked it or not, Chissel had a point.

"A number of the townsfolk have had the opportunity to participate as background extras," Chissel went on. "The new scenes we're adding in will mean more calls for extras, and we're already scouting additional locations. That will mean more location payments as well." He smiled. "I'm sure your constituents will be pleased enough when their checks arrive three weeks after we wrap."

"But you're extending your filming by what — a week? Two? Three? People are already expecting those checks — some are depending on them."

"There will be no payments until we finish," Chissel's voice got insistent, almost cutting. "As it is, we've suffered delays in our filming thanks to acts of sabotage and petty vandalism. We'd like to lodge a complaint with the local authorities."

Massini looked surprised. "This is the first time I'm hearing about anything."

Liza remembered the graffiti she'd seen. "Somebody did paint something nasty on one of the sheds by the docks," she said.

"That's just the most obvious act of sabotage," Peter Hake put in. "Over the last week, we've had pieces of equipment go missing or get messed up."

Now Massini looked doubly jolted. "Have you reported this to the town deputies? This is a little town and crime is so rare here it's almost nonexistent. I can't imagine that Sheriff Clements —"

"I can't imagine we'll get much help from a mere sheriff with a couple of deputies," Chissel said. "You're quite right. They have no experience in matters like this. Never mind making a report. Mr. Hake will deal with the situation. He has some security experience."

Probably from the other side of the law. The irreverent thought crept into Liza's head, and she found it hard to squash it.

"I'm still informing the sheriff," Massini said. But his voice was muted — it was obvious who had won this little skirmish.

The meeting broke up shortly afterward, with both sides offering polite and mutually insincere good wishes. Chissel and Hake headed for the door. The Mirage mogul glanced back when he realized Liza was following them.

"Is there something I can do for you?" he asked.

"That depends on whether you're heading for the main shoot or for the Killamook Inn," Liza replied. "If you're going to tell the crew what you just told the mayor, I

48

want to be with my client. If not, I want her to hear it from me first."

Chissel was indeed on his way to make his announcement of the changes he wanted in the script to the filmmakers. At least he was gracious enough to ask Liza to accompany him.

Hake drove a rental car with Chissel and Liza in the rear. They made a very awkward pair.

Every conversational line that Liza tossed out was cut off with a curt *yes* or *no* from Chissel. She finally subsided into silence. They went through the underpass beneath the coastal highway and into the industrial area down toward the harbor. The trailers for the film crew were parked along a side street.

A production assistant came running up to wave the car off, but when she saw Hake and Chissel, she ran off to one of the trailers.

"Looks like they're between shots," Liza said as they got out of the car.

Another PA came up, this time to convey them to the film's director. Lloyd Olbrich was a lanky man with a pouchy face and enormous black eyebrows that made him look as if he were always glaring. *Well, he doesn't look like he's trying to play any head*

49

games right now, Liza thought as the man greeted them. He was very polite to Chissel and wary when introduced to Liza.

"I sent some people out to gather everyone down by the dock," he said. "Whatever announcement we're going to make, we can do it from there."

"I'll do the talking," Chissel said.

Olbrich recoiled as though he'd been struck.

But Chissel was clearly in charge.

The director followed him without further comment.

They went to the dock, where the film crew had already been gathered. The film crew — lighting technicians, production assistants, sound techs, camera people, assistant directors, and so on — were sort of spread out. Another group huddled in a more compact knot — the actors. Liza recognized Jenny, and decided that she already looked pale and angry.

Olbrich introduced the big boss.

Chissel barely waited until the introduction was over before he began speaking. "I'm here today because I want to underscore how important Mirage — and I — consider this production to be," he began. Liza worked her way over to Jenny as Chissel went on to talk about additional filming and changes in direction.

Liza had just gotten to Jenny's side when the young woman broke into Chissel's remarks. "I've already heard about one of the new directions we're going in," she said. "One of the location scouts wanted to know exactly where I'd been held after being kidnapped — like I want to revisit that, physically or any other way."

Liza reached out to take Jenny's arm in a gesture of support and restraint. That statement wasn't exactly the way to talk to a studio head, even for a small studio like Mirage Productions.

On Jenny's far side, a tall, silver-haired man took the girl's other arm, more in a gesture of solidarity. Liza recognized Guy Morton, a veteran actor Derrick Robbins had recruited for the *Counterfeit* project. Morton had known lots of ups and downs in his long Hollywood career — a lot of experience showed in his laugh lines, frown lines, and squint lines, all characteristics that marked his once-handsome face.

The frown lines dominated now as he glared at Oliver Chissel. "We had a damned good movie almost in the can here," he told the studio boss. "Why do you want to come chiseling in now to turn it into crap?"

"Why don't you want me to pay your salary? You'll shut up and do as you are told. Or you're out of here. And I mean that for everybody here."

Nobody said a word. In fact, for a long moment, no one even blinked.

4

That speech managed to do an effective job of killing any buzz Oliver Chissel might have hoped to ignite in the crew with his pep talk. Apparently, the powers that be recognized this fact, too. Soon afterward, Lloyd Olbrich decided to wrap filming early that day.

Liza moved quickly to offer Jenny a lift back to the actors' accommodations at the Killamook Inn. She wanted to get the girl alone to talk a little about the facts of Hollywood life before the next time Jenny saw the crew.

One thing about Jenny — she wasn't dense. The girl glanced at Liza from the corner of her eye as they got onto the coastal highway. "You think I shot off my mouth too much," she said.

"I think you were very honest — which isn't necessarily helpful when dealing with people in The Business," Liza replied. "Sometimes it's better to keep them guessing — especially when it comes to studio execs."

"When I heard him talking, I just wanted to do something terrible to him. He made me feel furious — I wanted to smash in his face," Jenny said hotly. "By the time he and his stooge Olbrich get done with *Counterfeit,* it will be nothing like the movie Uncle Derrick planned."

"They bought up your uncle's company and brought in the money to keep the production going," Liza said. "That means they can do whatever they want. It's the Golden Rule."

Jenny turned to her. " 'Do unto others — ?' "

"No, that's the biblical version. The Hollywood version goes like this: 'Those who have the gold make the rules.' "

Jenny had to laugh at that, but there wasn't much humor in her eyes. "So what do I have to do now?"

"I don't think there's much we can do in the way of damage control," Liza said. "It comes down to two choices — suck it up, or take a walk and kiss any ideas of your career in the movies good-bye. A starlet who gets a reputation for being difficult on her first film isn't exactly an in-demand property in Hollywood."

"If I walk, I guess I won't have much use for a publicity agent." Jenny gave her a sudden grin. "So I guess if I want to keep you around, I'll have to suck things up."

Her grin wavered a bit. "A direct tie-in with what I went through might help to sell tickets, but . . . Liza, I nearly got killed out there. After the hospital decided I wasn't going to die from exposure, your partner asked if I wanted a shrink."

That was so out of character Liza actually glanced away from the road to look at her passenger. "Michelle never mentioned that to me."

"I told her not to after I told her no." Jenny sighed. "Maybe I should have, if I'm going to end up playing head games with Lloyd Olbrich. He's already been fooling around with new reaction shots for scenes that were supposedly all wrapped up. And I expect it's only going to get worse now that Chissel's here in person to put his mark on the production."

"It this is going to be too much for you —" Liza began.

Jenny cut her off. "Uncle D. wanted to get this picture made if it was the last thing he did — and it just about was. Maybe it won't turn out the way he hoped, but I'll go through with every frame of the shoot. I'll take the chance he offered me. I owe it to him."

"Just remember, if you need to talk, you do have friends," Liza told the girl. "I'm always available, if you need me. Michael's come up to town and so has Michelle. I expect we'll find them at the inn."

Her prediction was right on the money. When they pulled in at the entrance for the Killamook Inn, they found Michael waiting for them. He led them to a cabin discreetly off to the side, where Michelle had already established herself. Michelle's spies must have been working overtime. She knew all about the incident on the dock, and she had some stern words for Jenny about that.

"At least there weren't any cameras around when you decided to confront Chissel," Michelle finally ran down. "In the future, if you're going to shoot your mouth off, at least take a moment to look around and make sure of that. It'll get into the industry rags anyway, but only as gossip. Nobody likes Chissel, so you'll probably be okay. You may even come out something of a hero. But just bite your tongue and keep it inside the next time you feel tempted to take on a studio owner."

Having settled that point, Michelle then went on to the subject of food. Liza was always astonished that such a small person as her boss could pack it away and still remain petite. *She must have the metabolism of a shrew,* Liza often thought. *I guess it goes with the disposition.*

"I talked with your friend Kevin, and he assures me the kitchen here is better than decent," Michelle said.

"It's quite good," Liza replied. "I've eaten in the dining room a couple times." She noticed that announcement didn't fill Michael with good cheer. Well, he was the one who had walked out on her almost a year ago. He'd started the paperwork, too. If he was changing his mind about that, maybe a little competition was a good thing. It would keep him off balance and curious about her.

"Kevin also promised us room service, especially for tonight," Michelle went on. "I don't want to advertise that I came up here. Our official line is that filming is proceeding as normal —" She glanced over at Jenny. "Even if it isn't. Understood?"

"Understood," Jenny sighed.

After a perusal of the room service menu and a quick discussion, Michelle picked up the telephone and put in an order for all of them. Their food arrived hot, quickly filling the little cabin with delicious smells.

Dinner passed without any business talk.

Michelle then picked up the copy of the *Oregon Daily* that she'd requested along with their order.

"Checking my column?" Liza asked with a grin.

"No, the television listings," Michelle replied. "I wanted to see if some station up here in the wilderness carries *Evening Celebrity News*."

"You watch that stuff?" Jenny asked in surprise. "Most of their so-called 'news' is enough 'to make a wabbit womit,' as one of my old drama teachers used to say."

"True, but you've got to know what the enemy is up to if you want to properly counter them." Michelle rattled the paper. "It's been quiet in Tinseltown lately. No good gossip. No celebrities doing embarrassing jail time. No drunken arrests. Not even much fooling around. I'm betting Miss Jenny here makes the lead story. God, they put the prime-time schedule on early here."

Liza glanced at her watch. Yes, the show was almost on. She picked up the remote, powered up the TV, and input the proper channel.

Michelle expected no less.

In moments the cohosts of *Evening Celebrity News* appeared on the screen. The platinum and plastic female half of the team breathlessly spoke to her dark and hand-some partner. "Tonight, we have breaking news of conflict during the shooting of a major new film."

The male partner showed even, white teeth. "We hear shocking revelations from a veteran actor on location in Oregon — right after these messages."

"Uh-oh," Jenny said.

After the commercial, Guy Morton appeared on the television screen. "Today the head of Mirage Productions came to the set of *Counterfeit,* talking about a new direction. I know exactly what direction these chiselers are taking us — right into the toilet."

The camera focus tightened on the silver-haired actor. "I play a con man in the movie. These guys are con men for real. They want to take a clever script with lots of funny twists and a spunky heroine and turn it into just another teen-in-danger rip-off flick. Why? Because they think they can get some cheap publicity by having Jenny Robbins relive some of the crap she went through after her uncle died. Well, here's some publicity for them. They're ruining the film."

The interviewer's heavily collagened lips opened and closed like a fish's for a second before she got out, "We usually don't hear such, ah, frank remarks in the middle of production."

Guy Morton shrugged. "What are they going to do, fire me and reshoot my whole part? They're too cheap to do that. That's the problem they're creating — taking the well-plotted film they already have and tacking this stupid 'new direction' onto it. I came onto this project as a favor to Derrick Robbins — a friend who got murdered — to help Jenny learn the ropes of film acting. She's given a hell of a performance, but they're going to butcher that in the hopes of making a few extra pennies."

He thumped a finger against his own chest. "I've been around for a long time, and people have been telling me things. They want to turn my character into some kind of crazed slasher. Well, I've got no intention of becoming the psycho geezer. If they're not going to make the film I signed on for, I don't see any reason to play nice."

The scene switched back to the people in the studio, where the blonde reported, "There was no comment when we called the executive offices at Mirage Productions — except that CEO Oliver Chissel was not in town."

"Whew!" Jenny said as the show went on

to gossip about some other celebrity. "Guy certainly didn't pull any punches."

"No, he didn't," Michelle said, sounding surprisingly calm, considering the possible consequences of Guy's interview.

"Looks like Guy's back in form," Liza added.

"What do you mean? Guy's always been a team player," Jenny said.

Of course, Jenny only knew Guy as the sort of "foxy grandpa" figure he'd played since working with Derrick Robbins on a story arc in the TV series *Spycraft*. The show had given Derrick's career a new lease on life, giving him a starring role as an eccentric code wizard. Guy had come in playing a veteran secret agent dragged out of retirement. It wasn't much of a stretch — the network had dragged Guy out of retirement to take the part.

"In a way," Liza said, "this is like Guy's glory days on a TV series I watched when I was a kid. He starred in *Masked Justice* as a crime-fighter who went after rich and powerful lawbreakers — the kind who couldn't be caught by 'the system.' Though it only ran for five seasons, the show is still a classic cult hit. One reason for the show's continuing popularity is probably that Guy was a pit bull about script quality. When the writers didn't deliver, he'd threaten to rewrite the scripts himself. He did it several times."

"Yep, this isn't the first time old Guy has tangled with studio brass," Michelle said drily. "You have to give him credit."

"Guy has always stood up for what he believes is right," Liza said. "After his show got canceled, Guy went through a long dry spell. He made most of his income doing personal appearances as the masked hero he used to play. Cut ahead fifteen years, when some studio decided to do a movie remake — turning Guy's character into a psycho rather than a hero. The geniuses decided that as the original Masked Justice, Guy represented unwelcome competition. They filed suit to keep him from wearing a mask. What did Guy do? He kept making appearances — but instead of a mask, he wore specially designed sunglasses — in the shape of a mask.

"Incidentally, the movie version bombed. Nobody liked the changes in the hero."

"Well, it looks as if Guy feels the same way about the *Counterfeit* script," Jenny said. "And he's willing to fight for it. Does this change anything on the set?"

Michelle shook her head. "Officially, no. If Guy wants to tangle with Ollie the Chiseler,

I don't want you to get caught in the cross fire."

"Warfare by proxy," Liza said.

"Of course, the script is better left alone. I don't trust Chissel. If you were to bump into Guy around town, I wouldn't mind if you encouraged him a little," Michelle went on.

"As long as you can deny it," Liza said sweetly.

Michelle gave her the look she usually reserved for backward children. "Of course."

Their meeting pretty much broke up after that. Jenny went back to her cabin, while Michael followed Liza. "Would you mind giving me a lift? I came along with Michelle."

Liza gave him a sidelong glance. "Aren't you staying here?"

"I'm a poor freelance writer, not a Hollywood publicity maven," Michael replied. "Plus, the whole A-list on the film crew has pretty much taken this place over. I'm living in digs more suitable to my situation."

"I'm sure Kevin —" Liza began.

"Yeah," Michael interrupted. "Kevin and I are just like that." He held up two fingers together. "I think Kevin is the taller one." He tapped his middle finger.

Liza sighed. Michael and Kevin had

worked together to come up with a dramatic rescue. In the months since, however, they had gone back to their routine of being romantic rivals for her favors.

If only I could figure out which was Archie and which was Reggie, she thought. *Kind of hard when both of them act like Jughead.*

"So where are you staying?" she asked. "Somewhere here in Killamook, or over in Maiden's Bay?"

"In Maiden's Bay, actually." Michael hesitated. "I called Mrs. Halvorsen for some suggestions about bunking down in town, and she offered me her spare bedroom."

Liza whipped around, her mind nearly exploding with shock. "You're staying with my next-door neighbor?"

"The price was right." Michael shrugged and spread his hands. "Like I said, I'm a poor writer."

"Great. This should be interesting. Come on, then," Liza said. "At least I won't be wasting any gas."

The next morning, Liza woke up and started to roll over in bed. Obviously, it was too early to get up — it was still dark outside. Then her alarm began peeping insistently. She opened her eyes again, remembering why it was so dark — the bedroom curtains were drawn tightly shut. Usually, Liza didn't bother to close the drapes. Her bedroom was on the second floor, and her nearest neighbor was the elderly Mrs. H. Liza figured Mrs. H. had seen her in a nightgown — or without one — often enough that it didn't matter if she left her windows exposed or not. But last night, thinking of Michael next door, Liza had carefully pulled the blinds before getting ready for bed.

Shaking her head at the thought of having her soon-to-be-former husband next door for the foreseeable future, she sat up in bed, stretched, and took a deep breath. Then she stopped and took another. Odd. In fact, wonderful. Her nose wasn't stuffed anymore.

Well, thank heavens for some small mercies, she thought, padding over to the chest of drawers for a T-shirt, fresh sweats, and socks. She pulled on a pair of running shoes and headed downstairs. "Hey, Rusty," she called, "want to get out of here for a while?"

The response was an eager bark as her dog trotted to the foot of the stairs. Rusty was a mutt, of indeterminate breed, except that his coat color and his exuberance showed he had plenty of Irish setter in his background.

The dog eagerly circled Liza's feet as she went to the kitchen and drank some orange juice. Rusty was always energetic, but never more so than when he got out of the house, pulling on his leash. He also looked at going for a run more as a race than a bit of shared exercise.

Rusty danced around as Liza clipped on his leash. He didn't quite yank her through the door — quite. But Liza had to keep a good grip as they started out along the streets. They took a route that led to a footbridge over the railroad tracks and the highway, then headed down to the beachfront by the bay.

Liza let Rusty off his lead, and he dashed joyously along the sands. She jogged along after him, not trying to race flat out, just making sure he stayed in view. The dog led them toward the town's harbor area, in hot pursuit of interesting smells. Liza swung onto the hard-packed sand, increasing her pace as they came closer to the construction area — the planned boardwalk extension. Nobody was there yet, but she could see the pile driver rising up beyond the existing structure.

"Hey, Rusty!" she called. The dog stopped, but didn't come to her. That was unusual. He stayed where he was, his head going low, his ears flopping forward at full alert.

Liza put on some speed and caught up to the dog.

"Come on, boy." Liza almost tripped over Rusty as he slunk to one side, whining unhappily.

"What's the matter?" She leaned over, expecting to see a crab. One had nipped Rusty once. He'd had a nasty fear of them ever since. At least she knew it wasn't a dead bird or fish — otherwise the dog would be rolling on it.

Liza's first impression was that some sort of rock had spooked her dog. *Kind of big to wash up here,* she thought, *unless we had a typhoon overnight.*

She took a step closer, but Rusty got in her way again, making yipping sounds of distress. Maybe it was some kind of bundle that came in on the tide. She could see a starfish on the thing and some seaweed . . .

Liza suddenly stopped dead. That wasn't seaweed. What had at first seemed to be plastered-down ribbons of kelp was actually individual strands of something. And they were the wrong color to be seaweed, sort of a damp browny red.

She stepped round Rusty, getting a new angle on the mystery item — and sucked in a gasp. The strands resolved themselves into

67

overlong ginger hair straggling across a bald dome. She recognized it, even though it was pale now instead of pink.

It was a human head. In fact, it was the head of Oliver Chissel. And from the look of things, it had been here when high tide had come in and then receded.

5

For the second time in as many days, Liza found herself at the Maiden's Bay City Hall. This time, though, she was in the busy side of the building, the law enforcement side.

Not that Maiden's Bay was exactly a hotbed of crime. Judging from the police blotter in the *Oregon Daily,* the officers spent almost all of their time dealing with a fair number of working stiffs who had a few too many in local gin mills. That resulted in bar fights, not to mention drunk-and-disorderly arrests. The influx of Californians building expensive houses and filling them with expensive things had led to a few more burglaries in recent years. And, like everywhere else, some people took drugs.

Though not many. And not often.

But murder? Liza wasn't sure whether a murder had even happened during Sheriff Clements's time in office. She had met the county's leading law officer after the whole hoo-hah over Derrick and Jenny Robbins. But she'd seen him around the county since she was a kid. Bert Clements had been a deputy, a big, slope-shouldered guy in a plain khaki uniform. Newt McFarland, the sheriff back then, had looked more like a movie star than a cop, in a uniform that would have made more sense on some South American generalissimo than on a small-town sheriff on the West Coast. The look had only gotten more ridiculous as Newt got older, his good looks undermined by an additional chin. And more and more tailoring had been required to fit the fancy uniform over the years as Newt's gut had grown.

After Clements got elected, he wore the same plain uniform he'd worn on the beat, except for the addition of a gold badge. He still did.

Bert Clements was a big, bearlike man, a calm, authoritative presence. Of course, Liza had never been in an interrogation room with him before.

It wasn't even a real interrogation room, just a cramped space that doubled as an office. Clements's real office was in the county seat at Killamook, but he'd quickly come up the coast after Liza had called in her grisly discovery.

Clements didn't look like a huge pillar of calm right now. Instead, Liza found herself thinking of big, looming thunderclouds — just before the lightning came lancing down out of them, killing golfers and starting fires.

Clements had his cop face on today. His expression was sealed and self-contained, his eyes coldly inscrutable as Liza related what she'd done and seen on her morning walk with Rusty.

"And when was the last time you'd seen Mr. Chissel — before this?" the sheriff asked.

What's he expecting me to answer? Liza wondered. *Something stupid like, "Oh, it was a couple of hours before the tide came in, while I was busy burying him."*

"It was mid- to late afternoon yesterday," she said, "down by the docks."

"Where he made his announcement about extending work on the film here around town." Clements finished. "That upset a lot of people, including your client Jenny Robbins." He paused for a second. "You have to admit, you have a pretty public record of going the extra mile for that girl."

"So you think I just did away with this troublesome studio head?" The words sort of burst out of Liza. "Are you out of your mind?"

71

"Not currently. Could you account for your whereabouts yesterday evening?"

Liza couldn't believe what she was hearing. This was the guy who had shaken her hand not so long ago and complimented her on her investigative instincts. Now he was treating her like a murder suspect!

"They wrapped filming early. I gave Jenny a lift back to the Killamook Inn, had dinner with her and some business associates . . . and then I went home, did a little work, and watched some TV."

"Was anyone with you?"

Liza shrugged. "On the drive home, yes. Afterward, no. Just my dog. I got into grungy clothes, walked the dog around the block, settled in, and watched *House.* You can check with my next-door neighbor to see if I went out. Mrs. Halvorsen keeps pretty good tabs on the neighborhood." She paused for a second. "Also, my husband Michael is staying next door with her."

That made Clements blink. "Your husband?"

"We're separated. He came up from L.A. — he's one of the business associates I mentioned. I gave him a lift from the hotel — he can tell you that."

"Any other associates in town I should know about?" Clements asked.

"A few. Jenny you already know about. There's my partner, Michelle Markson. She's staying at the inn. Michael — my husband — is a scriptwriter. The Killamook Inn is a bit rich for his blood." She shot a look at the sheriff. "You don't think —"

"I don't think anything right now," Clements replied. "I'm just asking questions, trying to see who was where, and when. You find the body — you get asked the first questions. That's how it works."

One of the deputies, Curt Walters, stuck his head in the door. Liza remembered him from high school. He'd played football with Kevin Shepard. He'd also been one of the responding officers when Liza's house had been broken into. He'd impressed her then with his cool professionalism.

Curt didn't look as cool right now, interrupting his boss. "Uh, Sheriff, the mayor is on line two, wanting to know about the broken windows on Main Street. He'd like to talk to you right now."

"Walters, why don't you ask the mayor which he thinks will be worse for tourism — a few stores being vandalized in the shopping district or the dead body on the beach?"

"Uh — yessir!" Curt quickly disappeared.

The sheriff glanced over to Liza. "I understand you were with Massini when he met with Chissel yesterday."

"You understand a lot," Liza said.

"I hear things — it's part of the job. And it's also part of the job to ask questions until I understand things. You got a problem with that?"

Liza sighed. "No. I don't. The mayor wanted someone with Hollywood experience on hand when he talked with 'this Hollywood guy.' " She shrugged. "The mayor's words, not mine. He wanted the shoot to get wrapped up so he could get the boardwalk construction back on track. Not that I did him much good. Chissel had all the leverage."

"You never know. I think maybe you helped keep things businesslike and polite," Clements responded. "Massini and Chissel had another run-in later, at Fruit of the Sea."

Liza knew that was the nice restaurant in town, as opposed to Ma's Café. "I didn't hear about that," she said.

"You get too busy watching TV to keep up on the gossip, you never know what you'll miss." The sheriff looked down at some notes on his desk. " 'This Hollywood guy,' as you called him, stayed on in town after that first meeting broke up. He was making the rounds of all the location own-ers. He wanted them to know that their pay-ment wouldn't be forthcoming until the filming was finished. After they heard that, a lot of those people gave Massini an earful. The way I heard it, it didn't look like Mayor Massini was too happy about it. Then he goes out to supper and finds Chissel at the next table."

"Awkward," Liza said.

"Awkward and loud." Clements shook his head. "Ray Massini needs to learn a bit more about politics now that he's stuck his neck into the business. In his heart, I think he's still a Ranger sergeant, barking orders to his platoon."

Liza raised her eyebrows. "So will you be asking the mayor where he was last night, the way you did with me . . . and, I expect, with Jenny?"

"Sure. Not just them, but a lot of other people, too. Like I said, you find the body, you get first crack at the questions. But I've got a long list of other people to check in with."

"Hake?"

"Definitely. He stepped in to back Massini down at that dinner. Guy's got a nice line in subtle threats. They seemed to work. The mayor left."

"You know, you may just have one problem here, not two," Liza pointed out. "Maybe Chissel decided to celebrate his victory over the mayor. Maybe he got half a load on and ran down Main Street, breaking windows until an outraged local merchant stopped him. Figure out which window was broken last and you've got your killer."

That actually got a laugh out of Clements. "Wouldn't that simplify things?" he asked. "Unfortunately, I hear tell that murder cases don't tie up with such neat little knots."

"It was just an idea." Liza hesitated for a moment, then spoke. "I hate to bring this up, but maybe your eyes and ears already know about this. I saw Deke Jannsky get fired from being an extra on the film yesterday. He didn't take it too well. He started shooting his mouth off — it made me wonder at the time if he might not have something to do with the sabotage on the set."

Clements just looked at her, his face settling into a cop's mask again.

"Now there's more vandalism, this time on Main Street," Liza went on. "Is it all that different from the earlier sabotage?"

"I already planned to have a talk with Jannsky — after I get done with this piddling murder thing."

"They might be connected . . ." Liza said.

Clements rose, obviously dismissing her. "Thanks for your help. We may need to talk again."

"I know the drill," Liza said. *Like it or not,* she thought. *I've been here before.*

Liza stepped out of the room, getting a distinct whiff of *eau de drunk tank* wafting down the hallway — those subtle tones of vomit overlain with heavy-duty disinfectant were unmistakable. Hollywood publicists often found themselves visiting drunk tanks, but at least in Liza's case those visits had been strictly professional. Plenty of her clients overindulged in the juices of grape or barley. Unlucky stars wound up with disheveled-looking mug shots on TV. Very few of Michelle Markson's clients had ever faced such humiliation. But then, Liza considered, Michelle was picky. She tried to avoid signing clients who would make such asses of themselves in the first place. Once signed, Liza figured that Michelle's clients stayed sober out of fear that Michelle might kill them if they ended up on the celebrity scandal shows.

Speak of the devil, Liza thought as she pushed through the swinging doors to the front-desk area. Michelle sat on the first bench of the small waiting area. A deputy sat beside her, obviously placed there to prevent discussion with Michael, who had the next place on the bench.

Sheriff Clements obviously didn't want potential witnesses contaminating each other's testimony — or concocting any acceptable stories among themselves.

Like Michelle would leave such an important detail until after the fact . . .

Liza snorted. Her boss might scare people to death, but she'd never kill a client. It would be bad for business.

Michelle didn't need any words. The glare she gave Liza held an easily decoded message: *Well, here's another fine mess you've gotten us into.*

Doubtless there would be a major chewing out to come from her boss in her near future, but Liza was safe for now. Michelle wasn't about to tear her up in front of witnesses. Meanwhile, a couple of loud barks announced that someone was glad to see her. As the desk deputy untied the leash from his desk, Rusty wriggled so delightedly his dog tags jingled. He capered around Liza's legs as she took charge of him once more.

In spite of the show of pure joy Rusty was

putting on, Liza's attention was on the next bench, where Jenny Robbins and Guy Morton sat with another deputy. Standing behind them were Lloyd Olbrich and Peter Hake. The director continued to complain loudly about lost shooting time. The deputy with him apparently couldn't care less.

Liza glanced again at Jenny, who gave her a crooked grin and a shrug. Well, the girl had spent enough time with cops going over the story of her kidnapping to learn how to deal with them. That hadn't exactly been an interrogation, but the experience should do her some good. Saying anything to Jenny right now would just make the local police unhappier. Liza contented herself with a wave and a reassuring smile and headed for the street, Rusty leading the way.

In fact, it was more being towed out the door than it was making an exit under her own steam.

She took a deep breath of fresh air and reached down to pat her dog as the door shut behind her.

"What now, Rusty?" she asked the dog. "You've already gotten me in over my head today."

Rusty looked up the street and whined.

Apparently Ma's Café was doing a land-office business — and the aroma of the blue plate specials being served there was wafting down the street. Her dog trembled with the urge to check them out.

It was as good a direction as any. She and Rusty started walking along Main Street. The business district looked pretty crowded for a weekday, although Liza wondered whether more shopping than gawking was going on. Lots of store owners were busy trying to arrange some sort of cover for the holes in their windows.

The sheriff's Main Street vandal had been busy — it looked to Liza as though at least five stores had been hit. In a quiet town like Maiden's Bay, most merchants didn't bother pulling heavy grates down over their windows at closing time. Whoever it was apparently had the sense to stay away from windows that might have alarms, like the bank branch and the local jewelers. Ma's Café had been a target, and across the street the army-navy store and Schilling's Pharmacy had taken hits.

In fact, the whole Schilling family was outside working on repairs. Nora Schilling struggled to hold a sheet of plywood in place while Gary knelt with a hammer and nails.

Liza crossed over. "Let me give you a hand with that," she offered.

"It's not heavy." Nora nodded toward the two pieces of scrap lumber bearing the weight of the plywood. "Just cumbersome."

Liza left an indignant Rusty tied to a parking meter and braced the other side of the plywood sheet. "The same thing happened to me a few months ago, and Curt Walters boarded up my kitchen door."

"That's right — you had a window smashed in that break-in." Nora sighed as she looked at her display window. "I'm afraid this will take a bigger pane." She managed a smile. "And it will be a big pain in the wallet, too."

"I suppose that's true," Liza said. "Do you have insurance?"

"Yes, but I have to talk things over with Ray Massini. We all probably should. A mass of incidents like this can have consequences. If the company will want higher premiums, it might be better not to report this and pay for repairs myself." She shook her head. "In that case, there goes the money from the movie people. I was planning on using it to upgrade the cash registers, but this is more important."

"That's a shame."

"We've all been struggling, even with the movie people in town. It's tough to keep a small business going these days. Too much competition from big box stores way out by the highway." Nora sighed. "The location money would have given us all a bit of a cushion. Things have changed so much in this business. I was going through some old records, from the eighties. Back then, you'd have prescriptions for five dollars, or even two bucks. Nowadays, you're lucky to see a ten-dollar prescription. More likely, it's fifty, or a hundred and something. Our poor customers are having to choose between medicine and food. Food keeps winning, I figure."

She held tight to the plywood as Gary began hammering. "We saw the same thing when my husband got sick. The doctors prescribed something for the nausea from his chemotherapy, but they had no idea what it was going to cost us. The retail price was something like forty dollars a pill! Matt used to joke, saying that was the active ingredient — money! He said he'd be damned if he'd throw up something as expensive as that."

Gary brought out a ladder and began work on the top end of the plywood sheet.

"People think we're getting rich selling them drugs just because paying for 'em is making them poor. But there's really not that much difference between the price we pay for drugs and what we charge our customers for the prescriptions. People think all that money they're forking over is sticking to our fingers, but we've got to cut our markup to the bone to compete. Otherwise, people go to the chains or do their business over in Killamook."

Or they order online or go to Canada, Liza thought. But she figured saying it out loud would only make Nora more unhappy.

Gary finished his banging. "I think that will hold," he said.

Nora and Liza stepped away, and the wood didn't fall down. "Looks solid. That's about the best we can hope for," Nora said. "Holding on."

Liza retrieved Rusty from his hitching post and headed home, thinking about the sudden crime wave in Maiden's Bay. Graffiti, broken windows, a body on the beach . . . Ollie the Chiseler was dead, but she found she couldn't scrape up much emotion over that. On the other hand, she had all the sympathy in the world for the other victims, the people on Main Street, cleaning up and holding on.

■ ■ ■ ■

PART TWO:
THE USUAL SUSPECTS

■ ■ ■ ■

I'd be the first to admit it's tedious to work out the candidates for the forty, fifty, or sixty empty spaces in a sudoku puzzle. Hey, it's also tedious finding all the spots you're supposed to color blue in a paint-by-numbers project. But neglecting all sudoku candidates can have a bigger effect on the final picture than missing a few blue bits.

Yes, it can be disheartening to find spaces with six, seven, or the whole range of the usual one to nine suspects. But many of the higher-order solving techniques depend on whittling down those candidate lists. Computerized sudoku-solving programs can take the drudgery out of listing candidates and updating each space as candidates get eliminated. Of course this can make people lazy when it comes to pencil-and-paper solving. Don't get me started on the subject of keeping your candidate lists updated! It's just like politics — a promising solution can be derailed if you don't pay attention to candidate bookkeeping.

— Excerpt from *Sudo-cues* by Liza K

6

Liza headed for home up Main Street with Rusty eagerly in the lead. The dog shot her some disappointed looks as they zigzagged along the street, trying to skirt the crowds taking in the vandalism repairs. From Rusty's point of view, Liza was cheating him out of some interesting smells.

They set off across Main again, avoiding one of the larger knots of onlookers. *At least I'm not risking our lives,* Liza thought. *There are no big film equipment trucks on the road, not with all the filming suspended for police questioning.*

Then she saw a familiar SUV pulling up ahead of her. Kevin Shepard's big black behemoth was hard to miss. Liza often teased him that it looked like a cross between a tank and an aircraft carrier.

"What are you going to do with that thing when gas prices go up again?" she called as he leaned out the window to wave.

"I was thinking of raising a mast and adding some sails."

Now across the street, Liza poked her head in the passenger side window. "You could find something a little less expensive to run."

"Sure. Heck, I could kayak across the bay from Killamook." Kevin's bantering tone got a bit darker. "Although God knows what I'd have seen if I tried that today. Stumbling over bodies is getting to be a bad habit with you."

Liza shrugged. "Just lucky, I guess."

"Are you going to put yourself in the middle of this one, too? From what I hear, this Chissel guy deserved everything he got."

"Look, I didn't ask to find Oliver Chissel, any more than I asked to find poor Derrick. I can't say I'm crying any tears over Ollie the Chiseler, either. But we've got friends involved, and they're questioning me as well. And I'm not the only one they're talking to. The cops are already looking at Michelle and Michael —"

Kevin looked less than broken up about that.

"They'll be after Jenny, too — not to mention some of your guests, like Guy Morton and Lloyd Olbrich."

"That's how I found out about all of this,"

Kevin said sourly. "Curt Walters called me at the office, trying to see if we could help him pin down everyone's comings and goings."

"You don't sound too enthusiastic about that."

His look got more sour. "I'm not. At the inn, we expect our guests to exercise discretion — and they expect the same from us."

Liza tilted her head a little. "Meaning?"

"We try not to pry — unless we see a guest bringing in something like a goat, or the makings of a bonfire —"

"Or hookers from one of the less select resort towns?" Liza suggested.

"That's not funny, Liza. There's a lot of stuff they don't discuss in classes about hospitality management. Like suicides."

Liza blinked. "What?"

"Not everybody decides to take a swan dive off a cliff," Kevin said grimly. "Some decide to pop off in a nice place. They check in, have a good dinner, go upstairs, and off themselves. It's not so nice for the housekeeping staff. And it doesn't help the reputation of the inn if guests see the old guy in room twenty-three coming out in a body bag."

"This was hardly a suicide. And it didn't happen at your hotel. Besides, I figure if you know where your guests are and can keep them off the sheriff's list, it would be a big plus for the inn. You can't give anybody an alibi?" Liza pressed, thinking of Jenny.

"The best tools Sheriff Clements has to pin down the time of the crime are the local tide tables," Kevin replied. "And that can't tell him when Chissel got planted. The whole thing happened at night, probably late at night. We can't vouch for anybody — certainly not for the entire night."

Liza watched Kevin closely, teased by a hint of something worrisome in the back of his voice. The last time she'd heard that tone was in high school, when he'd broken a date supposedly for a special team practice. Kevin had just neglected to tell her what they were practicing for — maybe frat parties? It had turned out to be a night out with the boys.

"If you can't alibi anybody, don't you have someone you'd like to nominate for Pest Exterminator of the Year?"

That flash of discomfort grew a little stronger in Kevin's eyes. "Did you ever watch that old show with Guy Morton?"

"*Masked Justice*?" Liza nodded. "Sure. I missed the full run when I was a kid, but I saw it again on Nick at Nite."

"Have you seen *all* of them?" Kevin leaned

across the center console toward the window where Liza peeked in.

"Well, I'm working two jobs, and that time of night is usually when I really get going with sudoku. So I've probably missed my share of the episodes. Why?"

"I'm guessing you missed the one where that Masked Justice guy catches a member of this kidnapping gang. He needs to find out where the crooks are holding this kid, but his guy won't talk. So the masked man takes the baddie out to the beach and plants him up to his neck — with the tide coming in. The guy holds out until the water is actually sloshing in his mouth, but he finally talks. Masked Justice digs the guy out and goes off to the rescue."

"Are you saying you think Guy did this?" Liza asked.

Kevin shrugged uncomfortably. "Hey, I like Guy Morton. But everybody knows he hated Oliver Chissel."

"Yeah. Especially after he mentioned it several times on *Evening Celebrity News*," Liza said.

"I'm not saying I know anything for certain. But what if Morton decided to take a page from that old script — and changed the end?"

Liza had nothing to say to that. She

looked away. Kevin followed her gaze to the window of Ma's Café, where the short-order cook was working with tape and cardboard to cover a hole in the plate glass, under the watchful eyes of the owner, Liz Sanders.

The original Ma, Ma Burke, had decided to retire in the wake of the Robbins murder/kidnapping. But she'd left the café in the capable hands of her younger sister. Liz turned out to be a younger, smaller version of Ma, definitely just as feisty. And she could cook better.

A definite win for the little town.

"Dunno why the hell they couldn't have put a hole in the window of that latte palace down the street," she growled. "If I catch the peckerwood who did this . . ."

Liza glanced up at Kevin. "Have you ever had trouble with people trying to mess up your place? I mean, a lot of this area is still pretty blue collar. I figure a fancy-schmantzy inn would be a fairly ripe target for the more, uh, unreconstructed locals."

"Or is that yokels?" Kevin laughed. "Sure, I had one teenager trying out the old 'boys will be jackasses' thing. He pulled a drive-by in our parking area with a paintball gun."

"What did you do?"

"I invested in one of those gadgets for myself, and waited till the little turd showed up again. I covered his windshield, gave his pickup a new color scheme, and unloaded the rest of my magazine on the kid's butt." His grin had a little bit of the wolf in it. "The velocity of a paintball is about a tenth of a rifle slug, but it still stings when it hits."

Liza shook her head. "Typical. You sound like all those Chuck Norris jokes I keep hearing."

Kevin laughed. "You mean, 'Before the boogeyman goes to sleep, he checks that Chuck Norris isn't under the bed'?"

"Nope, the one I was thinking about was, 'Chuck Norris doesn't sleep — he waits.' That sounds like you, lying in bed with a paintball gun, staying up for this jackass."

"I prefer to think of it in terms of Chuck's best movie quote." Kevin deepened his voice. " 'You just messed with the wrong guy.' "

Is that what happened with Chissel? Liza wondered. *Did he mess with the wrong guy?*

"What do you think about Deke Jannsky?" The words were out of her mouth before she really thought about them.

"For what? Messing up Main Street or doing in Oliver Chissel?"

"Either." Liza leaned farther through the window. "Both."

Kevin hesitated for a long moment before

he replied, looking sharply at Liza to make sure she was serious. Finally, he shrugged. "Deke is certainly a major lowlife around town. A lot worse than . . . some people I could name."

Liza nodded sadly, thinking of the ne'er-do-well friend they'd lost the last time major crime had touched Maiden's Bay.

"That said — I dunno. Deke would have to have a pretty big mad on to start wrecking the shopping district. After all, he lives here, too."

"The last time I saw him, he was pretty mad," Liza said. "He got fired from his job as an extra on the film because he wouldn't follow the rules."

She paused for a second, frowning. "In fact, he was acting as if he'd put in a lot of work, and that doesn't happen with extras. Most of the time, they're just sitting around, waiting while the shot is set up."

Her frown got deeper. "Suppose he *had* been working, screwing things up on the set so filming would be delayed and he'd get extra hours?"

"Now that would sound like Deke," Kevin said. "Has there been a lot of sabotage?"

"Chissel made it sound like there was," Liza replied. "All I saw was some impolite graffiti painted on a shed asking the film company, though not in so many words, to leave."

"What color was it?"

She gave him a look. "Glitter pink."

"Too bad," Kevin said. "Not exactly Deke's style. Now, if it had been blue —" He broke off when he saw the look on Liza's face. "I guess you weren't around the time Deke decided to redo his kitchen table and chairs on the cheap and easy. He brought them outside, opened a can of spray paint, and began spritzing away."

Kevin laughed. "Maybe he was hungover, or maybe he was just being Deke. Anyway, he didn't notice that there was a pretty stiff breeze blowing, and very little of the paint was getting on the furniture. By the time he finally got done, he'd barely touched his furniture, but he'd turned most of his lawn a beautiful shade of blue, except for the silhouette of a cheap dinette set in the middle. That lasted a few weeks last summer, and it almost became a tourist attraction."

In spite of her efforts to be serious, Liza found herself chuckling at the mental image. "I guess that story doesn't exactly enhance Deke's stature as a criminal genius. If he'd done the stuff I saw, the graffiti probably would have been blue — I can't see him hoarding pink glitter spray paint."

"Maybe he used that color to throw everybody off the scent," Kevin said.

"Deke? You think he'd plan that far ahead?"

"Oh, Deke does have a bit of animal cunning that helps him through most of his scams," Kevin said. "But he has a nearly terminal case of laziness. In fact, it's the main reason I can't see him running down the street smashing windows."

"But what if he did do it — and Oliver Chissel saw him, the big boss of the company that just fired him — ?"

"You're really piling it on, aren't you?" Kevin interrupted. "Sabotage, vandalism, and now murder — there's a theory that ties up everything in a nice, neat package. Problem is, real life is usually a lot messier than theory."

Liza shrugged and nodded. "Sheriff Clements said pretty much the same thing. But imagine if it happened the way I said . . ."

"Remember, we're talking about Deke Jannsky here," Kevin said. "If they'd found Chissel dumped in an alley with a tire iron stuck in his head, that would seem more like Deke's style. Hell, they'd probably find Deke's fingerprints on the tire iron."

He shook his head. "But we're talking

about considerable thought and effort involved here. I mean, who'd think of using the ocean as a murder weapon? Besides, just figuring out the tides would take more planning than Deke usually puts into his scams."

"Not so much thought," Liza objected. "You just told me, the basic idea for the body on the beach appeared on TV not too long ago."

"Yeah." Kevin dragged out the word, dripping in doubt. "And the magic of TV is that it certainly wouldn't show how much of a job it would really be — hauling the body from Main Street down to the beach, digging a pit in the sand, getting Chissel arranged properly without him trying to fight his way out of there — I'm still wondering how our killer managed that stunt. Besides, digging's more work than Deke would ever do, much less packing the sand back in —"

"The pile driver was right there. Maybe Deke used that to plant Chissel."

Kevin didn't even bother to hide the look of superiority on his face. "For a would-be detective, you've got a lot to learn. You can't get a body — dead or unconscious — to stand up at attention like a wooden piling. And if the killer buried Chissel up to his neck in sand, he had to manage that. It'd be a tough trick, whether Chissel was dead or alive at the time." He shook his head, trying to make the image go away. "I'm hoping, for his sake, he was dead."

"So you think he was dead when his killer buried him?" she asked.

"I can't imagine what it would be like to be alive, watching the tide rise. But in his shoes, I'd have struggled like anything — heck, like my life depended on it. No way a conscious man would go in a hole all neat and tidy like I heard it was. Ugh. I don't want to think about it anymore. I saw enough dead bodies when I served in the army."

"So you think he was dead when he got buried? What about rigor mortis?" Liza said.

"You'll have to pay more attention to those *CSI* shows," Kevin told her. "Rigor can take hours. A very long time in hot weather." That haunted look came back to his eyes. "Almost makes me pity the guy who killed him. Can you imagine spending hours beside a stiffening stiff? More important, can you imagine Deke Jannsky doing that?"

"When you put it that way, no."

He shook his head. "And even if the killer did wait until Chissel was stiff, I don't think the pile driver would work. More than likely it would squish him rather than drive him.

Bodies are pretty fragile."

Liza shuddered a little at that mental image.

"Hey," Kevin said. "You're the one who started this, with your questions. If you don't like the answers, we can stop right now."

"No." She raised her chin, determined not to look squeamish in his eyes. "Maybe the police will find the answer, but it can't hurt for us to ask questions. I don't suppose Sheriff Clements has dealt with many murders in his career."

"You might be surprised," Kevin said. "He started out on the Portland PD. Ended up in homicide before he came here."

"Really?" Then Liza shook her head, determined not to let Kevin distract her from her main point. "All right, the pile driver theory doesn't work. Where does that leave us with Jannsky and Chissel?"

"Just a little less improbable than Chissel being abducted by the saucer people and getting beamed down into the beach." Kevin sounded flippant, but his eyes were serious as he looked at Liza. "Your scenario makes a nice package, but I want you to think for a second: Is Maiden's Bay the kind of place where you find a killer behind every bush? Or should you be looking where Chissel did his business, made his enemies, and screwed people?"

Liza didn't want to answer. Kevin had a point. Maybe Hollywood was pretty far away from the Oregon coast. But there were plenty of Hollywood people here in town — the movie crew, Lloyd Olbrich, Peter Hake, Chissel's assistant, Guy Morton, Michelle, Michael . . . and Jenny.

Chissel wasn't exactly Miss Congeniality back in Tinseltown. She wondered who would show up for his funeral.

Maybe the killer really was an out-of-towner.

Judging from the people stacked up at the police station, Sheriff Clements was pretty sure as to where he'd find his killer.

Not a local among them.

Except for her, of course.

7

"I guess I know better than to ask if we're done here," Kevin said. "You never give up on a challenge, never have. Probably never will. So I'll put it this way — do you have any other theories?"

"No," Liza admitted. "Not now. Not, I guess, till I talk with the people who are down at the police station."

Kevin tapped his hand against the SUV's steering wheel. "This isn't some puzzle for you to solve. Just because you found the body, it doesn't mean that you're involved. We know right from the get-go that this is murder — and that there's someone out there who definitely *doesn't* want to be found."

He didn't hide the concern in his face — or his voice. "Why are you worrying about this one?"

"Because I found him. And the sheriff thinks I might have killed him."

"Not seriously," Kevin said.

"Maybe not," Liza agreed. "But I'm in the middle of it."

"Not like last time," Kevin said. "At least the last time you got involved, you liked the dead guy and there was something to be learned from sudoku scattered into the case. It's different today. Can't you leave this one to the police?"

"The sheriff has his job to do, and that's to put someone — anyone — away," Liza said. "I just want to protect myself and my friends. As for the whole sudoku thing, logic is logic. It doesn't matter whether you're figuring out if the number nine goes in a particular space, or whether a particular person could be in a particular place at a particular time."

"It certainly smells different. I promise you that."

"You've got a point." She grinned and shrugged. "But I'm right about the logic. And judging from the last time, I may be more willing to look into some places that the police wouldn't think of."

"It's your neck on the line," Kevin said. "I sure can't stop you."

"Exactly." Liza looked down at Rusty, still pulling on the leash. "Somebody else has his neck on the line right now. I need to get this pup moving."

She set off up Main Street with Rusty, leaving an unhappy Kevin behind her. Soon she'd reached the tree-shaded residential part of the street. Two turnoffs and she'd almost be home.

"Speaking of puzzles," she told Rusty as they walked along, "I'd better work up a couple more sudoku before I take off work to play detective."

Whatever Rusty thought of that idea, he was more intent on getting home and getting breakfast.

Rusty bounded into the kitchen, eager for his appointment with a can of dog food to be consumed in the square of sunshine coming in through the window. While he chowed down, Liza fired up her computer.

She called up a puzzle she had begun earlier but filed. "Now, what was I thinking when I started this?" she muttered. Soon she was lost in the throes of creation. She used the software to run a check — yes, only one possible solution!

In the groove now, Liza retrieved another puzzle from the computer's memory, but her concentration was shattered by the ringing phone.

She picked it up to hear a shrill "I suppose it didn't actually occur to you that you

			6		4	9		
		3		8	2			
					1		7	4
6	8							
1	2	9				5	3	7
							1	8
3	9		7					
			8	1		3		
		1	3		5			

work for a newspaper, did it?" Ava Barnes was clearly in a state. Her childhood friend and boss at the *Oregon Daily* sounded torn between amusement and aggravation.

"What do you mean? I write sudoku. And I just got home from talking with the police," Liza said.

"I run a newspaper. You work for me. So you should call me when you see news. Finding a dead guy up to his neck in sand on our beach definitely qualifies."

"Ava, you know the *Daily* is a morning paper — today's copies were already on trucks being delivered when I found Oliver Chissel. Besides, you bribe every dispatcher in the department with weekly donuts to keep you up on the gossip. You knew almost as soon as I did. And you always tell me no paper does extra editions anymore."

"You could have called in and had me tell you again," Ava said. "At least tell me you haven't talked to any of those TV vultures. We can run a great first-person piece for tomorrow —"

"Sorry. Sheriff Clements asked me not to talk to anybody," Liza said.

That brought the usual flood of newsperson's arguments from her managing editor, which Liza tried to deflect. She'd had enough practice the last time she found a body to be getting good at it. "Change of subject — have you got anything about the windows on Main Street being smashed?"

"Nothing. We've been asking around, but so far the theories include drunks, kids, and drunk kids from out of town."

"Do you think it could tie in with the sabotage on the movie that Chissel was complaining about?" Liza asked.

"Huh." That got her a moment's silence. "Maybe. I had Murph talk to the movie crew." Murph was one of Ava's best local reporters.

"I bet that was pretty easy to do with filming suspended."

"Yeah, but it didn't get me very far," Ava said. "Besides the graffiti, most of the dam-

105

age was annoying but not very technical. Cameras messed with, stuff out of place. Could have been internal, or it could have been local. Repairing things on a fishing boat would teach someone enough to disre-pair the film equipment."

Ava sighed. "Lot of people around town these days are good with their hands and don't have a lot of work."

"So, if you had a job as an extra, say, and wanted the gravy train to hang around a little longer," Liza began, "would you mess with petty vandalism to keep the film crew around longer?"

"That might make sense, but I don't see how it necessarily ties in with the current sabotage — unless they were planning to film a big scene on Main Street," Ava cut her off. "It certainly doesn't tie in with today's bigger local story, where you were an eyewitness. So when can you talk to the paper about what you found?"

"I'll talk to the sheriff and see what he says," Liza promised. "Meantime, maybe he'd appreciate a little help from a profes-sional publicist."

Clements had already lived through one media circus generated by a high-profile, Hollywood-related murder case. And that case had already been solved. Liza was willing to bet the guy certainly wasn't looking forward to daily press briefings for newspaper reporters from all over, local and network TV crews, and what Liza had already heard him call "the scumsuckers" — the tabloid press and television people eager for some scrap of celebrity dirt.

"Just make sure you get the okay for a story —" The call-waiting tone cut in on Ava's orders. Liza begged off, hit the flash button, and heard an equally ornery voice.

"I'd have expected you to be down here by now, ready to help us get out." Michelle Markson was definitely not in a good mood. "The media is assembling, and there are too many familiar faces out there already."

"Working on it."

"Work faster then."

"I'm on my way." Liza hung up on Michelle, said good-bye to Ava, and explained that she had to head back down to City Hall.

"I still want that story," Ava insisted.

"I'll do what I can." Liza hung up, shook her head at the unfinished puzzle on her computer screen, then looked down at the disreputable sweats she was wearing and shook her head again. No time to change.

She let Rusty out into the backyard and grabbed her purse.

Traffic on Main Street was backed up almost to her neighborhood.

Sure, there's probably a battalion of television vans parked outside City Hall already, Liza thought. She took a circuitous route that brought her around the rear of the civic building, taking the side entrance that led to the mayor's office. As she passed through the central lobby, Liza got a rear view of Sheriff Clements standing on the front steps, addressing the assembled media.

"Not the time to ask about Ava's article," Liza murmured to herself as she entered the police side of the building.

The same deputy as earlier manned the front desk, but the benches were empty. However, a knot of people stood gathered in a corner out of the direct view from any door.

"Finally!" Michelle Markson growled. She stood at Jenny's left elbow, while Michael stood at the right. From behind them emerged Alvin Hunzinger.

Alvin had been bestowed the title "lawyer to the stars" due to his usually successful representation of Hollywood's finest in various drunken misdemeanors and felony assaults, not to mention the occasional wrongful death or murder. Michelle had dispatched him to Santa Barbara when Liza had discovered Derrick Robbins's dead body hanging head-down from a tree.

This time around, Liza had thought her partner was taking things more in stride. But clearly that wasn't Michelle's way. She didn't merely subscribe to the old Boy Scout motto, "Be prepared." She operated more on the maxim, "In trying situations, always have overwhelming offensive fire-power on hand at all times. And don't be afraid to use it."

Apparently, Michelle's call had dragged Alvin off the golf course.

That was the only reason that Liza could think of to explain what he was wearing. Now, it was easy enough to discount Alvin's legal smarts due to his laughably Elmer Fudd-like face and physique. But Alvin in golf clothes . . . Liza had to strangle back a guffaw. A mere smile wouldn't cover it.

The man was wearing seersucker plaid pants in every shade of the rainbow, colors so loud that the glow could probably be seen from outer space. He'd matched the pants with a pair of white leather golf shoes, pinholed and wing tipped with a little leather kilt covering the laces. The matching belt cinched in an Easter-chick yellow polo shirt. To complete the ensemble, he wore a floppy hat with a tassel in still more of the plaid. The last time golf fashion had ever taken such a hit, Rodney Dangerfield had been filming *Caddyshack.*

Michelle, however, found very little to laugh about. "You could have given us a little more warning from the get-go," she accused.

"I called you right after I spoke to the police — something I wasn't supposed to do."

Michelle's glare indicated complete agreement. But Liza knew it wasn't because her boss wanted matters kept quiet like the nice police officer requested. No, Michelle thought Liza was *supposed* to call her first, even before she called the police.

"I barely had time to confer with our client before the deputies arrived. And since she declined to listen to any advice —"

"I don't *need* a lawyer!" From Jenny's tone of voice, this was just another chapter in a continuing debate. "I didn't see Chissel since I left the set with you guys."

"And can you prove that?" Michelle challenged. "What did you do after we got back to the inn?"

Jenny shrugged. "We all had supper and watched *Evening Celebrity News.* Then I went back to my cabin and hit my script. There were new lines to learn, thanks to the hack writers Lloyd Olbrich brought in." Her lips twisted in momentary disgust. "After that, I turned in. When you have to get up before the sun does, that's generally a good plan."

"And that's what you told the police?" Alvin Hunzinger interjected.

"Yes. And I signed a statement to that effect." Jenny glanced over at Liza. "It's the truth. I've got nothing to hide. I'll tell you this, though. Sheriff Clements wasn't a big old teddy bear like the last time I saw him. More like a growly one."

"I noticed the same thing," Liza said.

"So the police have your statement, and they'll go to work trying to disprove it," Hunzinger said. "And if they can challenge you on any part of it, they'll be all over you."

"But I told them the truth," Jenny insisted, "so I didn't need a lawyer."

A shocked Hunzinger looked ready to argue that case, but by now Michelle definitely had enough. "What's done is done. I'm sorry I called you up here for nothing, Alvin."

She doesn't sound all that sorry, Liza thought.

"It wasn't really too much of a problem for you, was it?" Michelle concluded.

For an instant, Liza thought the lawyer

111

might actually give an honest answer. Michelle was a petite, pixie type, and there wasn't much difference in their heights. On the other hand, Michelle was also the warrior queen of Hollywood publicity, the woman who knew where too many bodies were buried.

Alvin reverted to Elmer Fudd at his most craven. "Of — of course not," he said faintly.

Just an hour or two on his firm's jet — and a lost tee time. No problem at all. Liza tactfully kept her mouth shut.

But Michelle wasn't finished with the lumpy lawyer. "There is one more thing you can do for us." She glanced at Liza. "I expect you found a less public way in — and out — of here?"

Liza nodded. "I'm parked at the back of the building, an easy run from a less-used side entrance."

"Good." Michelle began giving her people orders the way a general might deploy troops for the big attack. The hapless Alvin got the job of being a diversion. Michelle sent him out the front door in his golfing clown suit. Even through the walls of the building, they could hear the roar of aroused media. It sounded something like a block-long, mile-wide, hungry beast.

While they were busily feasting on the

little lawyer, Liza led the others across the building, out the side door, and into her car.

Michelle, of course, took the front seat. "Not bad," she said, "except *I* had to call you. Really, Liza, you should have been more proactive. We were pretty well trapped there, without transportation, and with that wolf pack outside."

"Guess I've been more reactive today," Liza replied. "I'm a little scattered. Funny how that happens after I start the day by nearly tripping over a dead man's head."

She heard a gulping noise come from Jenny in the backseat, and fixed her partner with a warning look. If they needed to argue, they could do so later, without their young client around. Apparently, Michelle agreed, because she subsided.

"So, where to?" Liza asked aloud. "Back to Killamook?"

Michelle shook her head. "The place will be crawling with reporters by now, and we still have some things to discuss" — here she glanced at Jenny — "before we talk to the media."

Liza thought of her place. It would do for a meeting, she decided, then she thought of the cramped living room, the sagging couch — the empty refrigerator. "I don't know about you guys, but I'm starving," she said. "Suppose we go someplace to eat and talk?"

"I hope you're not thinking of that café up the street," Michelle replied. "I've been there, regrettably. So has the news media."

"Nah, this place is out of town." Liza swung round to avoid the massed media around the City Hall and got onto the coastal highway. The harbor area flew by, and then they were paralleling the coast of the bay.

Jenny stared out the window at the beach, her face a little green. "Is this where you found him?"

"Ahh, why do you ask?" Liza hadn't thought of that when she'd chosen her route. But apparently, Sheriff Clements had been busy. The crime scene wasn't just marked off with tape; it was covered by a large tent. With the crowd of people working the scene, it looked like the circus had come to town.

"Nothing to see," Liza murmured as they continued past. Would they have dug Chissel out of the packed sand by now? Or would the crime scene people still be picking around the area, looking for clues?

Michael seemed to read her mind — perhaps the prerogative of an almost ex-husband. "They won't have all that long to work. The tide has to be coming back sooner or later." His writer's imagination seemed to kick in. "In fact, it may have wiped away any evidence when it came in the first time."

"Interesting," Michelle rapped out, "but not germane to our situation." She then proceeded to drill Jenny in the techniques of being as charming as possible while saying absolutely nothing.

"If you need to, don't hesitate to blame the police." She finished. "Tell them the sheriff told you not to say anything."

"But he did," Jenny said.

"So you'll be telling them the absolute truth. I like that in the right circumstances." Michelle's stomach made a low, growling noise.

She directed a look at it that would — and had — turn Hollywood veterans to jelly.

Her stomach unconcernedly rumbled again.

"Would this restaurant happen to be in Vancouver?" Michelle asked.

"The proper question is, 'Are we there yet?' " Liza told her. "And the answer would be, 'It's the next exit.' "

Michelle cast a dubious look at the weather-beaten building not too far from the beach. "It's a —"

"Divey-looking place," Liza finished for her. "Appearances are deceiving. They make great clams, which, oddly enough, you don't find along this stretch of the coast. And don't worry, Michelle. The plates probably won't match, but they'll be clean."

8

Liza led the way into the restaurant. Delicious smells greeted them as they came through the doors. Michelle sniffed appreciatively. "Maybe I was too quick to criticize," she said.

"Boy, she *must* be hungry," Jenny muttered.

They sat down at a linoleum-topped table. "How are the clams?" Liza called over to the waitress.

"Good as ever," the woman replied.

"That's good enough for me," Liza said.

"Me, too," Michael added. Jenny and Michelle decided on the same, too — along with beers.

When the waitress returned with their orders, Michael laughed. "You called it, Liza."

"About the food or the plates?" she kidded back. None of the tableware on the tray matched. But what arrived on them only added to the delicious smells in the place.

Silence fell over the table as everyone attacked the food. At last, Michelle sat back with a sigh, taking another sip of beer. "So, do you intend to get to the bottom of this whole situation with Chissel?" she asked.

"You make it sound like a new service from Markson Associates," Liza complained, "like that crisis management group you brought in for clients in serious trouble."

"You didn't call them in for me," Jenny said. "Does that mean I'm not in trouble?"

"Not yet," Michelle replied. "The crisis management people are supposed to spin things when you're arraigned — or convicted."

That shut Jenny up.

Michelle turned back to Liza. "Well, are you going to look into this or not?" she reiterated.

"Like you have to ask." Michael shook his head, further tousling his too long, curly hair. He tended to forget about getting it cut unless he was nagged. Since he and Liza had split up, apparently no one was around to nag him.

"I think people might talk to me differently than they'd talk to the police," Liza said.

"They'll tell you to buzz off a hell of a lot quicker," Michael pointed out.

"Since your last case, I've been talking with Buck about your investigating things."

"My last case?" Liza said. "You make me sound like Nancy Drew."

"And as a professional PI, not to mention a former cop, I bet Buck Foreman was delighted at the idea of an amateur sleuth," Michael put in.

"But Liza did find out who killed Uncle D., not to mention stopping that crazy plot — and saving me," Jenny said.

"Well, I'm not thinking of turning into Nancy Drew." Liza smiled.

"But it wouldn't hurt to think about how investigations are done," Michelle insisted. "I read a lot of mysteries. The key to solving a case is MOM."

"It's an acronym," Michelle continued. "It stands for —"

"Motive, opportunity, and means," Liza finished for her. She nodded at Michael. "I spent several years of my life with a writer who, among other things, did mysteries. Hopefully, I learned something."

Michelle waved that away. "Fine. Going on that formula, I think we can throw motive out the window. Chissel had at least two communities where most of the people

119

hated him — here in Maiden's Bay, and in The Business."

"Not to mention all the businesspeople — with a small B — that he screwed over with his financial dealings," Michael pointed out.

Michelle plowed on. "As for means, well, that looks like something out of a bad pirate movie."

"Or an old TV show."

"Interesting, but irrelevant." Michelle rode over Liza's voice. "What I'm trying to say — in spite of the interruptions — is that opportunity is the way to go. Why did Chissel get killed in this small town?"

"Because he came here?" Michael deadpanned.

"That's not as funny as you imagine," Michelle said. "Coming here, Chissel stepped out from behind his usual defenses. Think about it. If you wanted to come after him in L.A., you'd have to get past his house staff or a million and three assistants at his office."

"Out here, he only had Hake," Liza said slowly. She turned to Michelle. "You said Hake was a pretty bad guy. How bad?"

"Why do you ask?"

"Well, you also said that Chissel's finances were pretty dodgy. Suppose Hake decided that the golden goose wasn't going to be coughing up any more eggs — and wanted to get what he could in an early retirement?"

Michelle's face closed down for a moment as she pondered Liza's words. Then she was back, as vivid as ever. "Nice idea. I've already got Buck looking into Chissel's dealings. He can also get background on Hake — and check to see if anyone interesting flew up to these parts in the last few days."

Silence fell over the table for a moment. Then Michael asked, "When Michelle talked about means of death, you mentioned an old TV show. Why?"

Reluctantly, Liza explained about the interrogation scene from the episode of *Masked Justice.*

"I loved that show." Michael deepened his voice, reciting the voice-over from the show's intro. "Justice may be blind — but I wear a mask."

Jenny, though, jumped right to the heart of the matter. "You can't think that Guy Morton killed Chissel." She almost rose from her chair, her face coloring. "That's ridiculous!"

"Speak of the devil," Michael murmured as the restaurant door swung open and in walked Guy Morton himself.

He halted for a second, taking in the group, then gave them a genial grin. "And here I thought I had this discovery to myself."

"We had a native guide," Jenny said, smiling up at him. "You met Liza yesterday."

"Certainly," Morton said with a nod. "Liza Kelly. And everyone in The Business knows Michelle Markson." He grinned over at Michael. "How you doin', Mike?"

"Guy and I worked together on some epic that went direct to DVD," Michael said. "I can't even remember the name of it."

The older man laughed. "Come to think of it, neither can I."

"Why don't you join us?" Liza invited.

That got her a challenging look from Jenny. "Yeah, we were just discussing whether you killed Oliver Chissel."

"Were you deciding whether to give me a medal?" Morton asked.

"If you'd done it, I guess it slipped your mind when you were talking to the cops," Michael said.

Morton shrugged. "Well, you know, the years add up, you start to forget things . . ."

"This isn't something to joke about!" Jenny's voice took on a shrill note.

"It's not something to get all upset about, either." Guy Morton took Jenny's hand, and his authoritative manner of a second before softened. "It distracts you from your work — and it gives that skinny turd Olbrich a lever to use against you."

This guy is a professional to his fingertips, Liza thought. *Working one film with him will teach Jenny things that years of classes couldn't. And he seems genuinely fond of her.*

Jenny smiled. "And don't go pulling that old crock act. Guy is pretty damn sharp. When we run lines together from the script, he's usually the one who's prompting me. I just wish you'd been around last night to go over the new scenes —"

She faltered.

Morton shrugged. "Right now, I wish I had. It would have made my conversation with the cops a little easier."

"We saw you on *Evening Celebrity News,*" Michelle said.

"Yeah, I enjoyed taking a little jab at his high and mightiness." Morton's order arrived, and he took a long pull at his beer. "In fact, I enjoyed it too much. Went out to celebrate with a few drinks too many — not the best idea when you have to take pills to ward off the aches and pains from a misspent youth. Things got kind of blurry. I woke up in yesterday's clothes and had to move right quick to get on the set by call time."

His habitual grin broadened as he took in the expressions around him. "Not the best alibi you've ever heard, is it?"

"You don't remember?" Jenny said in a little voice.

"I expect that if I killed Chissel, it would have concentrated my memory some," Guy replied. "And I expect I'd be hurting a lot worse, even with my pills. Chissel was a big, fat windbag, and there was as much fat as wind to him. It would have been quite a bit of exercise, taking his carcass down to the beach and burying him."

He smiled at Jenny. "Don't get all upset, kid. If the cops had any real reason to suspect me, I wouldn't have gotten out of that little interrogation room."

The girl subsided, and Guy Morton tucked into his clams. "Now this is good eating," he said. "Even when I was riding high, I wasn't much into that whole 'elegant dining' thing. I'd rather have a decent steak — or a mess of clams — than anything by Wolfgang Puck."

His evident gusto brought a smile to Liza's face. "I can see why Derrick wanted you on this project," she told Guy.

The older man shot a smile at Jenny.

124

"Derrick was a good guy. He got me that job on *Spycraft,* you know. It was a case of stunt casting. They were looking for someone from one of the old-line action shows to play the spy sent back into the cold. Derrick had watched my show when he was a kid and was a fan, so he suggested me. And when we actually worked together, we clicked."

"You wound up doing an entire story arc," Michael said. "That must have paid off nicely."

"More than just the money, although the paychecks were pretty good," Guy responded. "I'd had a long dry spell. It was good to be working again, not to mention having the chance to sorta reinvent myself. You probably wouldn't remember it, but Fred Astaire wound up on a sixties spy show, playing the hero's father. After that he got all sorts of work playing larcenous grandpas."

Guy shrugged. "It's not the sort of stuff that wins awards, but it's work. Kind of a niche career. When Derrick was trying to set up the *Counterfeit* project and asked me to come aboard, I didn't even look at the script. But it's a good part for me."

He nodded toward Jenny. "And working with this one, it's like going back to the sixties when I was starting out. God, I'd do anything to get on a movie set — unload trucks, tote equipment, work tech. I did a lot of stunt work — those were the days when a stunt guy who could also act a bit had a shot. I usually played the hero's tough friend who gets killed in the second reel. Even had one producer looking at me for some Tarzan movies — I looked pretty good with my shirt off in those days."

"What happened?" Jenny asked.

"The project never went through. Then *Masked Justice* came along."

"And the rest was history," Michelle said with an ironic smile.

"Except that after five seasons, I was history, too." Guy gave them a rueful grin. "Guess I got typecast, and there aren't all that many roles that call for the hero to be wearing a mask."

"And later on, the studio didn't even want you wearing the mask," Michael said.

"Oh, you remember that whole ruckus?" Guy laughed out loud. "When I appeared in *People* magazine wearing the mask-shaped shades . . . you wouldn't believe the amount of mail I got. People who remembered the show, telling me how special it was to them, how they were behind me a hundred and ten percent."

His reminiscent smile grew more malicious. "And then there was the chorus of corporate dipwads at the studio, soiling their imported Armani shorts."

That expression turned to a troubled frown as he glanced over at Jenny. "It's like I keep telling you, never trust any of those studio clowns with your back."

"Would 'studio clowns' include directors?" Michelle wanted to know.

"Terry Hamblyn did a great job on the film, especially with Jenny," Guy Morton said. "As for that slimy bastard Olbrich . . ."

"Enough said." Michelle laughed.

Morton didn't join in. "Hardly," he said, his voice harsh. "Did you ever hear of someone named Jonathan Sanders?"

The people round the table shook their heads.

"He was just a kid. *Masked Justice* was his first job. He played a wisecracking street hustler — the exact opposite of what he was in real life." Morton looked around. "You come across people like that in The Business. They're quiet — shy, even — until you put a script in their hands. Then they literally become another person. That's what Jonny was like. When *Masked Justice* wrapped, he had a shot at the big time, an artsy little film directed by an up-and-coming director — Lloyd Olbrich."

Why do I think this won't have a happy ending? Liza asked herself.

"The film was a critical success, although not much of a moneymaker," Guy went on. "Olbrich made his bones — the reviewers all raved about Jonny's performance. But the mind games Olbrich played on him to get that performance put the kid in the booby hatch —"

"And he never acted again," Michelle finished for him. "The story has been around for years, but I forgot the name. Another bit of Hollywood trivia."

"And a kid's whole life trivialized," Morton added.

Michelle's raised eyebrows might as well have been semaphoring the letters M-O-T-I-V-E.

Yeah, it's a really solid motive, Liza thought, *but for murdering Olbrich, not Chissel.*

"Sounds as though you wouldn't mind messing up Mr. Olbrich's directing work," Michael said.

Morton laughed. "Are you talking about the sabotage on the set?"

Michael just shrugged. "You also talked about doing tech work when you started out in The Business."

"Very good!" Guy Morton slapped a hand

on the linoleum tabletop, laughing out loud. "The only problem with that theory is that the sabotage leaves me stuck dealing with the bastard even longer."

9

Guy Morton's blunt comment pretty much set the meal stumbling to an end. Liza ferried Michelle and Jenny back to the Killamook Inn.

"I'll just be getting my car," Michelle said. "A quick checkout, and then I'll be heading back to L.A." Her eyes hinted at the numerous things she planned to chase down once she got back to the office. Liza figured her boss would have most of Hollywood trembling before the sun set tomorrow.

"The sheriff didn't tell you to stay in town?" Jenny burst out, surprised. "That's what he told me."

"No, he didn't. But then," Michelle said, "I didn't open my mouth and flame a murder victim the afternoon before he died — in front of witnesses."

Jenny nearly ducked, as if the words that Michelle had flung at her were physical weapons, not merely an observation by a notoriously sharp-tongued woman.

As usual, Liza picked up the pieces.

"It's all right, Jenny," she said. "It's just standard police procedure. I went through it when I was dealing with your uncle's death. The police will find out who really did this, and everything will be fine." She glared at Michelle where Jenny couldn't see it. "Right, Michelle?"

"Right," Michelle said, but Liza could see that her boss didn't believe in letting things work their way to a natural conclusion. "Make it so," she told Liza, before stalking off to organize her exit from the hotel.

Liza figured that she wasn't the only person in the car who heard that as a threat.

"Thanks," Jenny said to Liza. "It helps to have you on my side."

"Just keep your mind on your work. We'll get through this."

After Jenny got out and headed into the inn's grand, if rustic, entrance, Liza turned to her remaining passenger. "Aren't you heading back to civilization with Michelle?"

Michael got out of the back and came round to take the passenger's seat. "I'm thinking of spending a little more time up here. No projects to worry about right now — maybe I'll take a minivacation."

"I might believe that if you were staying

here." Liza waved a hand to take in the main building, the cabins, the tennis court, pool, and other amenities. "But in Mrs. Halvorsen's spare room? The house is overheated, and that room in particular is so stuffy, I'm surprised you can breathe."

He shrugged. "Older folks like to keep things warm. And it's not been so bad, once I got the window open."

Probably cracking half a generation's worth of paint, and maybe your back, in the process, Liza thought. She was so engrossed with the image of Michael struggling with a stubborn casement that she almost missed what he said next.

"Best of all, I like the view."

For a second, she shifted her eyes from the road to glare at him. "Oh, yeah, scenic Hackleberry Avenue. Across the street is a big spruce that blocks everything in that direction. If you stick your head out and work at it, I guess you can see my driveway —" She stopped. "You're talking about looking at my bedroom, aren't you?"

"What do you think I am, some kind of perv?" Michael managed to sound honestly offended. "I just like seeing all the country greenery. It's beautiful up here. Speaking of which, maybe you could direct me someplace where I could hire or borrow a car. I wouldn't want to keep imposing on your generosity."

Some days I think you've been doing that for years, she thought. *Nothing like a marriage to invite that.*

"There's a car rental agency in downtown Killamook," she said aloud. "Want to go there right now?"

After dropping Michael at the car rental place, Liza drove home alone.

As she went along the coast, Liza found herself passing the crime scene again. The tent was still in place, but the beach looked empty. *No work going on,* she thought, *either on the film or the pile driving. Ray Massini must be delighted.*

She remembered the eyewitness account she was supposed to write for Ava. Well, there were still hours before the paper's deadline. Liza came home to a friendly welcome from Rusty. After checking his food and water bowls, she sat at her computer and began typing. Liza kept it short and sweet — just the facts as she recalled them, and even there she was economical. "No need to mention corporate shenanigans or dissension on the movie set," she told herself.

When she finished, she ran the story

through spell-check and then eyeballed it on the screen, looking for typos the computer might have skipped over. Ever since she'd written the immortal line "There are *faucets* to sudoku that even experts struggle with," when she'd meant to type the word *facets,* she'd learned the hard way to take that extra last-minute go-through of her work quite seriously. It wasn't too bad this time. Just one *his* that came out as *is.* That was a quick fix. Then she saved the story to her backup computer and a floppy disk and printed it out. Armed with the copies, paper and electronic, she set off for downtown again.

The swarm of news vans had deserted City Hall. This time Liza had no problem walking into the police side of the building. The proper thing to do would have been to call Sheriff Clements, but that would have allowed him to dismiss the idea of the story without even seeing it.

Coming in to see Clements, on the pretext of having him review the finished work, presented him with a fait accompli — or as Michael jokingly put it on a similar occasion, "a fat accomplice."

It worked. The duty deputy let Liza in to see Clements, he read over the article, and then he gave his okay.

"Nothing in here to compromise our investigation," he said. "No commentary or speculation — I'm not sure about your future as a journalist, Ms. Kelly." He gave her a look that was almost friendly.

"My nose for news prefers things logical and factually supported. That's why I wound up doing the sudoku column, I guess," she joked in reply.

The sheriff looked at her with interest. "I'd imagine that after your recent experiences, you might have a theory about Oliver Chissel's death."

"Of course. In fact, the problem is, I've got too many theories," Liza said. "The most interesting one came from my partner Michelle. She pointed out that this could have been a major crime of opportunity for somebody from Tinseltown with an axe to grind. Or a body to bury — under the circumstances that's probably a better metaphor."

He snorted, and motioned for her to continue.

"Coming here, Chissel had moved out from behind his usual defenses. No gated community. No bodyguards at every point of entry. No cameras taking background shots of the building exteriors twenty-four/ seven. He was vulnerable here in a way that he wasn't back in the city. I thought she might have a point. She's checking into it. She intends to see if anybody with a grudge against Chissel was on any flights in this direction from Los Angeles."

"Tell her to call me if she comes up with anything. I'd had a similar notion. I've already got a deputy on that, but she'd know the lay of the land back in L.A. considerably better than one of my boys," Clements said. "I like the theory just because it would be very nice to imagine that Chissel's killer came from somewhere outside of my turf. But it will take more than just checking flights to prove it. We'll have to check strangers in cars and passing boats or yachts — in our copious spare time. Which is getting steadily less copious, thanks to all your film people and their problems. I should get back to work."

He opened the door of the office/interrogation room where he'd been going over papers. As Liza stepped into the hallway outside, she paused for a moment. "About the broken windows on Main Street. Have you considered Deke Jannsky?"

"Jannsky was one of the first people we talked with," Clements replied. "Although, he has an alibi — of sorts. Deke was drinking with a buddy. His buddy agrees.

Though, considering the amounts of hootch consumed, it's not exactly an ironclad alibi. Deke's pal could have blacked out and not even been aware of it."

"Jannsky was pretty furious when he got fired from the film," Liza said.

"Deke Jannsky? Is he considered a suspect for the murder?" a voice cut in. They turned to see Ray Massini coming down the corridor. He wore another good suit, but severe harassment showed through the bare spots in his air of command.

"He was being nominated for the vandalism on Main Street," Clements told the mayor, "but I don't think he's a contender."

"Well, I'm glad to see you've been talking with a professional publicist like Ms. Kelly," Massini said. "You could use the pointers. Several media people got in touch with me. They were less than impressed with the briefing you arranged."

"Give it a rest, Ray. I'm sure they'd love it if we could arrange a shoot-out and nab the killer in front of their cameras," Clements replied. "I don't think it's likely, though."

"I also hear that you intend to use a young female deputy to conduct tomorrow's briefing."

"Brenna Ross is smart, articulate, and she's a lot more tactful than I am with bull

—" The sheriff glanced over at Liza, coughed, and changed direction. "Bull-oney questions, especially from the gossip columnists masquerading as journalists."

"I still think that you should be present —"

"Unlike some police chiefs, I'm not in love with seeing myself on TV, nor do I see the need to prance in front of the cameras for political purposes," the sheriff said. "I need to catch the killer."

"The public has a right —" Ray started to say, but the sheriff cut him off.

"Oh, is this the famous 'right to know' speech?" Clements asked. "How about the department's responsibility to conduct an investigation? That may include keeping details of the case secret just to rule out all the cranks and wackos calling in with misinformation." He shook his head. "Not that we've got much in the way of details to conceal yet."

The mayor was definitely not happy. "Sheriff," he said, "the people expect transparency from this administration."

"Especially the media people." Clements gave Massini a long look. "And that's an interesting attitude to take — considering that you haven't been exactly forthcoming with your own movements after your run-in

138

with Chissel last night."

Massini glared, speechless. Liza took that as an excellent cue to run away. Obviously both men had forgotten she was even there.

She tiptoed out of the office before either man even noticed she was gone and walked back to her car.

She drove out of town, to the satellite office of the *Oregon Daily* — a pretty grand title for a fairly cramped organization shoehorned into a second-floor office at a strip mall.

Ava Barnes greedily seized the disk with Liza's story and fed it into her computer. "Not bad," she said, reading the piece over. "Maybe it could use a little pizzazz —"

"I think you should save that for the editorial page," Liza told her boss.

"What, you don't like wild speculation in large type? What kind of newspaper professional are you?" Ava reverted to managing editor mode. "Now, what about your column? We only have a couple days' worth of material in the can. You've got to start building your cushion back up, Liza."

"I know," Liza said. "I'm working on it."

"Don't let this mess distract you," Ava cautioned, gesturing toward the story on her screen. "We're on the verge of getting your column syndicated. Papers from Arizona to Connecticut are seriously considering it." She scratched her head. "You may not know how serious that interest is. It's a shame you couldn't come to the convention in New York and see firsthand the way that people were lining up for it. You're an attractive young woman —"

"You left out articulate," Liza told her. "Although most conventioneers would probably be more interested in my cleavage than my conversation."

"Don't laugh it off," Ava insisted. "If we pull this off, it will be a big deal for you, not just for your status in — what do you call it? Sudoku Nation — but financially as well."

"I could use a little cushion there, too," Liza admitted.

"Who couldn't?" Ava said, then made shooing gestures. "So go! Work!"

"I'm going, I'm going." Liza headed for the door of Ava's glass-bowl office. But she hesitated for a moment. "One more thing. What can you tell me about Ray Massini?" she asked.

Ava looked at her with raised eyebrows.

"I met him yesterday for the first time in almost twenty years," Liza responded to the unspoken question. "Just now, when I was over at the sheriff's office, Massini was crabbing at Clements. I was just wondering what kind a guy Ray had grown up to be."

"Successful," Ava replied. "I suppose you could even say dynamic. Ray came back from the army after Desert Storm as a war hero — killed a bunch of Republican Guardsmen with his bare hands or something. Everyone was surprised when he took a job at Tuttle's Insurance. The agency was on its last legs, but Ray completely turned it around. When old man Tuttle retired, Ray bought him out. Massini Insurance is one of the town's success stories."

" 'Dynamic,' huh?" Liza had noticed the slight flush on her friend's face. "And just in the insurance business?"

"He also pretty much rolled through the female population of the county," Ava admitted, the flush growing deeper. "I went out with him for a while when I was a senior at Coastal University. He had looks, money, a nice car, clothes . . . and, um, he was pretty dynamic."

"I'm surprised you didn't hook him," Liza teased.

"If I'd been thinking about financial security back then, I would have. I made a bad enough choice in husbands." Ava made a face. "But I was smart enough even as a kid to see that Ray had a roving eye. He wound up marrying one of the Enderby girls — a damned good catch for the son of a fisherman."

If there were such things as first families of Maiden's Bay, the Enderbys would be at the top of the list. Oh, some of the Californian newcomers settling here probably had more money. But the land they purchased for their new stately homes probably came from the Enderbys. Much to Pa Enderby's disgust, the last generation of the clan had been all girls. So, except where it was chiseled in stone on various town monuments, the Enderby name was about to become extinct.

Pa Enderby had been extremely vocal on that subject. His wife had been on Valium for decades.

"Ray ran for mayor as the new broom, with the paper's support. The old guard was pretty much under the thumb of the boys from Killamook."

Liza nodded. The business and tourist interests in Killamook had pretty much run the county for as long as she remembered.

"At least Ray is trying to stir up a little life around here," Ava said. "So far he's started some worthwhile things. And he's good for some colorful copy."

So, Ray was colorful, dynamic even . . .

but no match for Oliver Chissel. A local boy who wanted the town to make it big, but his two biggest coups — the boardwalk restoration and bringing the movies to Maiden's Bay — had just about canceled each other out. Chissel had created a lot of financial resentment in town, but the one who might be hurt worst in the long run, and certainly with his peers, was Ray Massini. The mayor could be facing a lot of disappointed voters next year.

"Ray knows how to kill people with his bare hands. He didn't give the sheriff much of an alibi for the night Chissel was killed," Liza said.

"I can see him killing somebody in the heat of battle, but not the guy who is about to bring home the bacon for the town, and not in cold blood. Ray needed Chissel alive and functioning. Besides, I remember Ray as a boy with a gleam in his eyes — for me. I refuse to believe my old college flame is a killer. If you're finished trying to embarrass me, how about going back to work?" Ava said.

Liza did.

She spent the afternoon finishing several puzzles and the evening working up columns around them. *Cushion expanded,* she thought. Feeling tired but virtuous, she staggered off to bed early.

The phone rang around midnight.

Liza had grown up in the belief that late-night calls meant bad news — grandparents dying, car crashes, that sort of thing. That was the primal fear that gripped her heart as she blearily picked up the phone, squeezing out a shaken "Hello?"

"I didn't wake you, did I?"

Liza wasn't sure which was more annoying — Michelle's incredulous voice or the party noises going on behind her.

"What's up, Michelle?" She tried to keep the growl out of her voice.

"Buck just called with an interesting factoid about our friend Peter Hake," Michelle reported. "He picked it up from a financial columnist. It seems that early in his wheeling-dealing career, Hake wound up doing a deal with a regional retailing group — some of the store owners were franchisees who didn't like what Chissel was offering. Mysteriously, the holdouts began having bad things happen to the plate-glass windows of their stores, with what looked like the early makings of a serious fire hazard tossed inside. Arson wasn't ever committed, but the threat of it had the holdouts sweating bullets. Hake was found at the scene of one of these 'accidents' with a hammer, but the store owner wouldn't press charges. The guy who told Buck the story said the old boy broke out into a cold sweat just remembering what happened. The franchisees gave in, and Chissel got what he wanted."

Liza sat up in bed, silently processing what she'd just heard.

"Are you still there?" Michelle demanded.

"Yes," Liza said shortly. "I'll pass this along to Sheriff Clements" — she squinted at the clock — "later this morning." Michelle made speaking noises like a teakettle about to boil, which Liza interpreted correctly from long practice. "No, we can't claim this as proprietary information. Withholding it, if it proves useful, is probably a felony. Besides, the sheriff may have it already. He'd already glommed on to your 'Hollywood insider' theory. We do have computers up here, too. Good-bye, Michelle."

She put the phone in its cradle even as Michelle's protests still erupted into the air from it.

She dropped back to her pillow and closed her eyes.

She hated it when she got dragged out of a sound sleep. It was always so hard to get back into dreamland. When sleep finally came, though, it wasn't restful. First Liza

145

dreamed that Ray Massini had buried Oliver Chissel up to his neck, then turned his head completely around with his bare hands. Next Peter Hake appeared with a huge sledgehammer.

But when he swung it, Chissel's head exploded into a million glittering fragments.

10

Liza felt far from bright-eyed and cheery as she hauled herself out of bed the next morning. In fact, she felt more as though she were nursing a hangover. And she hadn't done a thing to deserve it. Staggering down the stairs, she winced at Rusty's exuberant greeting.

"No run today," she croaked at the dog, fitting the reel-in leash on his collar. She stood in the open doorway and pointed.

"Go over to the bushes, do your business, and come back here."

Rusty did as ordered, although he sent several reproachful looks her way as they went back into the kitchen.

"Empty the dog, fill the dog," Liza grumbled as she put bowls of food and water down.

Rusty gave a cheerful bark of agreement as he dug into his breakfast with abandon.

She turned on the little black-and-white

portable TV on the kitchen counter, hoping that a dose of news would help get her back in sync with the world.

As luck would have it, the interim head of Mirage Productions was explaining how the company would continue on course despite the loss of Oliver Chissel. Everything, he said, was going well for the film. Mirage was doing fine. The conscripted board member looked like a deer caught in the headlights, while his delivery sounded like a kidnapping victim reading the abductors' demands.

Not the most convincing performance I've ever seen, Liza thought. *And I've seen a few of them.*

She opened the refrigerator, whose shelves were still bare. Liza blinked. Had she eaten last night? Sometimes, in the throes of sudoku creation, she tended to forget about such mundane details.

She couldn't remember cooking, much less eating.

"Maybe I feel like crap because I'm really hungry as well as tired," she consoled herself. But her spirits fell again when she discovered that she was out of coffee, too.

"Only one thing to do," she said, climbing the stairway as if it were the final approach to the summit of Everest. "Throw on some clothes and go to Ma's."

Maybe no one at the diner would recognize her if she laid low in one of the back booths.

Liza sat hunched over the remains of eggs and toast, her hair in a ponytail under a baseball cap with the brim pulled down to cover her face. She reached for her coffee cup when her seat jumped as if a level three earthquake had struck. It hadn't. What she'd felt was just the impact of two bodies dropping into the booth behind her.

"Coffee please, Liz," a familiar voice yelled up to the front — Curt Walters. He carried on in a more conversational volume. "Much more, though, and I think my bladder's either going to burst or rust through. I tell you, man, double shifts just aren't fun anymore."

"Were they ever?" an even more familiar voice asked. That was Kevin Shepard — Liza was sure of it. She hunched a little lower, willing them not to notice her looking so awful.

"Says the man who used to pull all-nighters before final exams," Curt scoffed.

"That was one night," Kevin said. "Sound like you'll be pulling a lot more overtime before this case is finished."

"Yeah. Clements is busting everybody's butts," Curt reported. "The state police offered their crime scene and forensics people to help with the case. He's even been trying to push them."

"But you always say that stuff takes time."

"I know that, and he knows that, but the idiot reporters only know what they see on TV shows. There everything's done and the crime is solved in under an hour."

"Minus commercials," Kevin joked.

"The only useful thing they've given us is that when they removed the stiff, the crime scene techs found broken glass all around him."

That was so like the image from Liza's nightmare that she couldn't help gasping.

A second later, she heard Kevin saying, "Liza?"

She turned. Kevin had one knee on his seat, looking over the tall back of the booth at her.

He wasn't smiling, and Curt looked nervous. He probably wouldn't have been talking about the crime scene at all, except that he looked out on his feet — or his seat, actually. Tired people talked too much. It was a truism in TV shows. It probably applied to real life, too.

"What's the big deal?" Liza said, carefully

keeping her voice low. "That beach is probably the burial ground for about a million broken beer bottles."

"Yeah, but glass that's been in sand for any length of time would get etched — scratched and rounded." Curt shook his head. "These pieces were fresh."

He broke off, looking annoyed at himself for blabbing more.

Kevin fixed Liza with a disapproving stare.

"Curt, maybe you'd just better head home and get some sleep," he said. "I'll pay for your coffee."

"I think you're right." Curt got out of the booth. "See you around, Liza."

And if you do, you'll probably be ducking me, Liza thought.

"Bye, Curt," she said aloud.

She took a sip of her coffee, aware of Kevin's eyes still on her. "Broken glass."

She suddenly remembered her joke about Chissel breaking the windows on Main Street and getting taken out by an enraged store owner. Well, Hake had a history of plate-glass vandalism . . .

"You're just going to keep it up." Kevin's voice had a snap to it now.

"You know, this all seems to point to someone here in town — someone opposed to the filming . . . or angry at the filmmak-

151

ers, especially Chissel," Liza said.

"Goddammit, Liza!" Kevin really sounded angry now.

"So who had Chissel gotten angry up here in Maiden's Bay? Well, he's been holding up payment for the extras and the people who rented out their homes and businesses as film locations. Getting hit in the wallet — that's pretty bad."

She looked up at Kevin. "But there's someone with a lot more reasons to be fuming at Oliver Chissel, who put his prestige on the line for the whole film project up here, who was played and bamboozled from the get-go. There were nicer accommodations for most of the film people in Killamook, so the locals didn't participate in that profit stream, their food got trucked in by an out-of-town caterer, so the restaurants in town didn't pick up much business, and now Chissel screws up the boardwalk redevelopment schedule with his additional shooting. The one who's really hurt — the one with the most against Oliver Chissel — is your buddy the mayor."

"Do you know anything about collateral damage?" Kevin almost spat the words. "We saw a lot of it over in Iraq. An artillery shell lands on somebody's house instead of an enemy gun emplacement — that's collateral damage. Civilians run out from a doorway into a firefight — they're called collateral damage."

He leaned over the booth back, glaring down at her. "That's what you're doing, when you play detective around town here. You think it will all turn out well, but innocent people get hurt. It happened last time —"

"You can't say he was exactly innocent," Liza protested.

"Maybe not. But his life was ruined, then ended. You can ruin somebody's life this time, too."

Like I'd rat out poor Curt for working his mouth about something he shouldn't when he could barely keep his eyes open, she thought angrily.

She opened her mouth to say so, but Kevin abruptly turned his back to her, thumping down so heavily the whole booth shook.

He clearly wasn't in the mood to talk anymore.

Liza finished her coffee in silence and went up to pay the check.

Walking along Main Street to City Hall, she tried to sort out the thoughts playing leapfrog through her brain. Images of Chissel smashing windows — or Chissel and

Hake committing the vandalism — danced in her mind's eye. They were really hard to accept. Chissel didn't strike her as the kind of guy to get his hands dirty. Then why had there been broken glass on him?

Suppose he'd tried to *stop* someone from smashing the windows?

Hmm . . . It was at least possible.

Obviously, that didn't work out well, Liza thought. She was just passing Schilling's Pharmacy with the disfiguring plywood still covering half the display windows as Nora Schilling came out the door.

Nora sighed. "It's an eyesore, but we're still not sure whether or when we can get a replacement window up."

Liza's anger at the vandal flared up. These weren't big retail-chain mall stores, where a broken window might represent a fraction of a percent of the bottom line. They were mom-and-pop operations hanging on with their teeth and toenails.

"You'd have to have a sick mind to do something like this," she said.

Nora blinked, as if struck by the thought. "I — I suppose you're right," she said.

As she continued walking down the street, Liza tried to recover her train of thought. Right — Chissel trying to stop the vandal. Her mind immediately threw up a hard-to-dismiss objection. Why would an out-and-out scumball like Chissel stick his neck out — literally, as events proved — to help the Main Street merchants he was screwing over?

Did he hope it would make him some kind of hero? Liza wondered. *Or . . .*

She suddenly envisioned Hake, taking a tactic from their old playbook, smashing the windows. Chissel moves to stop him. An argument ensues, and Chissel ends up stretched out on the pavement.

The only problem was that if this scenario were true, Chissel should be carrying a mark from whatever was breaking the windows. Liza hadn't noticed any.

"Of course, I only saw his head," she told herself. "Maybe the blow that took him down landed somewhere else on his body."

Liza slowed up, realizing she was suddenly surrounded by news vans. "Great time to come down here," she groused, "right in the middle of the daily briefing." Still, she decided to join the rest of the locals checking out the show.

The natives might not be restless, but the newspeople definitely were. At the top of the stairs leading to the City Hall entrance, Brenna Ross looked harassed as annoyed questions bombarded her.

"You can't tell us the cause of death?"

"Is there a reason why the Sheriff's Department is withholding so much information?"

"Doesn't the public have a right to know?"

"The Sheriff's Department is attempting to conduct a thorough investigation as quickly as possible," Brenna replied. "Much information is not available yet. In the meantime we continue working to protect and serve the citizens."

Behind the glass doors of City Hall, Liza made out Ray Massini, his face like a thundercloud.

He ought to be glad he's not the one having to field questions, Liza thought. *Brenna is doing a damn good job with very little ammunition.*

A heavy hand on her shoulder spun Liza around. "You're the bitch that shoved a bug up Massini's shorts about me breaking the windows on Main Street." Deke Jannsky's angry face was almost nose to nose with her. In a weird way, the wash of beer-and-cigarette breath brought Liza back to the days when she was a little kid and her dad came home after a couple of quick ones with his fellow Pacific Bell linemen.

Of course, Dad apparently bathed and brushed his teeth a lot more.

"So stop screwing around with me, or you'll regret it." Jannsky stormed off down the street even as people in the crowd began to turn their way.

Moments later, the briefing ended in mutually insincere good wishes. Liza made her way around to the side entrance. Massini was nowhere to be found as she entered the sheriff's office.

Sheriff Clements leaned back in his chair, his hands behind his head, watching a portable television where two talking heads discussed how terrible it was that his department didn't gush more information.

"So," Clements asked, "come to complain about Deke Jannsky running his mouth at you?"

"I can't believe the cameras caught that." Liza nodded toward the TV. "So I guess you have great sources."

"The mayor's been politicking the DA to get after Deke, and your name leaked out somewhere." Clements sat up straighter. "Since you didn't answer with an immediate 'Yes! Squash him like a bug, Sheriff!' I imagine there's something else you'd like to discuss."

"It's just something my partner passed along — you may have it already." Liza related the story Michelle had told her about Hake's ploy to bolster Chissel's negotiating position with the store franchisees by smashing their display windows.

"Supposedly he was caught near one of those vandalism sites with some sort of tool, but the store owner declined to press charges." She finished. "I wasn't sure if that would actually go into a record somewhere. Anyway, I thought it was something you ought to hear."

"As a matter of fact, we didn't get a hit on that. Can you tell me where this incident took place?" Clements asked.

"Alleged incident, I guess," Liza said. "My partner got it from an investigator friend who got it from a business columnist. I don't know where, but I do know the name of the chain store."

She gave it, and Clements nodded with an odd smile.

"I think it's more than merely 'alleged.' For one thing it explains the odd way Mr. Hake acted when we first questioned him. He was as cool as the proverbial cucumber when we asked him about the death of his boss. But he got a little rattled when we mentioned the store windows being broken."

Clements shook his head. "Not that he broke down in tears or anything. He's talked

158

to too many cops over the years to give much away. But I picked up something, and so did the other people working the inter-rogation. He got very emphatic about being away from Maiden's Bay when the windows would have been broken. He says Chissel sent him out of town on the corporate jet — he had to take care of some sort of important business. He'd have been more convincing if he had actually said what that business was, especially since this alibi also happens to cover the murder."

The sheriff hunched forward with a grunt. "As it is, this is an alibi with a lot of give. Even if he missed the excitement on Main Street, a quick turnaround could have brought him back up here before high tide."

Clements looked more bearlike than ever. Maybe it was the sunken red eyes showing the sleepless hours he'd spent since the body had been discovered. "You know we're already checking departures and arrivals. We're being especially careful regarding Mr. Hake."

■ ■ ■ ■

PART THREE:
BAFFLED?

■ ■ ■ ■

It usually happens after you picked up a few sudoku tricks. You solve some problems, but you have a hard time climbing up the learning curve. When you try solving sudoku rated beyond the level you've mastered, your puzzle-solving machinery seems to break down.

This is not the time to give up — it's time to upgrade your machinery. Most sudoku starters instinctively grasp the basic three moves in the Twelve Techniques for Solving Sudoku — hidden singles, naked pairs, and nominating candidates. It's trickier to recognize Column and Box and Row and Box interactions and possibly eliminate a candidate from several spaces at once. And only practice can sharpen your eyes to spot hidden pairs or triplets, much less X-wings and swordfish.

So, if you hit the sudoku doldrums, try a little theory to enlarge your arsenal of techniques, and then a lot of practice.

And always . . . persevere! Run through your full repertoire of tricks and techniques for every space before admitting you're licked. Sometimes you'll find a way to crack that puzzle wide open!

— Excerpt from *Sudo-cues* by Liza K

11

Leaving the sheriff's office, Liza had that good-news/bad-news feeling. The good news was that Sheriff Clements was at least talking to her as if she were a sane person. He'd thanked her for her information, though obviously he'd check it. After Derrick Robbins's murder, the lead investigator for the Santa Barbara police had treated her like some kind of nut.

The bad news? Well, she had to admit to herself that solving this murder was worse than dealing with diabolical sudoku. Instead of reducing the number of candidates, as accomplished by every successful move in sudoku, her list of candidates for Oliver Chissel's murderer kept expanding.

Even the crime kept expanding. The broken glass found with Chissel's body (which she could never mention unless she wanted to get Curt Walters in trouble) suggested that the murder and the Main Street vandalism were connected.

Liza froze halfway through pushing open the side exit door. Could it be possible that the sabotage, the vandalism, and the murder were also connected?

She got a sudden, vivid flash of Deke Jannsky yelling at her, his red face twisted with fury. Suppose the town's lowlife decided to jack up his extra salary by screwing up the filming of *Counterfeit*. But he screws himself up with bad behavior on the set and gets fired. None of the other citizens of Maiden's Bay back him up. He gets half a load on and goes on a rampage down Main Street. Oliver Chissel sees Deke — maybe he hears him carrying on about the town and the movie. Fearing a public relations nightmare, Chissel tries to stop Jannsky. Instead, Jannsky kills him.

As a line of logic, it held together.

Right, that annoying voice in the back of Liza's head butted in, *except for the ending.*

Maybe the disposal of the body stretched the logical chain a little. Hell, it left the chain twanging apart like an overstressed guitar string. Why in the name of anything would Deke Jannsky bury Chissel up to his neck on the beach? An unpremeditated killing would suggest a panic-stricken reaction. If Jannsky had snapped and killed Chissel, he'd have freaked and dumped the body as quickly as possible — probably in the harbor.

Liza headed back to her car. Like it or not, she needed more information, and the place to get it was the *Oregon Daily*. Finding a spot in the strip mall parking lot, Liza went up the outside stairs and entered the reception area for the newspaper's satellite office.

Janey Brezinski, the paper's official meeter and greeter, barely responded to Liza's hello — she was tied up on an obviously important call. Liza walked past the reception desk and into the newsroom. She was in luck — Murph was definitely in the building.

The oversized reporter had the high color and upturned nose that marked a true son of Ireland. The light from his computer screen put copper highlights in his auburn hair as he hunched over his keyboard, inputting a story. His typing style was idiosyncratic — he only used his two forefingers — but he maintained a swift, *rat-a-tat* cadence as he wrote his story.

Liza stood silently beside the reporter until Murph sighed and slumped back. He aimed a slightly suspicious glance up at her. "You want something, Kelly?"

165

"I understand you're following up on the sabotage reports from the movie set," she said.

He nodded, his expression turning more toward boredom. "Pissant stuff. A person might die from a million pinpricks, but it's kinda hard to make an exciting story out of it, you know?"

"I was trying to think who might benefit from delaying the film shoot like that. The answer I came up with was anybody being paid by the day."

Murph shot her a shrewder look now. "Like the extras, you mean? Especially since most of them were available to work the movie because they couldn't hold down regular jobs anywhere."

He shrugged massive shoulders. "I thought about that very thing, but it wouldn't wash. Things happened on the set even on days the extras weren't there. And it was fresh sabotage — wires cut after lights had been taken out of a truck and tested."

"Huh," Liza said. Well, maybe it was too ambitious to try tying all the crimes together — like the physicists at Coastal University trying to come up with a theory of everything.

"The one thing everybody agrees on," Murph went on, "is that the sabotage only started when Lloyd Olbrich came on board. Everything went smoothly when Terence Hamblyn was in charge. The movie was even coming in under budget."

"I guess that's not surprising," Liza said. "*Counterfeit* was Derrick Robbins's baby, and he handpicked everyone involved with the film. They were supposed to work together well."

"Well, that stopped when Olbrich came in." Murph stretched and moved his hands back to the keyboard. "Made me wonder if the trouble wasn't coming from some kind of twisted movie politics — somebody with a grudge against the new director."

"You could wind up with a long list, from what I hear," Liza told him.

"Yeah, but I'm trying to do a news piece here, not a gossip story. You know some of the actors don't like the guy."

"How about the crew members?"

Murph's fingers, poised to type, went back down to rest on the desktop. "Only a couple of them worked with the guy before, and as far as I can make out, they've got no beefs with him. Of course, now all of them are complaining that he's working them like a slave driver."

If Olbrich got the same message from the Mirage board as I got over the news, he might

167

be right, Liza thought. *Best to get the movie done before they cut off the money.*

Murph took advantage of Liza's silence to go back into his story, tapping away like a maniac in his oddball typing style. She stood sorting through the movie people who might have a beef with Lloyd Olbrich.

Jenny, of course, had opened her mouth very loudly about Olbrich. And Liza knew that Jenny had worked on a lighting crew for the tech side of her theater training. Lights aren't all that different on a theater stage and on a movie set.

Mayor Massini must have been fairly annoyed to have Olbrich come in and start reshooting scenes. But he didn't have a motive for sabotage and delay. He'd want the film people to finish up and get out of town so he could start the boardwalk construction.

Guy Morton had seemed very up front when Michael hit him on the sabotage issue. Maybe, though, that bang on the table had been a little too much of a performance. That poor young actor getting institutionalized — that was a strong motive against Olbrich . . . and maybe more. Suppose Morton had decided to ratchet up local feeling against the continued filming and Olbrich's changes by going on a glass-smashing spree

168

down Main Street. If Chissel had seen him and intervened, that might also become a motive for murder.

"Are you annoying my reporters?" a voice at Liza's elbow demanded.

She turned to see Ava Barnes giving her a quizzical look.

"I came to get some information, but I think I'm suffering from information overload," Liza admitted.

"So you don't have a solution to the problem of Oliver Chissel?" Ava asked with a grin.

"It's like when I got my first sudoku techniques down," Liza said, "but the whole X-wing thing was beyond me. I was vaguely aware that there were patterns — I just couldn't *see* them."

"It was a lot easier when we had secret messages to decode," Ava agreed. "This time, so much stuff seems off the wall. Like the way Chissel was found — why wouldn't the killer bury him all the way? It's like the misdirection in a magic trick — somebody is trying to get us all looking in the wrong direction."

Liza's boss suddenly went businesslike. "By the way, I liked the new stuff you sent in. That will cover us for about a week, but we'll need more, so get to work! That story you started about learning the X-wings — could that be a column?"

"Maybe," Liza said, hoping Ava wouldn't notice the sudden faraway look in her eyes. Being reminded of this job had unfortunately reminded her of her other job. She'd been staying away from the set — Jenny had to learn to handle some problems without always being able to run to a publicist.

Now, though, she needed some sort of read on the temper of the set, not just for her second job as a publicist, but for her third — finding Chissel's killer.

Liza headed home to clean up, then walked back downtown. The crew was shooting at the harbor again, with a complicated arrangement of tracks extending down the boardwalk for the camera to roll along.

There wasn't much in the way of an audience. The townsfolk were pretty much bored with filming by now, and there weren't any tourists around.

Liza stepped past a PA who waved her along. She carefully kept out of the way as she watched the scene being set up. Jenny and Guy Morton were to walk down toward one of the piers while the camera executed a tracking pan. Olbrich watched in silence while they went through two takes. Then he suddenly started berating Guy.

"Maybe that hambone style of acting worked when you were still a stuntman pretending to be an actor. But times have changed, Morton. You actually have to show something more than that constipated hero face from the old-time serials." Olbrich jerked his chin nastily at Jenny. "Keep teaching that crap to the girl, and the only job she'll get in the movies will be selling popcorn."

He gestured impatiently. "Let's try it again."

The same scene proceeded, but this time Liza was amazed at the difference still-raw emotions could make. Morton's steaming anger, even though he repressed it, leaked through as an air of menace.

And Jenny's upset, not so well masked, showed as a sense of unease and vulnerability as the two actors walked and said their lines.

Liza was suddenly reminded of a hundred-year-old story from the theater world about legendary producer/director David Belasco. The man had a clear, almost dictatorial view of how a production should go — and an unscrupulous manner of getting his way.

One of the director's favorite tricks was to work himself up into a serious rage about some argument over interpretation or characterization, consummated by yanking the pocket watch from his vest, throwing it on the floor, and stamping on it.

A second later, Belasco would gasp, stepping back in horror. "My father gave me that watch on his deathbed!" he'd cry.

Of course the chastened actor or actress targeted by the stratagem, feeling terrible, would give in to the great man.

Olbrich's scam, if anything, did Belasco one better. He'd get a couple of insurance takes in case his mind game didn't work. Then he'd drop a bomb to elicit the emotional responses he wanted.

If that's the kind of abuse he dishes out in his mind games, I'm not surprised Olbrich drove some poor kid to the booby hatch, Liza thought.

But she had to admit the director was smart, flaming Guy Morton to get two reactions for the price of one tirade.

The crew was already preparing for a different scene. Liza could see where Olbrich was getting his slave driver reputation.

Jenny spotted Liza and hissed. "You see what he's doing? We barely have enough time to get these new lines down. And before we even get comfortable in a scene, he starts screaming at somebody."

"Pardon me, Ms. Kelly — Jenny." Peter

Hake, in a black car coat and jeans, made his way past them.

"Do you think it's such a good idea that Olbrich is rushing us along like this?" Jenny demanded.

"I'll talk to him," Hake promised, "but he is the director."

And Hake is just the special assistant to the dead boss, Liza thought. *I wonder how long it will be before Mirage cuts him loose?*

She didn't even have a chance to talk to Jenny. Olbrich just blew Hake off, instead yelling for his actor for the next scene.

This time around Jenny stood alone at the end of a pier. Apparently, she heard something, because she turned, looking surprised and wary.

Again, they did a couple of takes. Liza made her way closer, staying behind the camera. She watched as Olbrich leaned over to his cameraman. "Focus in on her face," the director muttered, "and keep rolling until the second time I yell 'Cut!' "

They started the scene again, with one of the PAs yelling, "Sound cue!" for whatever noise would be inserted.

But as Jenny turned, Olbrich howled, "Cut! What are we even bothering with this for? We're just wasting film! Cut!"

Even with the whole pier between them,

Jenny could see Jenny's mobile face register shock and, yes, a little fear. In close-up, such a naked reaction could make a scene.

Brilliant, Liza thought. *But nasty.*

In fact, Liza was so caught up in the little game going on in front of her, she missed the first yells from behind.

She turned to see one of the big equipment trucks wobbling its way onto the pier. One of the crew members was trying to wave it back — until he suddenly realized there was no driver behind the wheel. The guy had to jump out of the way — and into the harbor.

Liza herself was checking out possible escape routes when the floating pier wobbled again, sending the truck rolling right into a camera.

The moment of impact was almost anticlimactic. Sure, the camera flew into the water, followed by the truck. But the weight of the vehicle, concentrated on one side of the pier, overbalanced the whole structure.

One side of the floating pier rose till it snagged on the chains and ropes holding it to the pilings set in the ground. So the people on the pier got flung up, then the footing beneath them didn't follow. A couple of people were thrown into the

174

water, including a cameraman and his camera.

Liza staggered considerably, but managed to keep her feet. Even as the pier sloshed around, she ran for the end, where Jenny lay clinging to the wooden boards.

"Are you okay?" Liza yelled.

"Yeah, except I think I picked up a couple of splinters."

Jenny glared at Olbrich, who crouched in a huddled lump near where the camera had been, his face slack with shock.

"Well, I guess that wasn't some crap *he* was pulling." She aimed a wolflike grin at the shaken director. "Huh. When he probably thinks about it, he'll wish he'd gotten some footage of this."

12

The film crew was making a lot of noise. People on the pier were calling to people in the water and vice versa, making sure that everyone was accounted for.

Guy Morton came charging onto the pier, heading for Jenny and Liza, moving a bit like a broken-field runner since the walkway was still sloshing around.

"Are you okay?" Guy had to raise his voice to be heard over the pandemonium.

Jenny told him about her splinters, but Guy wasn't going to get too excited about that. He laughed when Jenny made a jibe about Olbrich, who was only then getting to his feet. The director did a sort of belated double take when he realized there were no cameras around anymore.

"Well, it wasn't one of his fake outs," Morton said. "What happened, did one of the drivers get drunk and try to bring his truck out?"

"Nobody was behind the wheel," Liza said.

"You mean somebody just released the brake and let a truck roll down onto the pier?" Liza could hear the disbelief in Jenny's voice, but she wasn't particularly looking at the girl.

Her eyes were scanning the crowd that had gathered, some to gawk, some moving to help get people out of the water. And at the back end of the crowd, disappearing around the first intersection, she saw somebody in a hard-to-miss piece of clothing.

Even in Maiden's Bay, you didn't see a hat in hunter's orange on everyone's head. But a disreputable example of the type graced one native's head. Liza had seen it earlier, its fluorescent orange making an interesting contrast to the brick red of Deke Jannsky's furious face.

So, she thought. *Does this mean one mystery down? It's almost too good to be true. Deke might as well have been carrying a sign saying, "Me! Me! Me!"*

On the other hand, this was the criminal genius who had decided to threaten Liza right outside the local office of the county sheriff.

Guy had helped Jenny to her feet. The floating pier had stopped shifting so vigorously. Olbrich was standing on the side where the camera had gone overboard, in deep discussion with the dripping cameraman.

Liza took a look at Jenny's palm, where several good-sized slivers of wood had stabbed deep into the flesh. They weren't exactly life threatening, but Liza was sure they were pretty painful.

"Come on, let's get over to First Aid and see what they can do about those splinters." She looked to where Olbrich still stared down into the roiled waters. "I'm pretty sure this will be the end of shooting for the day."

The sound of sirens cut across the hollering and yelling. By the time Liza and her friends reached the boardwalk, the local volunteer ambulance had arrived, along with a police cruiser.

As Jenny's hurts were being tended to, Sheriff Clements arrived on the scene.

Liza watched as Clements listened to reports and supervised the scene. When things calmed down a little, he stood to the side, shaking his head — the image of a bear with a sore toe.

Taking a deep breath Liza walked over to him.

"Enjoying the show, Ms. Kelly?" the sheriff asked in an ominous voice.

"I was part of it," Liza told him. "Although luckily I didn't end up treading water."

"Well, that's one good thing." Clements watched his deputies taking statements. "As if I didn't have enough balls in the air, juggling the murder and the nonsense on Main Street."

"This is a lot more serious than some cut wires," Liza said.

Clements nodded. "Damn right. This stupid stunt could have gotten someone killed." He sighed. "It will certainly bring the news vans back to report the growing lawlessness in Maiden's Bay." He glanced at Liza. "By the time this is over, we may need to hire you to win back the town's good name."

She hesitated for a moment, then said, "Things got pretty chaotic for a while. But I saw something I think you should hear about."

Clements listened in silence as Liza described her glimpse of the figure in the distinctive hat.

"Deke Jannsky, huh?" he finally said. "Well, you'll make Ray Massini happy. He's been trying to install Jannsky as public enemy number one since he overheard us the other day."

"Does the mayor have something against Deke?"

The sheriff shook his head. "Not that I know of."

And he's shown he knows most of what's going on around town, Liza thought.

"If it's not personal, why is the mayor so eager to get Jannsky arrested for something?"

"In your line, you've got to know that politics is just as much about perception as performance," Clements said. "If the mayor can announce an arrest — for anything — people will think we're at least dealing with this sudden crime wave. And looking like we're doing our jobs will help get us re-elected to do our jobs some more."

Liza noticed that the sheriff had the honesty to include himself in that election campaign comment.

"But you're not happy to arrest Jannsky?"

Clements shrugged. "Let's say I'd be a lot happier if you had seen Deke Jannsky's face instead of his hat."

With a nod to the sheriff, Liza went off to collect Jenny and Guy. The girl was looking in some annoyance at her right hand. Overly enthusiastic first-aid types had wrapped it in so much gauze that Jenny looked as if she were wearing a white mitten.

"You were right," Jenny told Liza. "They've stopped shooting for the day. But I don't know if I can drive with this thing."

"Just leave your car. I'll give you a lift," Liza said.

"I think I'm going to stay in town for a while and celebrate," Guy Morton said. "It's not every day you see a director manage to lose two cameras. Hmm . . . wonder if *Evening Celebrity News* would find this as interesting as I do."

Liza and Jenny walked up Main Street, through the industrial area below the highway, using the pedestrian bridge to reach the business section of Maiden's Bay.

"My car's over by the café," Liza said. "Let's make a stop at the pharmacy first, though."

Liza just wanted some throat lozenges, but Nora Schilling went into full pharmacy mode when she heard about Jenny's injury. She even brought Gary out from behind the prescription counter to get his advice. The young pharmacist turned bright red at the prospect of talking to a pretty girl, but he and his mother agreed that careful washing, an antiseptic cream, and a much smaller bandage would suffice to protect Jenny's palm while it healed.

"Glad to hear it," Jenny said. "I figured

181

the continuity people would freak if I showed up on the set wearing this tomorrow." She held up her heavily gauzed hand.

"That's right, you're in the movie," Nora said. "We saw you standing outside on Main Street filming in front of the store here." Her smile dimmed a bit as she glanced at the plywood blocking the store's window now. "I guess your continuity people would have problems with us now, even after the window gets replaced. We had the old flasks my husband's grandfather used in our display, but they were broken when the glass was smashed."

"Now that's a shame," Jenny said. "A window can be replaced, but a family heirloom —"

"We've got to be practical," Nora said. "The whole pharmacy is an heirloom — an inheritance, from Grandfather Gustav, to my husband Matt, to Gary here."

Jenny was subdued after they paid for their purchases and left. "I guess this movie is my big inheritance from Uncle D.," she said. "It's been the center of my life for the past few months — we haven't even straightened out the rest of the estate."

"Have you been back to Derrick's house much?" Liza asked.

"Just a couple of whirlwind trips since the

cops unsealed the place," Jenny replied. "Otherwise — well, my mail is being redirected to the Killamook Inn."

"What a surprise," Liza said. "That's our next stop."

They drove along the coast of the bay in silence for a while. Then Jenny said, "I'm glad you came to the set today. If I'd tried to tell you what Olbrich was doing, it would have sounded like whining."

"Different directors have different methods," Liza said carefully. "Some look on their work with actors as collaboration. Others feel they should definitely be the boss. Still others like to deviate from the script and encourage actors to improvise."

"And others alternate between staring at us as if we were bugs and screaming at us." Jenny shook her head. "All in all, I prefer the way Terence Hamblyn did things."

"But being a professional means working with all these kinds of directors," Liza said, "and others. Hang in there, Jenny. You handled what happened today — especially the truck — like a pro. That's what we'll be telling the media. I'm also going to make sure the inn screens your calls. If anyone gets through, you have no comment — refer them to us." She grinned. "And take it easy. Tomorrow could always be worse."

After dropping Jenny at her cabin, Liza arranged with Kevin to have the girl's incoming calls run through the front desk. On the way home, Liza used her cell phone to get hold of Michelle and bring her up to speed.

By the time she got to Hackleberry Avenue, Liza felt as if she'd gotten part of a job done right. As she parked the car, she saw that Mrs. Halvorsen was in her garden.

Liza walked to the fence and leaned over. "Hi, Mrs. H."

"Hello, dear." The older woman's round face had an unexpectedly serious expression. "Did you hear about what happened on the docks?"

"I was there."

"My, my. Tell me everything, dear." Mrs. H. smiled like a fisherman about to cast a line into a record salmon run.

Mrs. H. took an innocent pleasure in gossip, and Liza was glad to give her the straight eyewitness scoop.

Bet you Ava would like this story, too. That annoying voice from the back of Liza's mind spoke up with the notion to phone the boss.

Liza resolutely paid no attention. She had other fish to fry with Mrs. H. "I hope Michael isn't being too much trouble."

"Not at all," Mrs. Halvorsen replied with

a smile. "I'm working him like a slave. Who do you think weeded all the flower beds?" She complacently took in her pristine lawn. "He even agreed to do a little painting around the house. Such a nice young man."

"Try living with him for a couple of years," Liza muttered. Then she suddenly stopped and gave her neighbor a suspicious look. "You said Kevin was a nice young man, too." Mrs. H. was an inveterate matchmaker. In fact, she'd schemed to reunite Liza with her former high school boyfriend.

"And so he is, dear." Mrs. Halvorsen smiled and nodded. "But when it comes to nice young examples of the opposite gender, it doesn't hurt to have a selection. After all, Solomon had a collection of a thousand — seven hundred wives and three hundred concubines."

Liza grinned. Mrs. H. was also a fervent student of the Bible, though she put her readings to somewhat unorthodox uses.

"I see you stopped off at Schilling's Pharmacy." Mrs. Halvorsen nodded at the bag in Liza's hand. "I hope your cold isn't still giving you problems?"

"It was just an excuse to get Jenny into the place." Liza went on to explain about the splinters and how Nora Schilling had made suggestions. "She really is a nice lady."

"I expect she was well taught when she was younger," Mrs. H. replied. "Nora was an heiress, dear — not at all like that dreadful Hilton girl, though. She was a Timmons — that was an important name in California once. They had ranches and orange groves where some of the big studios are now." The older woman shook her head. "The Timmons clan went from owning land to having money — and they slowly lost it all to a bunch of bloodsuckers who wanted a share of it. Brokers and business advisors, entrepreneurs and out-and-out swindlers — by the time they were done, Nora didn't have much of an inheritance left. She came here to make a new start."

The older woman's smile mixed reminiscence with a bit of irony. "I was years older than she was, of course, but I still remember being a little jealous of her clothes. They were done by real designers, not these made-up names you find in stores today. Yes, Nora made a big splash in our little town. But she only had eyes for Matt Schilling, and her nest egg went into the pharmacy."

"I guess there's a lot about little towns you never learn until you get beneath the surface. Who'd imagine that Maiden's Bay had an heiress and a war hero —"

		2	6	9				
	8				1		5	
1		7						9
				1	5			7
	1	3		8		6	2	
7			9	2				
8						3		6
	7		8				9	
			3	9	4			

"Not to mention a sudoku genius," Mrs. Halvorsen added with a smile.

"Who should be working on more puzzles for her managing editor," Liza said guiltily. "See you around, Mrs. H."

She went into her house, greeted Rusty, and headed for the computer. The work went well — Liza now had a moderately difficult puzzle to add to her cushion file.

She yawned and went upstairs to bed feeling virtuously tired.

Unfortunately, her subconscious managed to mix the day's events and words into another disturbing dream.

This time, Deke Jannsky pushed huge trucks into the harbor as if they were toys, while Ray Massini rampaged along Main

Street, a torch in one hand and a hammer in the other, smashing windows. Along came Oliver Chissel, his face suddenly huge in the torchlight.

Liza woke with a start just as Massini swung his hammer and Chissel shattered like Humpty Dumpty. Yes, it was just a weird dream, but the strange logic underlying it kept Liza from getting back to sleep.

Suppose Jannsky was indeed responsible for the sabotage, but Massini had committed the vandalism on Main Street. If it could somehow be blamed on the Hollywood people, everyone in town would want the film crew out, and the construction project on the boardwalk could begin.

But if Chissel saw Massini, then the mayor would have to eliminate the inconvenient witness — and would need a convenient fall guy.

The morning's weather matched Liza's mood — gray and threatening. Even Rusty caught the vibe, being uncharacteristically subdued when Liza took him for a brief walk.

Liza got showered and dressed with a little more care than usual. She had no intention of turning up at Ma's Café looking like a slob again. But Liza especially wanted to make sure she wasn't giving away any points in advance when she saw Kevin Shepard.

13

Liza marched resolutely from her car to the café. She paused for a moment by the front counter, where most of the town's characters sat in a row enjoying their breakfasts.

Yes. She spotted Kevin sitting in one of the back booths. Even though he lived and worked in Killamook now, Kevin often made a morning visit to Ma's . . . especially if he wanted to catch the early gossip.

His greeting was less than effusive as Liza walked down and plunked herself in the seat opposite him. Liza didn't care. Things were likely to get downright unfriendly before they were done.

She plunged right into it. "What are you hiding about Ray Massini?"

He almost did a spit take with his coffee, looking wildly around the place. But Liza had kept her voice low. None of the patrons or staff even looked their way.

"I thought you were bent out of shape

yesterday because I had eavesdropped on Curt talking to you, and you were worried I'd get him into trouble. I should have caught on when you began talking about 'collateral damage' — that's a military term, something you probably learned with your army buddy Ray Massini. You're afraid that if I keep looking into Chissel's murder, I'll find out something about your pal the mayor."

The unease she had noticed days before in Kevin's eyes now came out all over his face. "Liza, please," he begged in a low voice. "Let it go."

"How can I let it go if Massini is involved in a murder?" Liza leaned across the table.

"He's not!" Kevin fought to control the tone of his voice. "Can't you just trust me on this?"

"Were you with him the night of the murder?" Liza bored in. "Because otherwise he's got bushels of motive — this whole movie thing has turned into a political liability. He hasn't been forthcoming with an alibi, so that's opportunity. As for means, well, with the way the extra filming was delaying Mr. Mayor's pet project, I bet Ray would have loved to plant Chissel like one of the pilings for the boardwalk project."

"He had nothing to do with what happened to Chissel," Kevin hissed. "I know that."

"You know that because you were with him?" Liza asked.

"I know it because I know where he was." Kevin's shoulders sagged. "He was in a supposedly empty room at the inn with . . . somebody."

Liza looked at Kevin. *This is why Michelle refuses to get involved in politics,* she thought. *Here's a guy, successful, dynamic. A successful, dynamic politician. A successful, dynamic politician with a socially prominent wife.* She remembered Ava's comment on the way Massini had gone through the ladies. Evidently, he still was.

"And you were keeping quiet while he dipped his wick."

Kevin winced at the way she put it. "We literally went through the wars together. He trusts me to . . . protect him."

"He wouldn't need protection if he kept his pants zipped," Liza hissed. "I can't believe you'd let yourself get involved in something like this."

"Ray's an old friend — he's trying to do things for this town," Kevin whispered miserably.

"Gee, and you can't think of anybody else who was going to do great things for his country until he got messed up by his extracurricular affairs?"

"Yeah, well, it didn't work out too badly for that guy." Kevin looked down, his face wooden, his voice going flat. "I figure Ray should get a little running room, too. I told you before, there are things you learn running a hotel that they never teach you at hospitality school."

"I guess so." Liza rose, waving away Liz, who was finally coming with her order pad. "Sorry. I'm afraid I'm feeling a little queasy all of a sudden. I think I'd better not try anything."

She walked very quickly to the door and got out of there. Outside on Main Street, Liza took a very deep breath. *You think you know a person,* she thought.

Behind her the café door slammed. She turned to see Kevin coming after her. "Liza —"

"Don't worry," she told him, "it's not the worst thing I've heard in my career. And like hoteliers, publicists are supposed to be discreet."

Kevin made a gesture as if he were throwing all of that aside. Then he grabbed her hand. "And us?" he asked. "Are we okay?"

Liza carefully got her hand back. "I'll have

to think about that," she said in a small voice.

Kevin nodded. Liza remembered her father nodding the same way, when the doctors told him about the cancer.

Then Kevin silently headed off along Main Street. Liza followed him with her eyes until a voice said, "I couldn't help noticing."

She turned. Michael.

All of a sudden, the strange, empty feeling inside her was replaced by flaring anger.

"You couldn't help," Liza repeated, her voice shaking. "Why don't you try helping, Michael? You'd be a real big help right now if you'd just walk away!"

"Okay, I get that you're upset with your boyfriend, although I don't know why you should take that out on me," Michael was into his own angry mode now. "But I heard something that affects your job with Michelle — something that may be bad for Jenny."

She looked up at him. "What?"

"Olbrich is filming at a new location today — Bayocean. And I don't think he told Jenny."

Changing currents had literally swept the town of Bayocean out to sea. The remaining ruins had served as Jenny Robbins's prison after she'd been kidnapped.

"He couldn't —" Liza broke off, hit by a sudden, stabbing headache.

"You know he could," Michael said. "I just found out. Since yesterday's excitement, the crew is supposed to keep any plans secret — greater security."

"Olbrich will *need* 'greater security' by the time I get done with him!"

Liza stomped off down the street. She got into her car, started it, and jammed it into gear. Luckily, there was no traffic as she screeched onto Main Street.

No time to stop at the pharmacy and get something for her headache. She'd just head out to Bayocean and give one to Lloyd Olbrich. Liza's eyes and mind were totally on the road ahead as she came to the next intersection.

She never saw the rock that came flying across the street to smash her windshield.

Unlike the plate-glass display windows on the stores, Liza's windshield was safety glass. It didn't shatter, it just cratered and fell in on one side. The shock of the impact and the sudden spider web of cracks spreading across the glass caused a distraction that nearly made Liza lose control of her car. She went slewing wildly onto the wrong side of Main Street. Steering into the skid, Liza narrowly missed a car pulling into a parking spot on the far side of the street before she managed to get in her proper lane again.

She brought the car to a stop and spent a long moment leaning on the wheel, hyperventilating.

Then she heard someone running up. Taking a deep breath, she frantically pawed through the impedimenta on the front seat, looking for something, anything she could use for a weapon.

"Liza, what happened?" A worried Michael appeared in her driver's side window. "Are you all right?"

Liza pressed her hand to her forehead and told herself to get it together. Now. She said shakily, "I think I'll feel a hell of a lot better after we get some cops around here."

If her well-being truly depended on the number of law enforcement people who arrived, Liza would soon have been feeling fabulous.

Not only did they get the cops, they got the sheriff himself. Clements met with them in the interrogation room at City Hall. "You know, I've got a real office in Killamook, a nice big desk chair. I'm beginning to wonder if I'll ever see them again."

Liza was not in the mood for humor. "When that rock hit my windshield, I was

196

wondering if I'd live to see anything again."

Clements raised his shoulders. "I suppose you didn't see anything."

"I was too busy trying to keep the car from wrapping around a light pole. Or taking out somebody else and me both."

"Not even the trace of an orange hat then." The sheriff nodded. "We went to pick up Deke Jannsky yesterday, but he wasn't haunting any of his usual haunts."

"Well, you might want to make a start looking around the intersection of Main and Spruce," Liza said.

"We thought maybe Deke was just lying low after stirring things up with that truck stunt." Clements sucked his lips in. "Now I'm wondering whether someone tipped Deke that you could place him at the scene."

"Not exactly. Only his hat." Liza scowled. "Well, if Deke Jannsky thinks this is the way to scare me off, he's made a bad mistake."

"Well, we'll do what we can to discourage him," the sheriff said. "I'll make sure to have a cruiser passing by your house on Hackleberry Avenue. But you'd best be careful. Don't go off alone, keep some friends around."

"I'm staying next door," Michael said. "I'll keep an eye out."

By the time they'd finished with Clements

197

and had a report typed up, Liza's stomach was making some very loud complaints.

"I missed breakfast, and now it's almost time for lunch," she complained, pressing a hand to her noisy middle.

"Want to stop for a bite?" Michael asked. He'd already offered to drive her over to the film shoot after her car went into the repair shop.

"No," Liza decided. "The sooner we get out to Bayocean, the better." She grinned. "Besides, we can always raid the craft table."

Following Liza's directions, Michael took his rental car down along the coast of the bay, then farther down to the next inlet. After they left Killamook behind, the scenery began to get wild and rugged.

"This is all state park," Liza explained.

"Which means picturesque, but possibly hard on the suspension," Michael said as they left the highway.

His prediction proved pretty accurate. They went from paved highway to gravel road to a bumpy path that led out onto the peninsula where the lost town was situated.

"I don't know how well we'll do on dune grass," Michael warned. "If we have to drive much farther, we may be calling in a tow truck, rather than inspecting a movie location."

He needn't have worried. As they came to the end of the looping path, they found a phalanx of trucks and a caterer's van. "I guess they legged it from here."

But Liza and Michael didn't have far to walk. The whole film crew had gathered back at the parking area, tucking into a catered lunch.

As Michael pulled up, a production assistant came running up, clipboard at the ready.

"I guess this is Olbrich's idea of 'heightened security,' " Liza snorted. She applied a couple of the gentler techniques she'd learned the hard way from Michelle and quickly discovered which of the trailers Jenny was using as a dressing room on location.

After knocking and getting no reply, Liza knocked on the trailer next door. A yawning Guy Morton appeared.

"Sorry," he said. "I figured I'd just close my eyes for a few minutes till they called us back."

"You haven't seen Jenny?" Michael asked.

The older actor blinked. "Olbrich wrapped us for lunch. The last I saw, he and Jenny were still talking out in the ruins. It was going to take her a couple of minutes to get moving anyway. We're doing the scenes where she's tied up —"

Liza whipped away before Morton even finished, hurrying over to the assembled crew. No Jenny in evidence. She did see Olbrich leaning against the catering van, a plate in one hand, the other bringing a sandwich to his mouth.

The director almost choked when he saw her. "What are you doing?" he sputtered. "This is a closed set."

"My client is available to me at all times," Liza grimly quoted. "That's a standard part of the Markson Associates contract, and it was incorporated into Jenny's contract with the production company. So where is she?"

Olbrich turned a sickly pale color, as if his sandwich suddenly wasn't agreeing with him. "I'm afraid, ah, she's the victim of a little joke," he began, glancing out at the headland.

"Why aren't I laughing?" Liza swung away and hurried out to the ruins where the filming was actually taking place. There really wasn't much left of the town — flimsy bungalows and summer cottages had washed completely away. Even the big resort hotel was gone, except for a corner of its foundation.

"What did he do?" Michael asked worriedly as he labored to keep up.

"I don't want to think of it," Liza replied.

At the sound of her voice, they heard kicking noises and a muffled moan.

Liza cut to the top of a dune, using the slight elevation to look down into the brick-walled hollow below. Jenny lay on her back on the damp sand floor, bound hand and foot, a tape gag over her mouth. She was still making wordless cries and kicking at the wall with her running shoes.

"Omigod, Jenny!" Liza flew down to the girl, bringing her to a sitting position, gently removing the tape as Jenny raised her head, her eyes streaming with tears.

Jenny coughed as the tape came free of her lips. "He — he said I wasn't getting the scenes right."

"Olbrich?" Liza asked.

Jenny nodded. "He sent everybody to lunch and sat beside me. Told me I — I was only remembering what happened out here. That I had to *feel* it, and he would help me do that. Then he jammed that tape over my mouth, and . . . and he left!" The girl shuddered heavily within her bonds, on the edge of hysteria.

Liza turned to Michael. "Have you got a knife? We've got to get her out of these ropes."

"You know me, always prepared." He dug

in his pocket and produced a tiny Swiss Army knife.

Michael sawed through the rope with it. It took a little while, but as soon as she was free, Jenny rose to her feet, shivering. "It feels even colder than when I was out here before," she said, teeth chattering.

Michael slipped out of his jacket and wrapped it over her shoulders.

"Let's get back to everybody else," Liza said grimly.

Interested onlookers had now trailed about halfway to the ruins. Lloyd Olbrich was in the lead. Whether he was trying to get there first or trying to wave everyone else back, Liza couldn't quite make out.

But she didn't mince words when she got to the director. "This was your idea of a practical joke? Leaving this poor girl tied up in the cold and wet while you have lunch? It's not enough that this is the place where she almost got killed. She also nearly got pneumonia out here — and the weather's a hell of a lot more raw now!"

Now Guy Morton pushed his way forward. "You left her tied up?"

"A — an acting exercise," the director tried to bluff.

"With a gag over her mouth so she couldn't call for help," Michael added.

"You sadistic son of a bitch! I'm going to kill you!" Morton might be an older man, but he was still pretty fit — and he definitely had a good right jab. His fist shot out, and Olbrich toppled back on the sand, blood spurting from his nose.

"Stop him!" Olbrich screamed. "He means it!"

"Yeah, I'm a real method actor." Morton came after the director, his arm going back again.

A couple of teamsters from the film crew grabbed hold of the enraged actor while others helped Olbrich scramble to his feet. "I — I'll have you up on charges!" the director's voice went up as he gobbled like a castrated turkey.

Liza thrust her face forward till she was nose to bleeding nose. "You've got problems of your own, Olbrich. Everybody knows about the little tricks you play on your actors. But this is pushing things way beyond the line. Once the news gets out — and when Michelle Markson gets done with you — you'll be lucky to find a job directing commercials for local car dealerships."

Olbrich recoiled from her, his face slack. Behind her, Liza heard Morton call out, "Hey, where's the kid?"

She turned to see Michael glancing

around in confusion. "She was right here —"

His voice was cut off by the sudden roar of a car engine.

Michael flapped his hands at hip level. "The car keys — they were in my jacket!"

They all turned to see Michael's rental car throw up a rooster tail of sand as it swerved around and took off like a bat out of hell.

14

"Come on!" Michael yelled. "We've got to stop her!"

Lloyd Olbrich wrenched himself free of the people holding him, suddenly the boss again. "Let her go! The hell with her — she's breaking her contract." He rounded on his subordinates, pointing at Guy Morton. "Get that maniac back in his trailer. And anybody who helps these two gets fired!"

"I think any reasonable judge would say that trying to keep us in this isolated area would constitute unlawful imprisonment," Michael said coolly. "And since you're already guilty on one count of that —"

Liza didn't know whether Olbrich knew if Michael was a writer or a lawyer. Right now she was more interested in running through her phone's memory, calling up Sheriff Clements's cell number. He'd given it to her on a courtesy card when they first met, and Liza had installed it as something potentially useful.

Always good to have a direct line, she thought.

Soon enough, a police cruiser arrived, Curt Walters at the wheel.

Even Olbrich wasn't stupid enough to mess with the local law. Liza and Michael got into the rear of the patrol car as the crew members slowly dismantled their equipment.

"What's the sheriff doing about Jenny?" Liza anxiously asked Curt. "I tried to explain over the phone, but I don't know if he understood —"

Images of some public relations nightmare like the pursuit of O. J. Simpson's white Bronco kept running through her mind.

"He understood that the girl took a car that didn't belong to her and that she's mighty upset," Curt replied. "The sheriff is trying to reach out on the quiet to some of the neighboring counties, seeing if we can get a line on where she's going without spooking her."

"It's a 2006 silver Toyota Camry, license plate —" Michael rattled off the string of numbers and letters from a piece of paper in his hand. "I kept the rental agreement in my wallet — which, thankfully, was *not* in

206

my jacket."

"Saves us a call to the rental agency," Curt said, relaying the information.

Liza wasn't sure what answer she'd get, but she had to try. "How is the sheriff taking this?"

Curt shrugged. "He's not delighted to have the girl blow town in the middle of a murder investigation. But he wants to talk to you, which means he's also willing to listen."

The spartan little interrogation room was becoming far too familiar for Liza's comfort. But Sheriff Clements didn't ask questions. He just let Liza and Michael tell their stories.

After he'd absorbed the high points, Clements leaned back in his chair. "Wouldn't know if you'd heard this," he said, "but I have a teenage daughter over in Killamook. Anybody tried a stunt like that with her, he'd be eating through a straw, and I wouldn't care if it meant me getting busted back to grunt cop somewhere."

He rubbed the back of his neck as if he were trying to get some stiff muscles to loosen up. "Too bad Jenny's not around to make a complaint. I wouldn't mind giving this Olbrich guy a little time in the tank."

"I'm more worried about Jenny," Liza

said. "Do you think you'll be able to find her?"

"It's kind of iffy, going on the cops' grapevine," Clements admitted. "But I don't know if it will do that girl much good to go all official and put out a BOLO on her. Better, I think, to check into places she might go — maybe even waiting till she cools off and contacts you."

Liza sighed. "Unfortunately, it's not just her business, but a lot of other people's."

She'd have to get in touch with Michelle ASAP to start spinning this development. No doubt Lloyd Olbrich was already busy trying to cover his ass.

Leaving the set in the middle of filming was the Hollywood version of a soldier going AWOL in wartime. Studio brass could ignore a lot of things — talent could sleep with other people's wives, teenage daughters, even sheep. Stars could shoot up or snort down all kinds of insidious chemicals. They could even espouse all sorts of outré lifestyles and political beliefs. But the one mortal sin, the unforgivable misstep, was to cost the studio money.

Olbrich was already feeling the heat, having to stop work for a murder investigation and sabotage. Losing a truck and two cameras probably took him from the frying pan right into the fire. If he could lay some of the blame for his problems at Jenny's door, he'd definitely do it.

On the other hand, a well-known director playing sadistic mind games on a young actress . . . The celebrity gossip vampires would think that was the most delicious blood they'd tasted in a dozen news cycles.

She and Michelle could play that angle like a Stradivarius violin, spreading the music all over Hollywood.

Liza was already going over who and what to tell as she and Michael left City Hall.

"Did the people in that garage give you an ETA on a new windshield?" Michael asked.

"It's going to be a couple days before I see wheels again," she replied. "I'm not so sure about your situation. I'm hoping Jenny will cool off and show up ASAP."

"Me, too. Thank God it's a short enough walk from here to get home."

Liza smiled. "Another difference between Maiden's Bay and L.A."

They walked in companionable silence up to Hackleberry Avenue. As Liza's house — and Mrs. Halvorsen's place — came into sight, Michael cleared his throat. "I just wanted to say, I'm sorry if I upset you this morning. I mean, coming up after I'd seen you obviously fighting with Kevin."

With all the stuff that had hit her since — including a rock — Liza had almost forgotten her uncomfortable moments with Kevin. Now she wished she could forget them again.

"Michael," she said, "that's something I don't want to talk about right now. Can you let it go at that?"

"Sure," Michael replied. "I just hate to see you look unhappy, that's all."

They parted company, and Liza went into her house. Rusty barked a greeting, and Liza's stomach just about barked back in reply.

A look in the refrigerator left Liza shaking her head. "Damn it, I've *got* to get to a store!"

First things first, though. She put through a call to L.A., to Markson Associates. Luckily, Ysabel Fuentes hadn't quit yet this week and put Liza directly through to Michelle. For the next hour-plus, Liza was lost in the world of top-level publicity as more and more associates joined in an ever-growing conference call. The crisis management team threw around some ideas. Michelle called Buck Foreman. She even brought Alvin Hunzinger into the loop to deal with a possible auto theft charge. Though, since Michael didn't plan to press charges, it wasn't an immediate worry.

By the time Liza got off the phone, she felt as if her brain as well as her stomach had been sucked completely empty.

Liza stretched and looked down at her dog lolling on the floor. "Wanna go for a walk and get some food?"

That sentence contained two of Rusty's favorite words. He barked in agreement and all but levitated to the front door.

After clipping a leash to Rusty's collar, Liza opened the door and stepped out. She got about five steps before a voice came from next door. "Hey, Liza! Wait a minute, will ya?"

She looked up to see Michael trying to stick his head out the guest room window. Despite his best efforts, he still couldn't get the uncooperative window open enough to do that. So he wound up kneeling and holding his head sideways to the opening to get his words out through the space available.

"Just give me a chance to get my shoes on, and I'll come with you."

Shades of high school, Liza thought. "You don't have to," she called back.

"That's not what the sheriff said," Michael replied.

What had the sheriff said? In the last few days, she'd seen Clements so many times.

211

Oh. Right. Deke Jannsky.

"You don't have to bother," Liza said. "I've got Rusty. And he'll only make you sneeze."

Michael's allergies had banned dogs from their home in their years together. Rusty had become a family member only after Liza returned to Maiden's Bay to find a reddish dog wandering the neighborhood — a mutt she'd rescued from the local Animal Control officers.

Rusty tolerated Michael, but he really liked Kevin. Liza wished she hadn't thought of that as she hurried down the street, determined to escape before Michael could catch up with her.

This speed walking brought Liza and Rusty fairly quickly to Castelli's Market. The prices for staples might be more expensive here, but without a car, the supermarkets on the highway were just too far away to contemplate. Both she and Rusty were in no position to be picky. They had to eat. She'd buy a few basics to tide her over until she had wheels again.

There were major perks to shopping local, though.

The Castelli brothers and their mom did a whole lot of home cooking. Besides a container of milk, a small package of coffee, and a loaf of bread, Liza emerged with a stuffed veal chop, a little square of still-hot lasagna, and a container of marinated string beans. Her mouth had been watering so badly when she'd passed the "good food to go" counter, she'd been afraid she was going to drool on Mario Castelli's hand as he cut her portion.

She was still drooling when his brother had counted out her change.

The market was on the very edge of the business district. After half a block, Liza and Rusty were strolling along tree-lined streets. That was another big difference between L.A. and Maiden's Bay.

Liza was just crossing the intersection when she heard an engine crank twice and then noisily come to life behind her. She glanced over her shoulder to see an elderly pickup truck with a lot of body rot groaning its way onto the street.

A little belatedly, she thought of Sheriff Clements and his warnings. What kind of car did Deke Jannsky drive? Liza cudgeled her memory, but no picture came to mind. The wreck slowly moving behind her would be right in character, though.

"Rusty, heel." Liza wanted Rusty close — and not vulnerably out in the street — in case anything happened.

The dog gave her an "are you kidding?" look. But, seeing she was serious, Rusty gave an audible sigh and abandoned his pursuit of interesting smells to trot obediently at her heels.

Liza lengthened her stride, trying to figure what would happen next. Would the driver pull up beside her and attack? Could she expect another missile to come flying her way? Would the pickup make a sharp turn at the corner and go for a hit-and-run?

The muscles in her back grew stiff as Liza prepared herself for evasion. If Deke tried to lay his hands on her, she might give him a surprise. Since the last bit of excitement in her life, she'd gone back to practicing the moves from the self-defense classes Michelle had insisted that she take.

Here was the corner, and the pickup did turn — in the opposite direction. Instead of going right after Liza, the pickup made an asthmatic left onto Crabapple and disappeared among the greenery.

"You're getting paranoid, Kelly," Liza told herself.

Still, she didn't slow her pace until she got home. And as she came in, she not only made sure the door latched, she turned the dead bolt — an addition to the door since a break-in months ago.

Liza frowned as Rusty amused himself by rattling his leash and dog tags. "I guess in some ways, Maiden's Bay *is* just like L.A.," she muttered.

After reheating the veal and pasta from Castelli's, enjoying them and the beans with a glass of wine in the safety of her house, Liza should have calmed down. But as she washed the dishes and tossed the containers aside for recycling, she found herself physically satisfied but mentally restless.

Liza sat at her desk and began to go over the notes from her call with Michelle, trying to see if there were any other action items she could come up with, any other avenues she could explore. Instead, her thoughts mingled with all the unresolved questions from Oliver Chissel's murder.

While Michelle sometimes practiced stream of consciousness thinking as a creative tool, this time the stream seemed to dead-end in a stagnant swamp for Liza.

Sighing, Liza tried to switch gears to her other career. She called up several puzzles onto her computer screen and began trying to work them into shape.

She managed a fairly simple puzzle, adding it to her cushion file.

But the usual sudoku Zen didn't take her over, a fact she had to admit after she

				2				
4			9			2	3	
		9	8			7		
9								2
		1	4	3	8	9		
8								5
		3			4	6		
	9	7			5			4
				7				

completely butchered a more ambitious puzzle. Checking her work with the Solv-a-doku program, she got the disheartening news that her creation now had 1,732 possible solutions.

Turning off the computer, Liza turned to the television. But after cycling through all the channel selections twice, she found herself watching a comical thing about a dog that turned out to be a commercial. Nothing else came even close to holding her attention.

Killing the boob tube, Liza got up, changed into some old sweats, and started going through her self-defense routines.

"Maybe this will make my nerves feel better — and tire the rest of me out," she told herself.

Rusty was delighted, thinking this was a new game. He jumped around, then tried to imitate her, prancing on his hind legs while waving his front paws like a boxer.

Liza would have laughed if she weren't so annoyed.

When she wound up sprawled on the couch because he'd gotten behind her at an inopportune moment, she had to take a deep breath to keep from yelling.

"Dumb dog," she muttered, mopping her red face with the sleeve of her sweatshirt.

This was absolutely unfair. She'd had two nights of disturbed sleep. By rights, she ought to be curled up in bed already. Instead, she found herself pacing the living room.

Rusty whined, not liking this development.

When the phone suddenly rang, it was a toss-up as to who jumped higher, Liza or her dog.

"Hello?" She realized her voice was too loud even as she spoke into the receiver.

"Ms. Kelly, this is Armando Vasquez." The voice hesitated slightly at her silence. "From the Santa Barbara Police Department."

"Oh, Detective Vasquez." This was the

lead detective from Derrick's murder case. Had she ever known his first name? "What can I do for you, Detective?"

"I'm not sure." A harassed quality crept into the detective's voice, making him sound more like the man she had dealt with. "I got a call from an associate of yours, a Mr. Foreman. He asked if we would keep an eye on Mr. Robbins's house, to see if his niece might turn up there."

"Has she?" Liza's voice was getting loud again. "Did you see her there?"

"Not exactly," Vasquez said. "We got a call from her, but she's not at the house. However, she *has* just reported that someone had broken into it."

15

Liza had to restrain herself from holding the phone out at arm's length and staring at it like a crazy person.

"So, Detective, do you know where Jenny is?" she asked when she finally got her voice back.

"She's been driving around, calling in to us. We tried to get her to come in to the station, but she didn't seem to like the idea." Vasquez paused for a second. "Is there a particular reason for that?"

Liza sighed. "She sort of borrowed my ex-husband's car and ran off out of town."

"Is that sort of like grand theft auto, maybe?" The detective's voice was definitely sounding more like a cop's.

For a second, anger overcame Liza's worry. "It's the sort of thing you might expect from a young girl who's been working long hours on a film set, dealing with a director who likes to play sadistic games to get the performances he wants." She decided just to go with the facts. "Before she left the set, we found Jenny bound, gagged, and abandoned. The director left her stranded on the spot where she was kidnapped for real, just to get her more into the role of a kidnap victim — in spite of the fact that she was a kidnapping victim in real life."

Vasquez was silent for a moment. "They actually do stuff like that to get into the movies?"

"Some people try to push cruelty off as parlor games — and they push their games as far as they can. Take it from me, Detective, Jenny felt pretty abused today. She was freezing, shaking like a leaf. She might even have been in shock when she ran off this afternoon. And now it looks as though the safe haven she ran to doesn't look safe anymore."

She frowned, making a mental list of all the things she'd have to do after finishing this call. "If Jenny calls in again, tell her I'll be down there as soon as possible. The first thing is to get her to land in safe hands."

"Yeah. That's what this Foreman guy said when I called him first," Vasquez said.

So, Michelle should already be hearing Buck's report, Liza thought. *Good. I won't be breaking the news to her.*

As if on cue, the call-waiting tone beeped in her ear.

"This will be my partner. I guess I'll be seeing you soon, Detective."

"Guess so." Vasquez's voice wasn't exactly bursting with joy.

Liza hit the flash button. Michelle didn't even bother with the usual amenities. "You heard?"

"I just got off the phone with Detective Vasquez."

"Right," Michelle drawled. "Your friend on the force up there."

"I don't know about the friend part," Liza said. "But he agreed to try and get Jenny to stop bouncing around like a pinball. I told him I'd come to Santa Barbara —"

"Figure out the quickest way and bill it to the company," Michelle cut in. "We need to get Jenny calmed down and back to work as soon as possible."

Loud laughter came over the phone — probably from the party going on over Michelle's shoulder. Most evenings she could be found at a party somewhere in Hollywood.

The noise receded as Michelle apparently stepped farther away. "Well, I guess you'd better get on it."

The connection went dead before Liza even had a chance to respond. She hit flash again, but Vasquez was gone as well.

Liza returned to her mental list, then began to deal with it by dialing Sheriff Clements's cell phone number. He sounded as if he'd been on the verge of sleep, but he got considerably more alert as Liza gave her report.

"She's very skittish about coming in to the police. They didn't exactly treat her well when she was dealing with her uncle's murder," Liza finished, "so I said I'd get down there as soon as possible."

"Mmm-hmm." The way Clements said it, that wasn't just an "okay, get on with it" noise. He was considering something.

"It's a trip to Portland, and the earliest commercial flight won't be till morning," he said. "You don't have a car. And even if you put the pedal to the metal like some people must have, the drive would still take hours. Do you mind small planes?"

"I flew with Derrick Robbins from Orange County to Santa Barbara," Liza said, "and didn't lose my lunch or my mind."

"Good," Clements replied. "I've got a pilot friend. Let me check with him and get back to you . . ."

Fifteen minutes later, Liza stood peering

out the window as a police cruiser came down Hackleberry Avenue. She was already out the door as the car pulled up, to the accompaniment of Michael's voice calling, "Everything all right?"

"It's fine," she directed her voice to the lit upstairs window. "We've found Jenny. I'll tell you more when I get back."

It was only about a dozen miles to the Killamook Airport, but the deputy driving the car wasn't in full sirens-and-screeching-tires mode. Drifts of fog blew in off the bay and across the coastal highway, and the driver kept a sensible rate of speed.

Liza remembered what had happened to Terence Hamblyn along this same stretch of road and decided she approved of the deputy's caution.

They arrived at the airport to meet an older man with plentiful gray hair pulled back into a ponytail. He even had all of his teeth. He showed most of them in a devil-may-care grin. "Jimmy Perrine," he identified himself. "Bert Clements tells me you're in an almighty hurry to get to Santa Barbara."

"Liza Kelly. Pleased to meet you. I've got a friend down there who's in trouble."

Perrine nodded. "You're lucky I dropped the old crate here instead of over in Manzanita. No lights over there. Here the runways are lit. This place used to be a naval air station. They even have one of those huge hangars where they kept blimps —"

"I suppose you think a guided tour could help to calm someone who might be nervous about going up into the air with a total stranger aboard an overgrown kite with one engine," Liza cut in. "I'm not afraid of flying. I'm more interested in why Sheriff Clements suggested you, and how much it will cost."

"Clements has done some — favors — for me, and I've done the same for him." Perrine's grin didn't exactly hide that evasive answer. "And I don't expect to do this out of the goodness of my heart. When we land in Santa Barbara, I want to be able to top off my fuel tanks. Think of it as getting where you want to go for gas money."

I wonder how empty the tank is to start with, Liza thought. Then she shrugged. Michelle was paying. She'd consider it well worth the money. "Fine — as long as you've got enough to keep us in the air and get us there."

"That's the spirit!" The pilot laughed as Liza waved off the police car. Only after the deputy's taillights had almost vanished did she realize how quiet the place was.

"Not exactly a booming business this time of night," she said.

"Most of the flying round here happens in daylight, so that's when the field is attended." Perrine shrugged. "Over in Manzanita, the airstrip isn't attended at all."

Liza frowned, suddenly remembering that Oliver Chissel's private jet had landed at Manzanita. *You'd think a guy like Chissel would expect to go first class all the way,* she thought. *It's not like Manzanita's any closer. All things being equal, why would the head of a studio go with number two of two choices?*

Unless Ollie the Chiseler was up to something . . . then it might be useful to fly into and out of an airport with fewer witnesses to whatever was up.

The pilot's voice interrupted her thoughts. "Unless you're having second thoughts, we might as well get going."

Perrine's plane was older, smaller, and definitely more spartan than Derrick's air cruiser. There were no lounge accommodations, just a copilot's seat whose stuffing had seen better days.

As he taxied for a takeoff, Liza realized that the plane was considerably noisier, too. After they'd taken off, the pilot dug out a set of earphones with a built-in mike. "Sorry," his voice crackled slightly through the small speakers. "I'm usually up here solo, so I didn't think —"

Liza bit her lip to keep from screaming at him to keep his eyes on his flying.

They were high enough now to see patches of fog creeping across the highway like land-going clouds. The red of a car's taillights popped into view in the distance. Was that the police car that had ferried her?

Business had plunked Liza's rear end into many jets over the years. She knew how it felt to fly high and then come in over the diamond spray of city sprawl, highways like living necklaces of light. Flying down lower with Derrick had been a revelation, the terrain rolling out beneath her view like an animated map.

Low-level flying at night was yet another experience. Undeveloped areas lay dark and mysterious. Sometimes, Liza suspected they were over the ocean, but she kept her mouth clamped shut, not wanting to distract Perrine from his piloting. Flying over towns with streetlights and traffic, Liza had unashamedly gaped like a tourist.

At least no mountains suddenly appeared to blot out the sky (and them) before they reached Santa Barbara. Perrine brought them in for a sedate landing, and Liza had used her corporate credit card to arrange for a long, doubtless expensive drink for the big bird.

When they had gotten in range of the Santa Barbara control tower, Perrine had asked the controller to pass a message to Detective Vasquez with Liza's ETA. But when she came out into the small terminal, there was no sign of police or a police car.

Liza hoisted the small bag of girl supplies she'd brought along over one shoulder. *Damn the man,* she fumed. She was checking the overhead signs to find the way to a taxi when a voice called, "Over here, Liza."

Buck Foreman stood leaning against an empty counter. He smiled at her surprise. "Even though you flew, I was closer."

She rushed over to him. "Has Vasquez heard again from Jenny? Is she okay?"

"We set up a meet based on when you'd be arriving." Buck's usually hard cop face gave her a reassuring smile. "I've got my car outside. If you were going to be late, I considered heading out on my own — but I thought Jenny might find me intimidating."

"I think the Incredible Hulk would find you intimidating," Liza told him. But she smiled when she said that.

They got into Buck's SUV and drove through downtown Santa Barbara, ending at the parking lot of an ice-cream shop. Liza suddenly remembered that the last thing Jenny had done before her life turned upside down had been going on an ice-cream run for her Uncle D.

"Oregon plates," Buck spoke up.

"And that's Michael's silver Toyota," Liza agreed. She stepped out of the car.

As soon as Liza stood in the light from the store window, the driver's door on the silver car flew open. A second later, Jenny clung to Liza, babbling, "Sorrysorrysorrysorry."

Liza patted the trembling girl's hair. "I should have kept you out of the confrontation with Olbrich. But then, I didn't expect Guy to punch him in the nose."

"I just wanted to get . . . away," Jenny said. "When I finally got over freaking out, I was almost halfway here. Then, when I got to Uncle D.'s and found that someone had been in there . . ."

"You got freaked out again," Liza finished. "Well, the first thing to do is go to the police. After all, we both know a few of the detectives here. I'm sure they'll be able to help us."

Well, another cheerful idea bites the dust, Liza thought as she glared across the desk at Detective Vasquez. The moment they ar-

228

rived at the police station, he had reverted to his usual unhelpful self.

"How long were you in the house, total?" he asked Jenny.

"A couple of minutes. I — I don't know," she replied. "As soon as I got in there, though, I could see that things . . . weren't right."

The detective glanced from Jenny to Liza, his expression saying, "Oh, great, here's another one."

Still he managed to put more kindness in his voice than he'd ever bothered to with Liza. "Look. You were tired, you had a terrible day, and you're a . . . creative person."

What a nice way to say "overimaginative drama queen," Liza thought wryly.

"You don't understand," Jenny said. "Uncle D. was — not fussy, but pretty insistent that things should be where they ought to be."

Liza got a sudden flash of the library in his study, all those books about sudoku, puzzles, and cryptography carefully arranged by type and author. Derrick would have been able to lay his hands on any volume he wanted in an instant.

"And as soon as I came in," Jenny finished, "I could see that things were out of place."

Vasquez took a long, deep breath. Liza

had heard a lot of those whenever she'd tried to talk to him.

Buck Foreman spoke up, trying the cop-to-cop approach. "Maybe it's nothing, but maybe it's not. It wouldn't be the first time you've had trouble at that house. Why don't you dispatch a couple uniforms to go with us and we can all check it out?"

"All right." Vasquez picked up a phone and waved them from his desk. But Liza could still hear the detective as he lowered his voice behind her to speak to Buck. "You know it's gonna turn out to be a sloppy housekeeper."

Liza wondered where Vasquez had found the escorts that accompanied them. Police academy graduates? They looked more like a pair of high school kids in costume as cops for Halloween. Heck, they might even have been pulled from the junior high crowd of trick-or-treaters.

The tall, thin, fair one reminded her of Ichabod Crane. Liza wondered how he could move with the amount of equipment dangling from his belt. As if to provide more contrast, his partner was a short, stocky Latina. At least she had a no-nonsense look that reassured Liza.

Patrolman Ichabod surprised her by demanding the key when they arrived at Derrick's house — Jenny's house now, Liza corrected herself.

Her eyes went wide as the pair of officers took out their guns as they opened the door. Pistols and flashlights at the ready, the police went in.

"Santa Barbara Police!" Ichabod might look like a stork, but apparently he had the voice of a bull when he needed it.

Liza glanced over at Buck. "Hell, I'm ready to surrender, and I'm on their side," she muttered.

"Shhh," he replied. Liza noticed he'd dropped back a little, darting looks toward both sides of the house. He also had a hand under his jacket.

"The back of the house is a straight drop down over that cliff." Buck's voice was barely a whisper. "If anyone *is* in there, they either have to come out past the cops, or out the sides. In other words, right by us. Pays to be careful."

Moments later, Ichabod's bull voice called out, "Clear."

Buck stepped to the door. "That's our cue to come in."

As the lights went on, Liza glanced around. She wasn't sure what she expected — maybe one of Derrick's manly, comfortable armchairs on its side, or the stuffing

231

pulled out of the couch.

But the airy rooms she saw looked pretty much as she remembered them from her first visit — and a couple of subsequent ones with Jenny.

"Are you sure — ?" she began, but Jenny shook her head, pointing at the grandfather clock off to one side. "Uncle D. had that clock dead center on the wall. It's not now."

And why would a sloppy housekeeper bother to clean behind a large, heavy clock? Liza wondered. Jenny's suspicions were beginning to sound quite plausible.

They went through the house, and in each room, Jenny kept pointing out items — often little things — that were wrong.

The police officers were eager — this was probably a big chance for them to show their stuff to their boss — but they began to look disappointed.

Buck fell back to talk to Liza. "You know," he said in a low voice, "the killers went through here. So did the SBPD. They'd have to do the whole crime scene thing."

"But we tidied up after that," Liza said. "Jenny and I spent days —"

She suddenly broke off, heading for Derrick's former study. A good day and a half of her life had passed in there while she'd worked to restore order to Derrick's trashed library.

Okay, the effort hadn't been quite as altruistic as it sounded. Jenny had promised to give her the books when her uncle's estate was settled.

She faced the ranked volumes arranged on handmade shelves built into the wall. "Somebody screwed with these," Liza announced. "When I started in here, the books were every which way, some even jammed in backward. I wanted to bring it back to the way — the way Derrick had them. Cryptography along here, alphabetically by author, sudoku down by the desk —"

She stopped and pointed to a book. "That's out of place. And there's dust along here, when I had squared everything with the edge."

She turned to Buck. "This isn't messy cleaning."

He nodded. "I think it was a very careful, but very unprofessional, black-bag job."

.

16

"Black-bag job?" Liza turned to Buck Foreman in bafflement.

He looked at her. "You did publicity for *Spycraft,* and you have no idea what a black-bag job is?"

"What is it?" Jenny asked.

"Illegal entry, usually to get information or photographs. The FBI did it as a counter-espionage thing." The corner of Buck's mouth twitched. "And other law enforcement organizations have dabbled in it for other reasons."

Liza looked around the room. "And you think somebody did something like that here?"

Buck nodded. "Someone went through a lot of stuff in this house . . . and tried pretty hard to make sure no one noticed." He turned to the police officers. "I think we can tell Detective Vasquez that there's something to Jenny's report."

Liza could hear the doubting tone in the detective's voice even though she didn't have her ear to the receiver. This time, she was happy to leave the arguing to Buck.

"Detective Vasquez." Buck was obviously exercising considerable tact to say just those two words and not a whole lot of the others going through his head. "Your criminalists had to take lots of pictures of the crime scene, right? And the only people who were here afterward were just Liz and Jenny. You don't think two women would go through a major rearrangement of the place just by themselves, do you?"

He listened for a moment. "So your wife did how much, and how much did you end up doing?" Buck stifled a sigh. "Could you get hold of the general shots and bring them here? Yes, now."

About half an hour later, Vasquez arrived, his face doing its patented thundercloud impersonation. "I brought the pictures. Now what amazing things are you going to show me?"

"Have you got a shot of the living room with the grandfather clock?" Jenny asked.

The detective followed her, sorting through his collection of pictures. "Here," he said.

"And . . . here," Jenny replied.

Vasquez looked from the clock she stood beside to the photo in his hand and back again, a different kind of frown appearing on his features. "Step away," he ordered, looking at the picture again. "It's moved."

"It's been moved," Jenny insisted from the chair she'd just sat down in.

"Why would anyone move a big mother like that and then put it back?" Vasquez wanted to know.

"Probably someone who wanted to look at the back after poking around all the insides," Buck suggested.

"We think it was a black-bag job," Liza added.

That got her a skeptical look from the detective. "And what were they after? A collector's-item copy of the last *Spycraft* script? Derrick Robbins's autograph?"

"We don't know," Liza admitted. "But this is definitely not your ordinary break-in. There's a lot of valuable stuff around here."

"Like that clock," Vasquez sarcastically rapped his knuckles on the large wood frame. "Hard to fit in my car, much less carry out the door."

"There's expensive stuff that's smaller — a lot more portable," Liza argued back. "While we were waiting for you, Jenny and I went over the house. Silverware, artwork, electronics — they're all here."

She shot Vasquez a look. "If the break-in was the work of your friendly neighborhood junkie, he must have been pretty much out of his mind to overlook all that — not to mention remarkably neat. So who else could it be if it's not a black-bag job? Some perv? If so, he was looking in some pretty odd places for underwear to fondle."

"Well, it definitely wasn't our people," Vasquez insisted.

"I'm not saying it was," Liza said. "In fact, I don't think it was anybody official. The question is, who done it, what were they looking for . . ." She paused. "And was it connected to the death of Oliver Chissel?"

Now everyone was staring at her.

"I heard this Chissel guy got killed up in your hometown," Vasquez said. "Far, far, away from here. What, did you get some secret message saying that killing ties in with whatever happened here?"

"No, but there are a number of things in common between what happened here and what happened there. I found both bodies."

"Don't remind me," Vasquez said.

"There are other ties. Derrick worked on putting the film together before his death. I've got friends tangled up in that case — including Jenny," Liza replied. She looked at the girl. "You wouldn't even have known Chissel except for what happened to your uncle."

"I guess you're right," Jenny said. "Uncle D.'s plan was to produce *Counterfeit* on his own and then get a distribution deal. That way he could avoid interference from a studio —" Her voice got sour. "Like what Olbrich has been doing to the production now. Uncle D. said he wanted to fly under the radar as much as possible until he could premiere us at Sundance or someplace like that."

"That was shooting high, maybe." Liza frowned in thought. "But he had a solid production team and a good script."

She turned to Jenny again. "Where did your uncle make these plans — where did he run Counterfeit Productions?"

Jenny stared. "Why — from right here." She pointed down the hallway. "From his study, actually."

Liza smiled as they followed the girl to Derrick's plush sanctum. "Yeah, I run my business from home, too." She winced, mentally comparing this glorious space with the corner of the living room where she'd set up her computer. Liza still had a desk up in her bedroom, but that's where she'd done homework as a kid. She wasn't about to use it for either of her adult professions — publicity or sudoku.

Jenny pointed to a quartet of file cabinets set under a wooden working surface. "The one on the far right is correspondence. The one to the left of it is full of Uncle D.'s business papers. The other two were full of stuff for *Counterfeit*."

"Were?" Buck Foreman prompted.

Walking to the leftmost cabinet, Jenny pulled out the top drawer. It was empty. She did the same with the other three drawers. None had any contents.

"This used to be home base for *Counterfeit*," she said. "But when Mirage Productions wanted to come in and take over the film, our lawyer — well, Uncle D.'s lawyer, I guess — asked for all the papers."

Jenny carefully closed the cabinets, as if she were still concerned about disturbing her uncle.

Maybe being in here, where he spent so much time, makes Jenny feel she's stirring up his ghost. Liza stifled a sneeze. *Not to mention some dust.*

"Hey, Jenny," she asked. "When was the last time you were up here?"

"The last time you were with me," the girl answered promptly. "I've still got my place down in L.A. and enough to live on, and of

239

course I've been all over the place with the filming." She shook her head. "It just didn't seem right to move in here. I mean, it's not like the place is mine, after all."

Liza and Buck both whipped round. "It's not?"

"Not in the way you're thinking." Jenny tried to explain herself. "I inherit everything, but there's still a lot of legal mumbo jumbo before it's all official. And even then — this is Uncle D.'s place."

Frowning, Buck pointed to the third file cabinet. "Is your lawyer's address in there?" he asked.

"Sure." Jenny knelt and pulled out the bottom drawer, which was stuffed with an array of papers. She ran a finger along the tabs and finally extracted a fairly bulky file folder. "It's in here, along with his phone number. Do you think you need it?"

"I think," Buck said, "we're going to pay a visit to this gentleman bright and early tomorrow —" He broke off, looking at his watch. "Today. And now, I don't want him to have any idea we're coming."

"Yeah," Vasquez said. "Surprise is always the best tactic with lawyers." He squared the set of crime scene photos he still held. "I guess we're done here. Do you intend to spend the night, Ms. Robbins?"

Jenny stared. "I don't *think* so," she replied.

"Well, I'll ask patrol to beef up our presence in the area," the detective said. "But I think you'd better bring in some private security to keep an eye on the place." He gestured around. "As you say, there's a lot of valuable stuff here. And if there's nobody in the house —"

"I can recommend some people, if you like," Buck told Jenny. "And if we're not staying here, we'd better find a place to rest our heads."

With the three police officers in the lead, they headed out of the house. Buck leaned over to Liza as they waited for Jenny to lock up. "Why did you want to know how long it had been since Jenny was here?" he asked quietly.

"I'm not sure," Liza admitted. What she didn't tell Buck was that she had experienced the same surge of assurance when she was first teasing out the logical chain that solved a tough sudoku. There was definitely a long way to go, but Liza felt a certainty she hadn't before.

If only you knew what that meant, the critical voice in the back of her head pointed out.

They caught a little flack, three adults turning up at a hotel after midnight with only one small shoulder bag as luggage. But Liza's corporate card got them separate rooms.

Besides, the recollection of the desk clerk's mere disapproval shrank to nothing in comparison to Michelle Markson's reaction when Liza finally called her. Liza found herself competing with throbbing dance music instead of laughter — apparently, the party had moved to a club somewhere.

The change of scene hadn't done much to jolly up Michelle, however. "I've been waiting forever!" she said sharply.

Yeah, probably on the edge of your seat down there in Club Eardrum, Liza thought.

"You know this business stands or falls on information," Michelle went on.

And Markson Associates was always the firstest with the mostest. Of course Michelle was annoyed at what she saw as her partner holding out on her.

"We got Jenny, she's sleeping in the room next to me here in Santa Barbara," Liza reported.

"How quickly can you get her back to work?" Michelle asked, mindful of the wrath of the studio executives. And the bad press that followed it.

"We want to come down to L.A. tomorrow to see Jenny's lawyer," Liza began.

"Her lawyer? Are there legal troubles?"

Liza could only admire the way Michelle could lower her voice while making it sharper at the same time.

"Not in the way you mean. But did you know that Derrick Robbins's estate still hasn't been settled?"

"No." Michelle's voice was back to normal — just slower, as she considered what Liza had just said. "No, I didn't know that at all."

"I think there might be something interesting to learn if I poke around and see why it's taking so long."

"Hmm. Your hunches have a habit of proving out." Michelle abruptly shifted gears. "All right, but I want Jenny back on set by the afternoon. One of the people here has been talking about his private plane. I'll arrange something —" Michelle paused. "I don't suppose Virginville has an airport?"

"Maiden's Bay," Liza automatically corrected. "The nearest airfield is Killamook . . . or Manzanita."

Suddenly, she felt a renewal of her interest in where Oliver Chissel had been keeping his corporate jet. Might be interesting to check that out, too.

"I'll speak to you in the morning about any arrangements."

243

And that was that. Liza yawned and turned to the bed.

The next thing she knew, the room phone was ringing and sunlight was coming through a chink in the heavy drapes.

"This is your wake-up call." Buck Foreman sounded as if he'd been up and out for a run already. Liza tried to focus her eyes. Eight hours of sleep — just barely.

"Breakfast in half an hour, then we're out of here," Buck warned.

Liza and Jenny shared the supplies in Liza's bag and managed to beat Buck's deadline by a good minute.

"Could I get the car keys you were using?" Buck tactfully asked Jenny when she had finished her orange juice. "I made arrangements to get the rental back up to Maiden's Bay. Michael needs his wheels. We'll take my car to visit our legal friends."

The firm of Colberg & Gaskell wasn't one of those flashy, Century City practices. Their officers were in a fairly low-rise, staid, old building in a staid, older part of town.

So meeting Joshua "Call me Josh" Colberg was a bit of a surprise. Shaking hands with the effusive attorney, Liza found herself thinking of him as a Gary Schilling gone bad. Like Gary, Josh had thinning hair

244

(aggressively combed over in his case) and round, unformed features — the kind of face made for a collar and tie. Seeing the lawyer in ultramodish Hollywood casual attire was like watching Ron Howard trying to play Brad Pitt.

Josh's bright smile dimmed a bit after Buck handed him his card. "Private investigator?" Now his voice started to sound like Alfalfa from the Little Rascals.

"We're looking into certain irregularities in the affairs between Derrick Robbins and Oliver Chissel — both recently deceased." Even seated across a large desk, Buck somehow managed to loom over the hapless Josh.

"I can't imagine how you think I can help you," Josh almost whined. "Derrick Robbins was my father's client. Dad set up his will and handled most of his affairs. He and Max Gaskell conducted a general practice, while I handled entertainment law."

Liza's lips quirked, but she managed to keep from commenting. Translated from Josh-speak, that probably meant that Dad and his partner brought in the meat and potatoes for the firm, while Junior was off chasing rainbows.

"I'm surprised we're not speaking with your father then," Buck said gravely.

245

"Well, Dad's not with us anymore. He and Max Gaskell went flying — Max was an enthusiastic pilot —"

This is just what I need to hear right before going up again in a small plane, Liza thought.

Josh apparently misunderstood the look on her face. "It happened shortly after Derrick Robbins passed away. We had just finished the agreement with Mirage Productions."

"So you've been handling things since then?" Buck asked.

"Ah — yeah," Josh responded warily. "Not that there is very much to do."

"I suppose not," Buck's voice got grimmer. "Especially if you are dragging your feet over settling Mr. Robbins's estate."

"That's not the way it is at all," Josh protested, weakening his case by adding, "exactly."

"Then how is it — exactly?" Buck demanded.

"Certain executives at Mirage Productions . . . suggested a . . . postponement." Josh looked like a hamster backed into a corner of its cage.

Liza could just imagine — Josh, the would-be player, just about ready to jump through hoops for Mirage and Chissel. The poor boob probably looked up to Chissel as

246

a master of the deal.

"Forgive me." Josh turned to Jenny, apparently just realizing that his supposed client was also in the room. "I thought — I got the impression — that the Mirage people were afraid you'd be distracted."

"Not as much as you might think," Jenny said.

"I bet that's a big relief off your mind," Liza muttered.

"Besides," Josh added, taking refuge in his best lawyerly manner, "there's the problem of the assets."

"And what problem is that?" Buck's voice amazingly managed to mix gentle inquiry and threatening menace.

"When Mr. Robbins set up Counterfeit Productions — my father tried to persuade him not to use that name, by the way — Mr. Robbins liquidated a number of holdings for start-up money. If necessary, he was willing to capitalize the whole production."

"Breaking the producer's golden rule," Buck said.

Liza nodded. "OPM."

"What?" Jenny asked.

"Other People's Money," Liza explained.

"The cash was being held in a numbered account in the Cayman Islands," Josh rushed on. "Only Mr. Robbins had the number and the password. He didn't share that information with my father."

Certainly not with you, Liza silently added.

"Uncle D. never mentioned any of this stuff to me," Jenny said.

"So how much do these missing assets come to?" Buck wanted to know.

"Er — ah —" Josh ducked behind his desk, coming up a second later with a file folder. He spread it open on the desk and picked up a sheet of paper.

"In round figures —"

Buck reached over, took the sheet from Josh, and looked at it. His widening eyes betrayed what was behind his poker face as he turned to Jenny. "Remember last night when you were wondering what papers could be left over from your uncle's estate that needed looking into? I think we found them — about three-quarters of a million of them."

248

17

On the trip homeward, the plane was larger, but the ride was bumpier. Liza was somewhat relieved to arrive at the airport and meet the uniformed pilot and copilot waiting for her and Jenny. She had been afraid to find some sky-happy acquaintance of Michelle's who was going to loop-the-loop all the way back to Maiden's Bay.

Instead, Michelle had somehow gotten the use of some sort of corporate jet with executive amenities. Liza and Jenny strapped themselves into swivel chairs in a spacious lounge. Coming over the intercom, the pilot's voice apologized that there was no steward.

"Just as well," Liza called back. "We're on the Hollywood diet."

"We are?" Jenny asked. "What's that?"

"That's the loss of appetite you get when dealing with a studio that wants to make you throw up," Liza replied.

That turned Jenny's mind to what they had just heard. "I can't get over that Colberg guy doing what he said." She shook her head. "I mean, he was supposed to be Uncle D.'s lawyer."

I guess you've got a lot to learn about lawyers, Liza thought. Instead she said, "Josh is your uncle's lawyer's son. The chump was probably wetting himself at a chance to sit at the table with the great Oliver Chissel. Ollie the Chiseler would probably have eaten him for lunch."

"I don't think so," Jenny said. "Josh Colberg struck me more like a lightweight snack."

"An hors d'oeuvre," Liza suggested with a grin.

That bit of joking was the last lighthearted thing that happened on their ride. Almost as soon as they got to their cruising altitude, the plane began making sudden dips and jumps.

"I'm afraid we're catching some onshore winds," the pilot's voice crackled over the intercom. "It may get a little turbulent. I'll see if we can get above them. Please keep your seat belts on."

Whatever the flight crew tried didn't seem to work, though. The rest of the journey felt more like a roller-coaster ride.

Jenny's face looked as white as Liza's knuckles, which were clamped to her chair's armrests. Her mind kept going back to the other story Josh Colberg had told — the one where his father had gone up in the sky with an avid amateur pilot. Was this what they had gone through before taking the big plunge?

Liza shuddered and decided she'd better distract herself from such morbid thoughts. Maybe if she took a shot at trying to untangle all the information about the various crimes, organizing it logically . . .

It would be pretty ironic if you solved all of this, but crashed and died before you could tell anyone, that perverse, back-of-the-head voice commented.

Shut up, Liza told the voice. Then she put her mind to organizing.

The whole situation just seemed to keep growing. There was sabotage on the set, murder and vandalism — or vandalism and murder, given the broken glass found with Oliver Chissel's body. And now there was a big honking wad of missing cash.

Liza frowned. Actually, the cash went astray before all the rest. She remembered something Buck had once said, about all crimes in the end being about money or sex. Considering the way Chissel looked, even

251

before the tide got him, she decided to concentrate on the money angle.

That brought her back to the misplaced chunk of capital Derrick Robbins had raised to bankroll *Counterfeit*. As far as motive went, that was more of a reason to kill Derrick than anyone else. And Derrick had died for altogether different reasons.

Could someone have believed that Chissel had gotten hold of the missing cash? Could they then have tried to force its location out of him? That someone would have to know about the cash in the first place, of course. Derrick hadn't been blabbing around about it. Jenny never even knew her uncle had been raising the money for the film. *He sure didn't mention it to me,* Liza thought. It had taken a personal visit and a little intimidation to get it out of Josh Colberg. And Caymanian bankers had a reputation for being as secretive as their Swiss counterparts. So who might have gotten a whiff of the cash stash?

Derrick had been friendly with Guy Morton, involving him early in planning for *Counterfeit*. Could Derrick have told the actor about his backup financing plan?

Then too, there was that *Masked Justice* episode where Morton's character used the oncoming tide to loosen a prisoner's tongue.

But Guy had shown honest affection —
and a strong protective streak — when it
came to Jenny Robbins. Why would he go
after her inheritance?

Nah. It just didn't fit what she knew of
the man.

*Unless he's a much better actor than you
think,* that annoying voice suggested.

Liza ignored that idea for a more promising one. What if Morton thought he was
saving Jenny's money from Chissel? That
suspicion could prove pretty bad for Ollie
the Chiseler, especially if he didn't actually
have his hands on the money.

But would Guy Morton actually leave a
person to drown, even if that person didn't
tell him what he wanted to hear? That didn't
square with Liza's assessment of Guy Morton. Punching someone in the nose — as
he'd done with Lloyd Olbrich — that was
Morton's style. But to stand cold-bloodedly
by while someone died? Liza didn't think
so.

So who else might have known about the
money? Jenny?

Liza shook her head. The girl's surprise
had been too genuine. Liza had been around
Jenny at too many unguarded moments to
doubt that she'd been completely surprised.

Besides, Jenny was the one who'd pointed

out that the house had been searched, leading them to the discovery of the money in the first place. She'd told the cops first thing, despite the fact that she was afraid of dealing with the police. If she were searching for the big bucks, why let the cat out of the bag?

Besides, *when* could Jenny have searched the house? She'd been convalescing, then throwing herself into preparations for the film, and finally spending all this time away on location.

Liza frowned. There was the germ of something there, below the surface.

Another thought intruded. Suppose Jenny knew about the missing money, and so did someone else — someone who had secretly searched the house! They could be in a race to retrieve the fortune!

She shook her head, her stomach flip-flopping as the plane seemed to go in about three directions at once. Maybe this wasn't the time for higher thought, Liza decided. This might just be a time to live in her lizard brain, hoping for survival.

They jounced and shuddered through the air for a while more, then finally encountered calmer atmosphere. Neither passenger had to resort to the barf bags that the pilot had helpfully pointed out. But, for Liza at least, it had been a very close thing.

The pilot came on the intercom again, rather apologetically announcing that they'd be landing at Killamook. "I'm afraid the other field you suggested is unattended, ma'am."

Yeah, Liza thought, *that's why I wanted to get a look at it.*

Still, the guy up front had a boss to answer to, and he didn't want to risk an aircraft that probably cost a hefty chunk of change on a possibly empty airfield. Liza didn't object, and soon enough they had landed.

Only when they were on the ground — Liza managed to restrain herself from dropping to her knees and kissing it — did she realize they had no ground transport.

Jimmy Perrine came by and gave Liza a jaunty wave. "Looks like you've come up in the world," he said with a glance at the corporate splendor standing behind her on the runway. "But if you need to make the trip again, I'd be happy to oblige — at the usual rate."

Liza was almost tempted to ask him what a drive to Maiden's Bay might cost, but she decided to fall back on her cell phone instead. Michael picked up on the second ring and promised to be over there as soon as possible.

Jenny found them a seat out of the breeze, and they composed themselves to wait.

"Michael won't be too long," Liza assured her friend. "It's not as if he's fighting his way here on the 405," she mentioned a well-known, almost infamous, L.A. freeway.

Her phone rang, and Buck Foreman answered her hello.

"Our chat with good old Josh this morning made me start thinking about Chissel's money situation," he said. "So I got on the horn to the guys I had checking into Ollie's financials."

"From your tone of voice, I think you just found something." Liza forced herself to relax her grip, reminding herself that she couldn't literally squeeze information out of a phone.

"He was in trouble," Buck reported. "It's gotten worse lately. The Mirage deal sucked up most of Chissel's available capital. He's been running on fumes so long even his debts have debts. For the last couple of months, he's been juggling like a maniac to keep his financial house of cards from collapsing."

Buck's tone was almost appreciative. "The guy was good. He was milking company funds for all he was worth — hell, he even finagled his house staff onto the corporate payroll. But sooner or later, it was all going to come out. He needed a decent hit to help unload Mirage onto someone else and get his money back, or he needed an infusion of capital to finance some other scam."

"If he needed a hit so quickly, why was he extending the shoot on *Counterfeit* instead of pushing to wrap it up ASAP?" Liza paused for a moment, then asked, "Unless the extension was in itself a way to help him get his hands on some capital?"

"I don't think your local mayor could pay him enough to make the guy happy, not even to get him out of town," Foreman said.

"No, of course not. That wasn't what I was thinking. What if it gave Chissel a shot at gaining access to Derrick Robbins's offshore account?" Liza remembered the notion that had niggled her on the flight north — in between fierce moments fighting nausea and fearing for her life. "Since she's started work on *Counterfeit,* Jenny has had too much on her plate even to get down to Santa Barbara."

Jenny, who had been listening intently, nodded vigorously and said, "It's been crazy."

"Keeping her too busy on the set to even breathe left lots of time for Chissel and company to make a leisurely search of the house," Liza went on. "They didn't want silver or electronics. They didn't even take the jewelry. I think they were trying to find Derrick's Cayman account number and the password."

"I'm not ready to bet on that yet," Buck said, "but it was a pretty thorough search, if it went as far as moving that big monster of a grandfather clock," Buck said. "If Chissel found it, Jenny is screwed out of her uncle's legacy to her. No way to track numbered accounts without the appropriate number to access them."

But how to get the number? Liza wondered. The scenario of an avenging Guy Morton sweating information out of a thieving Chissel flashed through Liza's head, only to be blotted out by an even brighter flash.

"I don't think so," Liza said confidently. "I don't think Chissel found that number when he searched the house. The movie kept dragging on. The sabotage on the set didn't stop."

"I think you lost me," Buck told her.

"Chissel would have wrapped the instant he had the money in hand. He might have been looking, but nothing's turned up yet," Liza said. "Think of the film set . . . First, they tried slowing down the pace of work. I bet that's why the sabotage started. Then they got rid of the director who was helming the film. They had to, since Terence Hamblyn was getting finished ahead of schedule. So they bring in Lloyd Olbrich, someone guaranteed to start almost from scratch so he can reshape the film in his own image. But Olbrich must know how fragile things are at Mirage. He's been pushing like mad to get filming done. Maybe he had to be slowed down, too. So, more sabotage. And more serious sabotage."

"You think Chissel was capable of sabotaging his own movie?" Buck demanded.

"Sure. He had a rep as the kind of guy who'd sell his own family for a buck. I think Chissel was a gambler — all these big-money guys are. He was willing to bet on delaying his desperately needed film if it meant a cash payday to keep things going." Liza paused for a moment. "But I don't think he was doing the sabotage — or the searching. Ollie might be a chiseler, but he wouldn't want to get his hands dirty. He used a tool — and I think that tool was named Peter Hake."

"Chissel's arm-twister and bagman," Buck said.

"A guy with all the expertise not only to screw things up around the movie set, but also to break into the Robbins house and find a clue that would enable Chissel to loot Jenny's inheritance before she even knew she had it." As Liza made her case, the logic seemed stronger and stronger.

"But then Chissel died," Buck pointed out, "and if I remember what you were saying to me, the sabotage still went on. Didn't you nearly have a floating pier overturn on you the other day, post-Chissel?"

"I thought that might have been caused by somebody else," Liza admitted. Then she suddenly remembered the scene as Deke Jannsky got fired as an extra. He'd pointed to his trademark disreputable hunting hat . . . and somebody from the crew had produced a double. Couldn't the saboteur have done the same? Had she been fixated on Deke, when a film insider was really to blame?

As she told that story to Buck Foreman, another thought hit her. "What if Hake got tired of being a tool? If Chissel was losing it, maybe his pet thug decided to get rid of him . . . and take a shot at finding the money for himself."

■ ■ ■ ■

PART FOUR:
DEPARTMENT OF
DIRTY SECRETS

■ ■ ■ ■

Okay, maybe it's not as dirty a secret as you were hoping for. But it is a topic many puzzle creators don't like to discuss. I'm talking about the so-called "back door" in sudoku. All puzzles have a space where, if the correct candidate is filled in, the rest of the puzzle solves out with the simplest techniques.

The problem lies in finding that space and candidate, because it may involve the G word — guesswork. That's a horrible blasphemy to many in Sudoku Nation.

Sometimes, though, a solver can find a back door without the need for guessing. You can accept such a thing from computer-generated sudoku — the programming might have a blind spot. When it comes to puzzles made by hand, though, when the rating says a sudoku is fiendish, but it only takes three rounds of solving techniques before the puzzle rolls over and plays dead, that can be embarrassing for the creator.

For a solver, though, there's nothing like the moment when the whole puzzle opens up for you . . .

— Excerpt from *Sudo-cues* by Liza K

18

Liza cut the connection on her phone and turned to find a pair of big green eyes staring at her.

"You think Hake is the one behind all this?" Jenny blurted. "The break-in at Uncle D.'s place, the sabotage, all those broken windows —" Her voice lowered. "The murder?"

"It doesn't matter what I think. It only matters what the police can prove. There's a big difference between thinking a person did something and proving it, especially in court," Liza warned. "Logically speaking, though, Hake would be a good suspect. He's got a strong motive, checkable opportunity, and definitely the means for the break-ins. The same goes for the sabotage. As for the murder — well, there's plenty of motive."

Hake claimed he was traveling on important business for Chissel the evening of the mur-

der, Liza thought. *But he never told the sheriff exactly what that business was. Wouldn't it be funny if the alibi he didn't want to talk about turned out to be a breaking-and-entering job in Santa Barbara?*

"Hake actually got picked up once for breaking windows, so I guess you can say he's got a history. He was very insistent on not being around, so maybe he can prove that. And I can't think of any sort of motive," Liza admitted.

But the window smashing was related somehow to Chissel's death. The broken glass buried with Chissel seemed to point that out. Of course, the broken glass could be some sort of attempt to fix the time of the crime and help the killer create an alibi. Hake had been very insistent about not possibly being able to smash the Main Street windows.

And then there was the whole bizarre effort involved in disposing of Chissel's body. A professional like Hake would have to know the dangers of hanging around a corpse long enough for a fancy murder by drowning. Why take such a risk? Why not quietly dump Chissel's dead body in the bay?

Okay. Suppose Chissel was the usual brains of the operation when it came to breaking the rules. Maybe Hake didn't have the benefit of a Chissel plan in doing away with his boss. So he had to wing it. Or maybe he came up with some sort of over-complicated "perfect crime" that required broken glass and the body being found.

After the battering it had taken on the plane trip north, Liza's head was just not ready to deal with such logical curlicues. She also had no intention of sharing any of this with Jenny. The girl was fairly well freaked out already.

Liza's cell phone rang again.

"Proof?" Jenny whispered.

No. A very satisfied Michelle Markson spoke over the line. "I assumed you'd have arrived by now," she said.

"We just got off the plane," Liza assured her, "and now we are taking a minute to catch our breath. The trip was on the rough side —"

"But you made it." Michelle cut through the clutter in her usual style. "Now you'll have to get Jenny onto the set as soon as possible. They're shooting in the harbor again. I'm sure you'll know where that is."

"Of course. I expected — well, at least a little more trouble from Lloyd Olbrich about moving away from where Jenny was held after she was kidnapped."

"Oh, he tried to make some," Michelle said. "Puffed himself up about going to the union, fixing things so that Jenny would never work again."

Every nightmare I've had since Jenny ran off after Guy Morton decked Olbrich, Liza thought.

"One little prick."

Liza realized she must have missed the rest of what Michelle was saying. "Excuse me?"

"That's all it took to deflate that man," her partner went on. "If he was hell-bent on trying to nuke Jenny's career, I promised him MAD — mutually assured destruction." Michelle almost seemed to lick her lips at the old term of Cold War brinkmanship. "Besides the ammunition you gave me, I mentioned our new client — an actor turned author named Jonathan Sanders. He's emerged from seclusion with a new book about a young performer driven to the edge by the abuse, mental and otherwise, of a sadistic director. We were debating whether to market it as a roman à clef or as a straight memoir."

"You didn't really take on —" Liza sputtered.

"Take on a new client?" Michelle asked sweetly. "That's for me to know and for Mr.

266

Olbrich to sweat over. In any event, you and Jenny should find him a changed — or at least a more cautious — man."

Michelle continued, "In return for his co-operation, Jenny has to be seen as both responsible and professional — which means you have to get her back to work without delay."

"We're just waiting on a ride now," Liza said.

"Good." Michelle cut out.

Liza relayed her partner's news.

Before Jenny could answer, they had a new distraction — Michael arrived.

"Well, I'd say your car came through without any serious damage," Liza said, glancing over the rental as she climbed into the backseat.

"Except that the rental people are going to rake me over the coals for the mileage." Michael aimed a mock-reproachful look at Jenny, but relented at the girl's stricken expression. "Joking — just joking."

Liza sent a worried look at the girl sitting beside her in the backseat. "Are you feeling all right?"

Jenny put a hand on her middle. "I don't know if my insides got scrambled on that plane ride, or if it's the prospect of facing Lloyd Olbrich again. But the last time my stomach felt like this, I was getting ready to take my first screen test."

"Well, from what I've seen of your screen tests, you came through it all right," Liza reassured her. She turned to Michael and explained about their new destination.

"Michelle's wish is my command," he said, pulling away.

By the time they got to Maiden's Bay, Jenny had gone from pale to light green.

"I'm sure a few more minutes can't make all that much difference," Liza told the girl. "Why don't we stop off at Ma's? You could have some tea and toast . . ."

"I appreciate your wanting to help," Jenny replied. "But with all due respect, you're not my mother." She gave Liza a wan smile. "Besides, I think if I tried to eat anything, even easy food, it might come right back up." Tapping Michael on the shoulder, Jenny pointed across the street to Schilling's. "Could we stop off at the pharmacy? Maybe I'll be able to get something there."

Going inside, Jenny began scouting the aisle instead of consulting with Nora Schilling. Liza chatted with the older woman, nodding toward the front where sunlight again came in. "So you got your window replaced — that looks a lot better."

Nora nodded. "Ray Massini managed to

pry some money out of the insurance company."

Sure, Liza thought. *Mister Mayor doesn't want his downtown to look like some kind of war zone.*

"It's nice to be able to look out again." Then Nora shook her head. "But it won't be the same. I don't know how we'll ever replace Grandpa Gustav's glass vials."

The window space once occupied by the colored glass bottles and odd-shaped flasks with their brilliantly colored contents now stood empty. "They were original with the store," Nora sighed. "It's a real shame they went with the window."

"We have bigger problems than that, Mom." Gary Schilling came out from behind the prescription desk, looking harassed. Liza was a little surprised. She'd never heard Gary use that tone with his mother before.

She promised herself she'd ask Michael to use his Hollywood connections. Surely he knew a prop man or woman who could get hold of a few pieces of old, richly colored glass without paying a fortune for it.

Jenny appeared with a bottle of the extra thick, extra strength pink stuff and paid for it. When she got into her seat in the back of Michael's car, she opened the package and took a quick slug straight from the bottle.

Liza hid a smile as Jenny made a face. She remembered the taste of that stuff on too many mornings after junk food-fueled late-night study sessions in college.

She had better sense than to let stress get to her that way these days.

"Just remember to brush your teeth, or at least swish some water around in your mouth before you report for makeup," she warned the girl. "Turning up in front of the cameras with a bright pink tongue will give the continuity people fits — not to mention Lloyd."

That had the desired effect of making Jenny laugh as she got out of the car.

Liza didn't accompany her, though she watched from the car as the girl approached one of the production assistants. "As Jenny said, I'm not her mother," Liza told herself. "And she's not off for her first day at kindergarten."

Nonetheless, she quietly watched until the girl was out of sight.

Michael turned to her. "Where to next?"

"City Hall, I think," Liza said. Sheriff Clements should hear what she'd learned . . . and maybe what she suspected as well.

At least Liza didn't get the Armando

Vasquez bum's rush when she told the sheriff about the break-ins in Santa Barbara and the possible connection with Peter Hake and the events in Maiden's Bay. But Clements didn't exactly leap into "calling all cars" mode, either.

He ran a thoughtful finger along his mustache. "As far as I can see, you've got a whole lot of guesswork holding together a few chunks of fact here. As far as the sabotage goes, we might get lucky and catch whoever is doing it in the act — if he's still doing it. Your next strongest chunk of fact is for the B and E in Santa Barbara. That comes down to us doing a whole lot of legwork checking where Hake was when, making a case for a crime that happened in another jurisdiction."

"Yes, but if you got him on that, couldn't you use that as leverage to get more information out of him on the other cases?" Liza asked.

"As you yourself admitted, we don't have all that much linking Hake to either the vandalism or the murder," Clements said. "So far as we've been able to ascertain, Hake flew out of town early in the evening on business for Chissel." He grinned. "That could be good with your theories — possibly he headed down to commit some

271

minor burglary in California. He didn't get back until after the time of death — that's all we have proof for here."

"Could it be that he — or somebody else — is trying to play with the evidence by burying Chissel on the beach to throw off the time of death?"

Clements shrugged. "That happens more often on mystery shows than in real life," he said. "Much more often."

Liza sighed. "So, bottom line — does anything I had to say interest you?"

"Oh, a lot of it interests me," Clements replied. "The whole lost money thing raises a new motive — which is just what we need, but it's something to look into. For the rest, I don't think it justifies diverting my limited time and manpower onto just one suspect."

"Especially if the payoff is in Santa Barbara," Liza muttered.

The sheriff shot her a look, but then nodded with reasonable good nature. "Speaking of other jurisdictions, we got a line on Deke Jannsky," he said.

"You did?" Michael asked.

Clements nodded. "Apparently, he decided it was best to lie low out of town after the incident with your car's windshield. Seems he got himself into a fairly serious fight with a tourist over in Gold Beach. The upshot is that Deke will be a guest of another county — not Killamook — for the near future. Maybe that will give both of you time to cool down."

With that news, Liza and Michael were dismissed. They walked along Main Street to Michael's rental car, Liza frowning as she went point by point over the case she'd presented to Clements. Could she have made it any stronger?

"Speak of the devil," Michael muttered.

Liza looked up to find Peter Hake walking toward them.

"I'm surprised to find you hanging on up here, Mr. Hake," Liza said. "Now that the man who usually holds your leash isn't around anymore."

Hake responded with a growl that showed teeth, and a swagger. That disappeared as Liza went on.

"You know, things would be warmer — and richer — down in, say . . . Santa Barbara."

"Pardon?" But Hake stopped.

"I mean, why are you breaking your neck to screw up production on *Counterfeit* when it can't help Chissel anymore? If you're going out on your own, I think we should tell you that other people know about Derrick Robbins's missing money now."

"I'm afraid I don't understand." Hake's voice held puzzled curiosity, but his face had turned into the "give nothing away" mask it must have worn for a lot of police interrogations.

Instead of being happy that she'd forced him onto the defensive, Liza found herself getting angrier and angrier that she couldn't break through his macho façade and get to the truth. Her words got rasher.

"The better part of a million bucks — that could be motive for a lot of nasty things. I wouldn't be surprised if you find yourself moved to the front burner on the murder case. Maybe you decided to grab this score for yourself. However it turns out, you may end up just stuck with whatever severance Mirage gives you. And that probably won't be much, since the whole company is going down the tubes."

Hake turned to Michael. "Is this skirt of yours spouting some dialogue from your latest script? It might make a good potboiler mystery movie — but I don't see how it has anything to do with me."

He stepped away and continued down the street. Liza noticed, though, that Hake's big hands had clenched into fists.

"Well, that was pretty stupid, wasn't it?" she asked in self-disgust as she and Michael walked along.

"I think it was pretty optimistic of you, expecting him to break down and confess to anything, much less everything," Michael told her. "Dealing with intrusive questions has to be part of his job description, doesn't it?"

They drove back to Hackleberry Avenue. As they came onto Liza's block, she realized something was parked at the end of her driveway.

"Oh, dear God!" she groaned.

"Mrs. H. checked with the garage. When she learned how long your car was going to be out of commission, she decided to lend you her Oldsmobile. She had to struggle with her heart to let go of it for a while. But she's so fond of you. She means it in the kindest possible way, you know."

"Michael, that thing was old while Reagan was in the White House. The first term! And I don't think it was running right then."

"Well, it's sturdy — not to mention an interesting shade of greenish blue, too," Michael said. "Can't wait to see you behind the wheel. I'm planning on breaking out my camera to immortalize the moment."

Liza stomped off into her house. A few minutes later, she came stomping over next door. "I need the keys," she announced grimly. "I'm taking the Olds for a twirl around town. There's nothing in the refrigerator."

"Just let me get them for you . . . and my camera!"

After an errand run in the embarrassing car for supplies, Liza came home, made supper, and tried to do some more sudoku work. Rusty hoped for an evening walk, but Liza was already yawning. She only took him out as far as the bushes. Then she dragged herself upstairs and went to bed.

Liza didn't know how long she'd slept. It was still dead dark outside when Rusty's barking roused her. She pried her eyes open and called out, "What do you want, you crazy dog?"

Staggering to her feet, she went to the upstairs landing and looked down. Rusty wasn't jumping around as usual. He stood rooted before the front door, his hackles up, using a deeper, nastier bark, interspersed with low growls.

This was Rusty at his most serious — not the sort of barking he directed at the mailman, but at a burglar.

Burglar! Liza whirled back to her bedroom to peer out the window. All she saw was a confusing mass of shadows, but she clearly heard the sounds from some sort of struggle — grunts and thudding blows.

She stepped back, wrestling her way into an old, worn terry cloth bathrobe that had once belonged to her father. Scooping up her cell phone, Liza plunged back downstairs and turned on the lights. When that didn't stop the sounds outside, she hit the speed-dial button for 911 with one hand while grabbing hold of Rusty's collar with the other.

Liza shouted her address to the operator who answered, reporting an assault in progress. Then she flung the door open, yelling, "I've called the police!"

She stood frozen in the doorway, staring out at the scene illuminated by the light streaming out from behind her.

Peter Hake lay writhing in the driveway while Michael, her husband, stood over him — kicking the stuffing out of the bigger man.

Michael looked up, his face pale. "You called the cops?" he gasped. "Thank God! I don't know how much longer I can keep this up!"

19

"Michael?" Liza had to struggle to keep herself from screaming at her estranged husband. "What the hell are you doing?"

"Doing?" Michael stared up at her, then quickly turned back to Hake, who'd managed to push himself up on one arm. Rearing back, Michael lashed out with his right foot, which thumped into Hake's ribs, knocking him flat again.

"I think that's pretty obvious, isn't it?" He grunted as he kicked Hake again, making him curl up into a ball.

Liza stood there in horror as that went on for minutes more until a police cruiser arrived. Peter would swear and threaten to kill Michael, try to get up off the ground, and Michael would kick the supports out from under him. Hake would lay there and get his breath back, then threaten to kill Michael again, and the whole thing would repeat.

Liza was overjoyed when the deputies bailed from the vehicle, their pistols already drawn.

"Police! Freeze!" Curt Walters shouted.

Michael took a long jump back from the prone form in the driveway, then stopped all movement.

"Hands above your head!" the other deputy ordered.

Michael immediately complied.

"Now what's going on here?" Curt demanded.

Hake awkwardly pushed himself up on one elbow. "This man attacked me." His voice was rough with pain — and was that embarrassment?

Curt looked in bafflement from one man to the other. It would take about one and two-thirds Michaels to make one Peter Hake. "He attacked you?"

Peter Hake nodded, croaking, "From behind."

He shifted again, and Michael shouted, "Don't let him get up!"

Curt turned his pistol on Hake. "You stay." Then he glanced at Michael. "You tell me why."

"I've been staying next door, trying to keep an eye on things out here," Michael said. "Tonight, I saw this guy doing some-

279

thing under the hood of that car over there." He nodded toward Mrs. Halvorsen's Oldsmobile.

"So I came down to see what was going on, and he threw a wrench at me. I ducked, ran up, and slammed the hood on him a couple of times. He staggered around, and I managed to kick his legs out from under him. He kept threatening me about what would happen to me if he got his hands on me. I believed him. I knew if he got back on his feet . . ." Michael gestured, comparing the two of them. "You know Hake is a pro — a leg breaker. If he got up, I figured he'd kill me." Michael shrugged. "So I did my best to make sure he didn't make it up."

"By kicking the crap out of him?" Liza still couldn't believe it.

"You got a better plan? It worked. I'm still alive, and he's still around and breathing. He's right here for the cops to catch," Michael told her.

"I think you'll both be heading downtown," Curt said.

"Fine. But before we go, I'm not kidding about the car. He was doing something in there before I came up, and he dropped a tool or something when I interrupted him. And that's in addition to whatever it was he threw at me."

"I didn't —" Hake rasped.

"Yes, you did!" Michael whipped round on him. "You were doing something to that car, and you didn't want to leave finger-prints. Why else would you go for a walk in a quiet residential neighborhood — wearing rubber gloves?"

Hake stared down at the hand he'd ex-tended to bear his weight. It was torn and a bit tattered from scrabbling on the driveway gravel, but that was obviously a surgical glove he was wearing.

Curt's partner pulled up the hood of the Oldsmobile and, using his flashlight, peered into the cavernous depths of the engine well. "The tool you heard drop didn't fall — exactly," he reported. "The handle must have banged against something when it fell out of this guy's hand. Looks like some kind of ice pick, stuck through the brake line."

"When Terence Hamblyn had his car ac-cident on the highway, they were talking about brake failure," Liza spoke up.

"Maybe Hake was trying to see if history would repeat itself." Michael put his hands behind his back for the cuffs. Curt's partner put them on carefully.

Curt looked much less gentle as he re-strained Hake.

It took both deputies to get Hake to his

feet, and even so he staggered and groaned. Mainly, though, he glared at Michael.

"You know," Curt said as they led Hake to the patrol car. "We still have what's left of that director guy's Beemer in the impound lot. It was pretty well totaled, and he's still in the hospital. Might be worthwhile, though, to compare what happened there with what happened here. I bet we could try to match that ice pick to any holes in the hydraulic system. Pull a CSI on our friend's shenanigans."

Hake's shoulders sagged. Even a professional can only take so much.

As the deputies drove off with their prisoners, Liza went back into her house, one hand still holding on to a growling Rusty's collar, her other hand clutching her robe together. It had begun to gape embarrassingly as she'd watched the drama unfolding outside.

Just hope you weren't giving the boys a show of your own, that critical back-of-the-head voice told her.

She quickly went upstairs to get dressed, then called Ava Barnes to inform her of the story — and also to find out about a lawyer for Michael.

Ava gave her the home phone for a man she described as a good local criminal attorney who owed her a favor.

It must have been a good favor. At least when Liza mentioned Ava's name, some of the sleepy surliness left the man's voice. Then she made a call to the local cab company — no way was she driving the Olds. It was a crime scene!

The cab arrived and Liza was soon headed off for downtown.

She arrived at the police section of City Hall to hear Hake's voice echoing down the hallway. "I didn't kill Chissel! I couldn't — I was busy knocking over that actor guy's house in Santa Barbara, trying to find a clue about where the hell he stashed his money."

Caught in the act and likely to have at least something of the sabotage stick to him, Hake had apparently decided to cut his losses and cop to some minor crimes in hopes of escaping a murder charge.

"Let's not worry about what you didn't do then." Sheriff Clements's voice wasn't quite as booming. "Just stick to the things you did."

With that, the floodgates opened, and Hake gave a detailed rundown on his activities for thwarting progress on the *Counterfeit* set. Liza was surprised to hear him even admit to tampering with Terence Hamblyn's brakes to get the director out of the way.

"You understand that you're admitting being party to a fairly serious crime," Clements pointed out.

"It's better than facing murder one," Hake responded. "I didn't kill my boss. And I didn't break those windows."

"We have a record —" Clements began.

"I know — I did a job like that once for Chissel. But that was years ago," Hake said. "This time around, Chissel was trying to keep the suckers sweet — to string along the people in town who were looking for money from the movie. He figured he could either stiff them, or sell the studio and let the buyers worry about paying off."

"Sounds like a really charming guy, your late boss," Clements said.

"You wouldn't think it to look at him." Hake's voice got almost reverent. "Maybe that was the whole thing, you didn't expect it. But when he put his mind to it, Chissel could convince you of almost anything — that up was down, that black was white. For him, the bigger the lie, the bigger the challenge. He started out as a broker in L.A., and that's what happened to all his clients — they got broker. When he came back there to head up Mirage, I asked if he worried about meeting any of the people he'd conned. You know what he did? He laughed."

Hake chuckled himself. "Chissel said he was so far out of the league of those losers, they'd never get near him. And if they did, well, if he conned them once, he could do it again. All it took was a bit of carrot and stick."

Judging by the sound of things, by the time Hake finished giving his statement, she'd probably be able to take Michael back home with her.

The other thing she noticed — thug he might be, but Hake had an almost superstitious awe of Oliver Chissel. His confession cleared away some of the underbrush — the same way that eliminating candidates on a sudoku puzzle pruned the one true solution into view.

There were still lots of questions, though — Derrick's money, the Main Street vandalism, and, the biggest puzzle of them all, finding Oliver Chissel's murderer. The picture should be clearer. Liza felt like a sudoku novice wrestling with a puzzle over her head. With the right techniques she should be able to slice away the encumbering candidates and get to the real clues. Her puzzle master instincts told her so.

Instead, even more frustratingly, the patterns seemed just beyond her reach.

The lawyer arrived while Liza was giving her statement. By the time Sheriff Clements was done with her, Michael had been released. He rose from one of the benches in the outer office as she came out. "They tell me Ma's Café is open by now. Feel like getting something to eat?"

Liza splurged, allowing herself French toast, maple syrup, and sausages. "I'll run tomorrow," she told herself, chewing happily. "Hell, I'll run all week."

The tall back of the booth seats kept her from seeing Kevin Shepard until he was almost on top of them. Besides, there was no getting away from one of Ma's booths. Failing escape, what was she going to do, hide under the table?

"Sheriff Clements tells me one of my guests is now a guest of the county," Kevin said. "He also mentioned how he was arrested outside your house, monkeying with your car."

"Not mine. Mine had already been monkeyed with. It was Mrs. Halvorsen's car, actually. But the accident was meant for me," Liza said.

Kevin sent a doubtful glance over at Michael. "And he said that you took Hake down."

Michael shrugged, dabbing a bit of toast

into his runny fried eggs. "I grew up in a fishing town not all that different from up here. If somebody had a beef, we didn't debate using Robert's Rules of Order — or even the Marquess of Queensberry Rules. I've been in fights, and I knew that fighting Hake was biting off more than I could chew."

"So I cheated." His face got a little pale as he looked back on last night's adventure. "This was a fight I had to win."

"Yeah." Kevin's eyes went from Michael to Liza and back again. "I know what you mean." He nodded and headed out of the café.

Liza gazed after him for a moment, then returned to her French toast. The rest of breakfast was finished in silence.

Kevin's status as a knight in shining armor had taken a considerable dent with his revelations of the seamier side of his inn-keeping. How strange that Michael's dirty fighting had buffed up his tarnished armor considerably.

Liza returned home with only one thing on her mind — sleep. She yawned for the entirety of Rusty's quick walk. When she got upstairs, she'd make sure the bedroom curtains were arranged so no chink could allow sunlight in to stab her in the eye. Then she'd make like a dead person until some-time in the afternoon.

A muted beeping from the answering machine told Liza she'd gotten a call while she was out with Rusty. "Armando Vasquez again," the familiar voice came from the speaker. The Santa Barbara detective sounded considerably more cheerful than usual. "Your sheriff called to say he got the doer on my break-in . . . and that the guy hadn't found what he was looking for. So I started wondering — what if the thing he was searching for wasn't there anymore? I checked over our evidence list, and guess what? We've got a laptop computer that belonged to Derrick Robbins in our lockup."

There went all hopes of any rest. Liza got on the phone to Michelle, rousting her out of bed, and to Buck Foreman — he was up already. Then she called Sheriff Clements to inform him of what was going on if Vasquez hadn't, and to ask if Jimmy Perrine was available.

Liza got some sleep on the way to Santa Barbara, though she felt stiff and cramped from her position in the copilot's seat.

Worse than flying coach, she silently complained. *Of course, if you're flying the plane — or even helping — they wouldn't want you so comfortable that you'd be drifting off.*

Buck met her at the airport, but when they got to his car there was someone already inside. At first glance, Liza would have taken him for a car thief — he looked like a skinny kid in a faded black T-shirt, baseball cap crooked on his head, heavily tinted sunglasses making his eyes almost invisible.

However, Foreman introduced him. "This is Bradley." He didn't explain if that was a first name or a last. "Bradley's served as a technical expert on computers for several local police departments, including the SBPD."

"How ya doin'?" the man responded.

Liza looked at him with interest. Most technonerds she'd met had been of the chubby, high-water-pants variety. It was interesting to see one that aspired to cool.

"Vasquez will probably also have the cop shop's in-house guy available, too," Buck went on.

"Guy's a hobbyist," Bradley said with disdain.

Clouds of geek rivalry filled the room as soon as the two technical types saw each other. Vasquez simply ignored the fumes, pointing to the computer on the table. "The LAPD found this when they searched the apartment of Leo Carruthers. Remember him?"

"Hard to forget," Liza said. "He shoved a gun in my face."

"Yeah?" Bradley showed the first stirrings of real interest she'd seen since Liza had met him.

"Anyway, the L.A. guys noticed there was a plaque on the computer saying, 'To Derrick Robbins, who helped put the craft in *Spycraft.*' They figured Carruthers helped himself to it the night Robbins got killed. Anyway, they turned it over to us, and it's been in the evidence lockup ever since."

"Luckily it's an older-style model, without the latest bells and whistles. Otherwise, it might have walked," Bradley grunted. "What's it run, XP?"

"Bradley, you are an idealist," Buck Foreman muttered.

The geek in black shrugged. "Computer belongs to a dead guy, it's sat around for months, so it's not likely to be returned — dead guys being notorious for not needing Internet access and all. And stuff never goes missing from lockups, right?" he said skeptically.

The geek in blue, a heavyset kid with watery gray eyes, looked ready to dispute the point until Vasquez touched him on the shoulder. "On a preliminary investigation, the computer appears to be password protected."

"So we either need the password, or we've got to try and crack our way in," Bradley said.

"Robbins was the codebreaker on *Spycraft*," the police expert said. "Suppose we try a few related terms to start?"

He brought up the password request and typed "cipher," only to be rejected. "Encryption," "decryption," and "crypt-analysis" also failed.

"What if he encoded his name or something?" Bradley reached over his blue-clad counterpart and typed in "18 15 2 2 9 14 19." "That's 'Robbins' in a straight number-for-letter switch."

Liza glanced over, impressed that Bradley could do that in his head. However, the computer wasn't impressed at all. When Bradley tried a reverse of the code and failed again, the geek in blue snorted, "If it's a code, it could just as easily be something like this."

He typed in "1S52J852D3Y8-;0Wi*Y6I45&620." Of course, that didn't work, either.

"You aren't saying anything, Liza," Buck said.

"That's because I'm still angry at myself

for not asking about a computer earlier," Liza admitted. "It would make cryptography and puzzles — including sudoku — a lot easier."

She frowned. "Now, we're going on the idea that Derrick left some kind of message on here. The most likely recipient would be Jenny. She didn't share his passion for codes, so it would have to be something simple —"

Excusing herself, she stepped past Bradley and leaned over the shoulder of the uniformed officer, typing letters into the password window.

"Uncled?" The word came out in unison from both experts.

"No, Uncle D. That's how Jenny always referred to Derrick — and how she still does." She hit the Enter key. A second later, the computer had opened up.

20

The young tech officer looked up at Liza, openmouthed in astonishment at her success. Bradley was less impressed. "Lucky," he grunted as the computer's desktop floated into view on the screen.

"Don't mistake knowledge for luck," Buck Foreman reproved his protégé.

"Yeah." Vasquez unexpectedly rose to her defense. "She pays attention, and that paid off."

"Whatever." Bradley leaned forward to peer at the screen. "What's he got on this sucker?"

"There's a big Bible concordance program," the police tech pointed to one icon.

Liza nodded. Tracking down biblical quotes would have been a big help in Derrick's efforts to decode the messages he'd found embedded in sudoku problems that he thought were coded. Of course, that interest, that decoding, had also led to Derrick's murder.

She ran her eye along the ranks of icons. Most were code- or puzzle-related. Derrick even had an early version of Solv-a-doku on this machine.

"Bunch of programs I don't even know about," Bradley commented in his usual graceless way. "What the hell are we supposed to find in here?"

"I think we're supposed to be looking for a message," Liza said.

"Well, there's a buttload of Word documents." The young officer called up just one screen as an example. "And there's lots more."

Scanning the titles, Liza said, "Most of these look like correspondence or business. All of those files with 'Count' in the titles probably have to do with *Counterfeit,* the movie he was trying to produce."

"Well, looks like he didn't do much housecleaning on this machine." Bradley reached down to fool with the tracking device below the keyboard. "Yeah. More than three thousand documents cluttering up his hard drive."

"Well, we don't have to look through them all," Liza told him. "We just have to look for any that pertain to Jenny."

While the two technical experts verbally

fenced over the respective effectiveness of various search algorithms, Liza got rid of the Properties window and began scrolling through the ranks of documents. Derrick had elected to go for an alphabetical view, which made things considerably easier. Even so, Bradley and his antagonist had almost gotten to blows by the time Liza reached the *J*s.

"This looks promising." She pointed to one icon on the screen. The title below was in all capital letters — the online equivalent of shouting. It read: JENNY!

They opened the file to find a four-line message and an attached picture file:

Jenny,
This puzzle is tough, but it could be worth a lot if you remember my favorite sandwich and check the losing Democratic presidential candidates for 1984. If you need sudoku help, talk to Will Singleton or Liza Kelly.

"Oh, come on!" groaned the uniformed tech.

"Just as well this guy is dead — he's seriously beginning to bug me," Bradley said.

Vasquez looked at the message with an uncomprehending frown. "Reagan creamed

	8		6					
2				1		9		
9			7	2			4	
	1					3		
	7		2	4	3		8	
		8					9	
	6			7	4			5
		4		6				8
					1		6	

the Democrat in '84. That was — not Carter — Mondale. Walter Mondale."

"But it says candidates — plural," Buck Foreman pointed out. "Does that mean the running mate, too?"

"Geraldine Ferraro." Liza filled in the blank. She shrugged when they all looked at her. "What can I say? It was a big deal at the time. Besides, that was probably the first presidential election where I was old enough to pay attention."

She had whipped out a pad and began jotting down the numbers from the puzzle. Frowning, she asked the officer to bring up the Bible concordance program. "Has it got a listing for the books of the Bible?"

He frowned, looking through the program

menus. "Will this help?" The screen filled with information.

"Yes . . . and no." Liza sighed. "I had hoped that Derrick might have been using the same code he'd cracked to get the sudoku messages. But it's just given me gibberish."

"So what have we got?" Bradley demanded.

"We've got a clue," Liza replied. "And I have some things to ask my client." She turned to Vasquez. "What happens to the computer now?"

"It's back to gathering dust till Carruthers goes on trial," he said. "If you need another look, let me know."

He jerked his head at Bradley and said in a lower voice to Buck, "Next time, you can lose Mr. Jolly over there. Liza did well enough on her own."

Liza carefully copied the mystery sudoku into her notebook before they shut the laptop down. She spent most of her journey back to Maiden's Bay trying to extract the solution from the clues Derrick had given. *Maybe he made it easy for Jenny to find this sucker,* Liza thought, *but she'd have a real job finishing it. We're not talking entry-level sudoku here.*

In fact, her simpler solving systems didn't

even make a dent in this puzzle. Liza had to move much farther up the hierarchy of a dozen tested techniques she used to solve sudoku. At last, however, she started to get the upper hand.

"I thought you were trying to burn a hole in that paper, you were looking at it so hard." Jimmy Perrine's voice crackled in the earphones Liza wore.

"For that, I'd need a magnifying glass," she replied, sitting up straighter and looking out of the cockpit. "How much farther?"

"Unless something exciting happens, ten, maybe fifteen minutes," Perrine said. "You going to need a lift into town?"

"Actually, I'll need a lift into Maiden's Bay," Liza said. "I'll pay for your gas if you'll do it."

She arrived down at the harbor to find all the film people wildly celebrating. "We just wrapped the filming!" a jubilant Jenny informed her.

"At least the location part of it," Lloyd Olbrich corrected. But all in all, he seemed pretty subdued.

"I guess it's amazing what you can get done if there's no one around sabotaging the set," Liza joked.

Olbrich nodded. "I heard about that. But the main reason —" He hesitated for a moment, then went on. "I decided to stick more with Terry Hamblyn's original plan."

"Artistic inspiration?" Liza asked.

"More of a financial imperative," Olbrich sourly replied. "If I understand correctly, Chissel engineered an accident to get Hamblyn out and me in to prolong production up here." He sighed. "If we prolong much longer, there might not be a studio left to produce for."

"As bad as that?" Liza said quietly.

"Let's just say I'm not getting any straight answers." Olbrich didn't look full of confidence. "So we'll head south tomorrow. The interior sets have been sitting in the Timmons Grove production facility for weeks now. We'll get started as soon as possible, and hopefully bring the film in before anything extreme happens."

He glanced at his watch. "In fact, I've got to talk to a few people before the partying gets out of hand."

As he walked off, Liza followed him with her eyes. "So, is the big, bad wolf behaving himself?" she asked.

"He's a lot more schedule-conscious," Jenny said. "And I guess he's trying to be encouraging. It's a stretch for him. But he's getting a feel for the role. Are we really racing the clock as much as he says, or is that an attempt to make sure we know our lines?"

"I'm not sure," Liza admitted. "But I think you'd better take Olbrich seriously."

She'd been wondering how to broach the subject of her latest find with Jenny. Finally, Liza decided just to plunge right in. "I was down in Santa Barbara today."

"Was it about Hake?"

"No — we were looking in your uncle's computer."

"I knew it was gone," Jenny frowned. "Things weren't really sharp — or I wasn't — when I got kidnapped. But I think I remember one of the guys with the carrying case slung over his shoulder."

"You're right," Liza said. "The police wound up with it, and they're keeping it as evidence. There was a message on it for you. Whatever Derrick might have foreseen happening after sending his message, I guess it didn't include you and the computer being grabbed."

Jenny just looked down.

"I think the message may be connected to the missing money."

That brought Jenny's eyes up. "How? What did Uncle D. say?"

"The main part was a sudoku puzzle."

Jenny struggled not to roll her eyes. "I

know you're really into that, and so was Uncle D. But I sorta suck at it."

"I sorta got that idea," Liza said. "And I'll tell you, this is a hard puzzle. But does this mean anything to you?" She read out the text that had been set over the puzzle.

"Uncle D.'s favorite sandwich? Definitely a Reuben," Jenny told her confidently. "He loved to go to Canter's to get them — it had to be a real, old-fashioned Jewish deli. Then he'd go on a diet for two weeks."

"How about the rest of it?" Liza pressed.

"Who lost the election in 1984?" Jenny wrinkled her forehead in puzzlement. "I think Reagan won."

When Liza mentioned the loser, she only got a blank look. In Jenny's history of the world, Walter Mondale probably came in just a few weeks after Hammurabi bowed out.

"Doesn't much look like I'm being any kind of help." Jenny looked unhappy. "I hate the thought that Uncle D. is depending on me to find that money — and I'm letting it slip right through my fingers."

"You've got other things on your mind right now," Liza told her. "Derrick also wanted *Counterfeit* to be the best movie it could be. You've got to make sure that happens, so go get yourself ready for the move back to L.A. — and don't party too much."

That at least got a smile out of Jenny. "Don't worry," she said. "I'm not really in the mood."

"Save the boogie nights for the final wrap," Liza advised the girl.

She headed off the piers, just taking a moment to shake hands with Guy Morton.

"Olbrich says we'll be working almost like a TV shooting schedule when we get down to the studio," he said. "Is the studio really that tight?"

"I don't know," Liza admitted. "But Olbrich seems to think so. Will that be a problem for Jenny?"

"Nah," the older actor assured her. "She's the one who's always been most prepared. And now that Olbrich is laying off her, and following Hamblyn's lead . . . I think we're looking at a pretty good movie here."

"Let's hope," Liza said.

Coming up on the streets where the film company's trucks parked, she could see that Olbrich's time-is-money mind-set was already at work. Many of the tech people had already gone from celebration back to work mode, loading the last equipment aboard the big tractor-trailers.

Liza quickly made her way through the port-related facilities, small factories, and warehouses that made up Maiden Bay's other side of the tracks. She took the pedestrian footbridge over the highway and headed up Main Street.

She wondered where Michael might be, but then shrugged. Who needed Michael and his car? After all that time crammed into an airplane cockpit, she could use the walk.

Liza had just begun to stretch her legs, going a few blocks to work the kinks out of her joints, when she passed City Hall.

On impulse, she turned in. Sheriff Clements's intelligence system might not be as wide-ranging as Michelle Markson's, but he was certainly tuned to the local grapevine. Jimmy Perrine had probably told him that Liza was back, and she was sure he'd be interested in the latest wrinkles in the Santa Barbara end of the case.

Maybe he'd surprise her by offering some insight that the big-city cops had missed.

She inquired after the sheriff at the front desk and was sent right in.

Clements sat in the combination interrogation room and office, going through a fairly thick sheaf of papers. "Enjoy your trip?" he asked.

"Once again, it just left me with more questions and not enough answers," she replied, giving him the high points. "So, we think we found a really confusing clue to Derrick's hidden money." She stopped for a second, saying slowly, "Or maybe to the offshore account where it's stashed. What do they call them — numbered accounts?"

"That's right," Clements said.

"Well, I've got a puzzle here with eighty-one numbers."

The sheriff shook his head. "Have to be a pretty big bank, with an account number that long."

"It's a pretty tough sudoku — way out of Jenny's league. Maybe she wasn't expected to finish it." She started counting the clues. "There are twenty-six numbers given. That would probably be enough to give an account number and the password."

"Maybe," Clements said, "if you knew how to arrange them."

"Maybe that's in the message on top," Liza said excitedly. She dug out her notebook and read out the note to Jenny. "She told me Derrick's favorite sandwich was a Reuben."

Clements extended a hand. "Could I see that, please?"

Liza handed over the book. The sheriff read, frowning. "You copied this exactly?"

"Yes."

"So it refers to 'the losing Democratic presidential candidates.' Not the candidate or the running mate. Would you consider your friend Mr. Robbins to be a careful man?"

"When it came to puzzles, I'd say definitely yes," Liza said.

"Puzzles, perhaps — or codes?" the sheriff added. "Because either this is an inexcusable typographical error, or there's something more going on in those three lines."

Liza shook her head. "Seems like there's always something more in this case."

"Tell me about it," Clements said, "or maybe I'll tell you — provided you don't pass it along to the *Oregon Daily.*"

"I can keep my mouth shut," Liza replied.

Clements clapped a hand on top of his reading matter. "This pile of paper here is the medical examiner's report. It tells me a whole lot of stuff I already know or could guess. Stomach contents — Italian seafood. But we already knew Chissel had dinner at Fruit of the Sea."

Where he had words with Ray Massini, noted lover — and fighter, Liza thought.

"It says he drowned — there's a surprise. I didn't think Chissel died from old age waiting for the tide to come in."

The sheriff rattled some papers. "And

then we get a surprise."

Liza tried to look interested, figuring she was going to hear about the broken glass — this time from an official source.

"The ME found traces of adhesive around Chissel's mouth."

Liza's memory immediately flew to an image of Jenny Robbins lying in the sand at Bayocean, tied up . . . and with a length of duct tape slapped across her lips.

"Had Chissel managed to get it off?" she asked.

"As far as they can tell, the tape probably came off while Chissel was submerged," Clements went on. "Apparently it wasn't your standard duct or packing tape. No, it's just something more. Like you said, this case is full of that."

He looked at her and shook his head. "Why the hell would someone use surgical tape for a job like that?"

21

Exchanging mutual regrets over their mutual cluelessness (or rather, over-cluefulness), Liza and the sheriff said good-bye. She came out of City Hall and walked up Main Street to Hackleberry Avenue.

Arriving home, Liza got out of her publicist clothes and pulled on some more comfortable sweats. She made herself some dinner and fed Rusty. Then she took her dog out for a walk.

As soon as she opened the front door, she heard the upstairs window next door scraping open. Liza stopped and looked up at the guest bedroom. "Still keeping a watchful eye on me?" she asked.

"Only in a general way," Michael assured her. "Could I join you?"

"We're just going for a walk."

"I could use the exercise," he said. "While you were away, I spent the whole day hunched over my computer." He gave her a

307

half smile. "It's a nice house, but not exactly built for modern business. You either sink waist deep in the chairs or perch on the edge. Either way is murder on my back."

"Well, if you want to go." Liza gestured to the dog. "But Rusty is coming, too."

"I'll risk it." Michael disappeared from the window and came out Mrs. Halvorsen's door a moment later. "I mean, as long as we stay in the open. I shouldn't —"

He was interrupted by a huge sneeze. "I don't —"

Another sneeze hit him. Michael tried to bring his hand up to his face, but the next sneeze almost bent him double.

Rusty had jumped at the first outburst. As they continued, he barked, then growled. Rusty was willing to tolerate occasional thunderous noises from his human, as he had during Liza's cold. But from a comparative stranger, well, Rusty didn't like that. At all.

Michael managed to dig out a wad of tissues and wiped his streaming eyes. "What did you get there?" He managed to stifle the next in the sneeze cycle. "The super-dander dog muta—" Another sneeze hit. He managed to muffle it with the tissues, but he stepped back from Liza and Rusty.

Tugging on Rusty's leash, she moved even

farther away. "Sorry, Michael. I guess this isn't going to work," she said, regret in her voice.

"Where have I heard that before?" Michael asked ruefully.

He headed back to Mrs. Halvorsen's.

Liza allowed Rusty to trot around, sniff the smells, and do his business. Then she headed home, too.

Rusty got himself comfortable on the living room floor, and Liza took a seat in front of her computer. In a moment, she was online and trying her luck with an IM. The last time she'd tried an instant message to her Uncle Jim, he'd answered right away, even though it was an ungodly hour in faraway Tokyo.

Jim Watanabe had some sort of foreign service job in the US Embassy. At least that was what he told everyone. The fact that he'd served there for a good twenty years might have something to do with his knowledge of Japanese. Or, as Liza had come to suspect, it might have something to do with his knowledge of codes. All through the Cold War, Japan had been the staging ground for intercepting Soviet communications. In today's world, similar tabs would have to be kept on the Russian Federation.

If Uncle Jim was a spy, he was a pleasant,

jovial one. When Liza spent some time in Japan after college, he'd helped an awkward Hibernasian girl get along with her Watanabe relatives when they claimed her Japanese had an unintelligible Irish-American accent. In fact, Uncle Jim was the one who'd gotten her started with sudoku, as a sort of bridge between cultures made of numbers.

Hey, Uncle Jim. Are you there? Liza typed.

When the response window didn't show anything, she sighed. Well, too much to hope that she'd always be lucky. Maybe a more formal e-mail would help, forcing her to organize her thoughts.

Just as she was about to close the window, words appeared.

What's up, Liza?

I didn't think I'd catch you. Her fingers dashed along her keyboard. What time is it over there?

It's my lunch hour. I decided to do a little surfing.

Liza smiled at that image. What would Uncle Jim go trolling for — sudoku challenges? Secret coded messages?

That expression turned into a frown of thought as she typed away, trying to outline her problem while keeping the story short and snappy. How can I help Jenny make sense of all this, she finished, so she can find out where her uncle's money went?

Liza was sure that it would take her uncle a little while to take in all she had sent. But she waited long enough until she began to wonder if the connection had broken.

Finally, Uncle Jim's answer appeared. This is even harder than the last time you asked me about codes.

Back then, you thought someone was using coded messages to pass along orders to people. At least in that situation, both the one giving orders and the ones receiving them both know the code, he wrote.

Now you're suggesting that the person passing along information is putting it into a code that the message receiver has to figure out without any clues. I don't know how anyone can do that.

Liza jumped onto her keyboard. There was a note with the puzzle. She slowed down her typing, making sure she transcribed the note accurately.

Do you have an answer for the first question? Uncle Jim asked.

Jenny told me D.'s favorite sandwich was a Reuben. By the way, that is "candidates" in the second question. Either D. made a mistake, or is there a message in there?

Liza eagerly looked at her screen as her uncle's answer rolled in. If it is a mistake, the answer would be MONDALE. Interesting. No letters repeated in that name. And if you spell the

R	U	B	E	N	A	C	D
1	2	3	4	5	6	7	8
K	L	M	O	P	Q	S	T
14	15	16	17	18	19	20	21

M	O	N	D	A	L	E	B
1	2	3	4	5	6	7	8
J	K	P	Q	R	S	T	U
14	15	16	17	18	19	20	21

sandwich as RUBEN, no letters repeat there, either.

Why is that important? Liza asked.

We already discussed letter-to-number codes. Do you remember?

Sure, Liza typed. A = 1, B = 2, and so on.

Uncle Jim's answer came quickly. You can make it a little harder to crack by adding a word at the front of your alphabet, eliminating those letters later on. Say RUBEN goes in front. Then the code becomes R = 1, U = 2, B = 3, E = 4, N = 5, A = 6, C = 7, and so on.

Liza nodded. Okay, give me a minute.

She began jotting away on a sheet of paper, creating both codes:

The digits one through nine appeared in the puzzle, but no zeroes. That meant in the RUBEN code, there could be no *G* (the tenth letter) or *S* (the twentieth). Liza frowned. That would cramp any message-writer's style. The MONDALE code wouldn't have any *F*s or *T*s.

Though she was now feeling doubtful, Liza attempted to use the codes to "read" the eighty-one numbers in the finished puzzle. The result was gibberish. She tried the process backward, with the same results.

When she reported this to Uncle Jim, he responded, There are other ways to read through blocks of numbers, like going left on the first row, right on the second, and so on. Also, did you try reading down the columns?

Liza followed his suggestions and got a big, fat goose egg. She tried to apply the code just to the clue numbers in the puzzle, again getting nothing she could read.

Then Uncle Jim wrote, What if we aren't supposed to get letters, but numbers? You think the money is in a numbered account, right?

Puzzled, Liza typed, Right.

His answer came immediately, as if he'd been typing without waiting for her response. Maybe RUBEN and MONDALE are key words to find certain spaces in the sudoku? If you follow a straight letter-to-number transposition, M would mean space 13 on the puzzle, O would be space 15, and so on. MONDALE, as the longer string, would be the account number. RUBEN would be the password.

Liza ran through the grid, getting an apparently random set of digits.

More appeared on her screen. Possibly RUBEN is to be read from the beginning of the puzzle, and MONDALE, who suffered a reverse, should be read from the back. Also, RUBEN could be REUBEN. Too many variables.

Liza grimly nodded. How was Jenny supposed to figure this out?

She typed, And we get all of this because we suppose that Derrick made a perfect puzzle, and then was sloppy writing his message. Any suggestions on the "candidates" problem?

The answer screen quickly filled. Frankly, I don't know. If you take MONDALE/FERRARO together, you get a very long account number. If you take FERRARO as an additional key, I have no idea what it refers to.

The screen filled again, this time not with code theory but with reminiscence. I remember Mondale pounding away on Reagan's deficit spending, saying it was a swindle across the generations, robbing our children and grandchildren.

Liza stared as the word "swindle" seemed to jump off the screen, followed by "generations" and "grandchildren." Pulling herself together, she typed, Sorry, Uncle Jim, I just realized I have to take care of something. Do you mind if we postpone this discussion?

His reply was quick. It's okay. I should be

314

getting back to work anyway.

They signed off, Liza went offline, and then she began shutting down her computer. A strange line of logic was forming in her mind, ricocheting off disparate bits of information like a hyperactive pinball.

Peter Hake talking about Chissel's early career.

Mrs. Halvorsen's offhand mention of a piece of ancient gossip.

Broken glass found with Chissel's body — and the destruction of the windows downtown.

And finally, there was the point Sheriff Clements had gleaned from the autopsy reports, about traces of a gag on the corpse — a gag of surgical tape.

Liza glanced at the clock on the mantel. Would she be too late?

She quickly headed out the door, then called up to the window next door. "Michael?"

He quickly levered up the sticky window and peered out. "What's up, Liza?"

"I need a lift downtown," she said. "It's kind of important that I get there before the stores close."

"Okay."

A moment later, he joined her, car keys jingling in his hand. "Is it some kind of emergency?"

Liza wasn't quite sure what to tell him. "Just something I'd rather not put off till tomorrow."

They got into his rental car. As soon as they were sitting together in the enclosed space, Michael began to sneeze.

"I guess I still have traces of Rusty on me," Liza said.

"It's not as bad as him in person," Michael replied through some tissues.

In a moment, they pulled off onto Hackleberry Avenue, heading for Main Street.

When he brought the car to a stop in front of Schilling's Pharmacy, Michael said, "Maybe I'll come in with you, see if I can get a pill to clear my nose."

"I'll pick something up for you," Liza promised. "But I need to talk to Mrs. Schilling alone."

She walked into an empty store, except for Nora Schilling standing behind the rear counter. She was reading something and looked up in surprise. "Oh, you startled me, dear."

Nora glanced at the clock behind her. "You're lucky. We were just about to close. How can I help you?"

"I need something or I won't be able to sleep tonight," Liza replied.

"I don't suppose you have a prescription. Well, there are some over-the-counter sleep aids. I could ask —"

"I don't need a pill, Mrs. Schilling," Liza interrupted, "just some information, to prove or disprove this crazy idea I've gotten."

Nora frowned in puzzlement. "What's that, dear?"

"This whole town has been in an uproar since Oliver Chissel arrived to prolong the movie shoot and postpone payment for the extras and location owners. That caused a lot of hard feelings, but nobody in town could possibly suspect it was the scam Peter Hake now admits it was."

Liza carefully watched the widow. "Nobody, that is, except someone who had already been swindled by Oliver Chissel early on in his career, when he was a broker and you were Nora Timmons."

Nora stood behind the counter, saying nothing. But the answer was in her eyes.

Liza didn't believe her shot in the dark had hit home. "You killed him, Nora? How could you do it?"

"I'll tell you." Gary Schilling's voice was harsh as he stepped from behind the tall prescription desk, a pistol in his hand. "She had help."

22

Liza began to think that those antigun activists might have a point. Personally, she was getting pretty tired of having the damned things pointed at her.

Nora Schilling stared at her son. "Gary!"

"Mom, she knows." Gary's soft features had changed, the flesh drawn tighter over the bones of his face.

"She had no proof," Nora insisted. She too had undergone a subtle change.

After seeing the look on Nora's face, finding proof would only have been a matter of time. Of course, young master Gary had accelerated the process by producing that hand cannon he was waving around.

The pistol just looked ugly. It seemed crudely made of mismatched pieces.

Nora followed Liza's eyes. "Matt bought that blasted thing years ago, when the punks began robbing stores for drug money — and drugs. It was the cheapest thing he could find at a gun show."

A Saturday night special, bought to ward off thieves with weapons equally cheap and awkward. Or was the awkwardness not in the weapon, but in the way Gary held it?

His hands weren't shaking. Liza had already had that experience, where she had to wonder if the gun would go off by mistake. No, Gary looked as if he were holding a slimy eel, or plunging his hand into a bucket of dirty diapers. He was holding a tool he didn't like, but he would get the job done nonetheless.

"Mom," he said, "why don't you put the 'closed' sign in the window and lock up?"

Nora took a long, measuring look, then nodded. No, they couldn't let Liza go. So they'd try to buy some time.

The elder Schilling walked to the front of the store, turned the locking bolt, and set up the sign. As she did that, Liza heard a car engine start up.

"There goes my ride," she muttered.

"What?" Gary said. "What car was that, Mom?"

Nora angled her head, looking out the window. "A silver one. I don't recognize it."

Liza didn't know what Michael might have seen. But apparently something made him suspicious. She silently thanked God that he hadn't decided to come in and play hero. City Hall and the police station were only a few blocks away.

"He'll be coming back with the sheriff," she said.

"We'll be in the back with the lights off," Gary replied grimly. "Just another shop, closed for the night."

For a second, Liza wished she had discussed her suspicions with Michael so he'd have ammunition to convince Sheriff Clements. But it had only been suspicion — a hunch. She hadn't wanted Michael pouring cold water on her idea.

Then she went with Gary into the back of the store, among the shelves of various pharmaceuticals, while Nora turned off the lights.

"Do you miss being a Timmons?" Liza asked the woman as she joined them.

"I've been Nora Schilling longer than I was Nora Timmons," she replied. "To tell you the truth, I've never missed it."

"Mrs. Halvorsen mentioned the lovely clothes you used to have."

"Yes, there was a time when I could have anything I wanted, made to order." Nora laughed. "Today, I just look for the least expensive, least ugly things I can find. Losing my money — yes, that was a shock. But coming here, finding Matt, I can't say I ever much fretted about it — until recently."

Her voice grew a little muted. "Matt and I managed to live comfortably, with a little put aside. Only when he got sick — then I wished for more money. There were treatments we could have tried, but the insurance people wouldn't pay for them. We were already in debt; the only way to raise more money would have been selling the business. And Matt simply refused to do that."

She sighed. "And even then, we might have beaten the cancer, but losing this place would have killed Matt. It happened to my grandfather. After he sold our spread, he just sort of shriveled up and died. That's what my parents said."

"The Timmons Grove production facility," Liza said. "That's where the movie crew is going to finish up *Counterfeit.*"

"The name is new. Grandpa sold his land to Mammoth Studios — how long have they been out of business now?" Nora's voice mixed amusement and bitterness. "I got a letter telling me how they were trying to preserve the area's historic heritage. They're just looking ahead to the day when developers get all that land. Which would sound better? Mammoth Acres or Timmons Grove?"

"I guess it must have been hard on your grandfather," Liza said, "going from running a ranch and farm to managing money."

Nora gave a bitter laugh. "I can't say any of us did well at it. My parents tried — so did my older brother. It's as if selling our land put a curse on the family. Everyone died young, and the money just seemed to run between our fingers. Stock speculation, land development, everyone had a deal for us. When it all came down to me, I was determined to invest carefully."

"And you wound up with Oliver Chissel."

"I thought he was working hard, always moving my money around," Nora said. "Nowadays, I think they call that 'churning.' With every transaction, I seemed to lose a little more, while Chissel pocketed a healthy fee. He was doing it to other people as well. But by the time someone complained, he'd left town — and left me with a pittance."

She sighed. "But that was years ago. I'd come to terms with it, moving here, marrying Matt, putting my little bit into the business."

"Then Chissel had to come here," Liza said.

"I didn't even know he was involved with the movie," Nora told her. "We were all so glad when the film person — the scout —

offered to pay for our permission to film around the store. Of course Gary and I said yes. Frankly, we could really use the money."

Her voice grew darker. "Then Chissel came to tell us that all payments would be delayed. He didn't even remember me. But I recognized him, even though he'd gotten fat and bald. He had the same smarmy manner, too, trying to talk me into doing what he wanted."

Nora took a deep breath. "But not this time. I told him he'd have to meet the obligations he'd assumed in the contract with us. It was only fair that he should part with some of the money he'd defrauded out of me years ago. If he didn't, I'd make sure the whole town knew about the way he did business."

The last thing Ollie the Chiseler's financial house of cards needed, Liza thought.

"Then he got nasty," Nora said. "Who would people believe, a financier with a national reputation or some silly old woman? I told him I could just imagine his reputation, and that enough people around here would listen to me and make a stink."

"And then?" Liza asked.

"Then he started with the threats." Nora's voice got tight. "He said that nobody crossed him and got away with it. How would we like to have our windows broken or have adulterated drugs turn up on our shelves? He'd get some national chain to open across the street from us and force us out of business. Chissel even swore he'd buy up our debts just so he could squeeze us like bugs."

Plenty of stick, but not much carrot, Liz thought, remembering Hake's words in the police station.

"Then he turned on his heel and started walking out," Nora's voice quivered with rage. "But he stopped by the door, so sure I'd come after him, begging, pleading that I'd do anything he wanted. Well, I did walk after him — just as far as the cane display. I picked one up and hit him in the head as hard as I could."

"I was working here in the back," Gary suddenly picked up the story. "I wasn't really paying that much attention until I heard the crash. He — he'd fallen into the display window, smashing all of Grandpa Gustav's old bottles."

"Broken glass," Liza said. "That's why you went up and down Main Street, taking out windows."

"Starting with our own," Gary admitted. "I ran around like a maniac, trying to spread the damage as far as possible. It was around this time of night, the stores were closed, and no one was on the street."

He jerked, bringing his gun up as his story was interrrupted by the sound of rapping fingers on the store's front door. "Hello," a deep voice called. "Anyone still in there?"

Outside, Michael watched as Sheriff Clements tried to peer into the darkened pharmacy, then rapped on the door again.

"Nothing moving that I can see." Clements glanced round at the deputies who had accompanied them. "Any of you spot anything?"

That got him a chorus of head shakes.

"Sheriff," Michael said, "I drove Liza Kelly down here. She was especially anxious to get here before the store closed. I saw her go in, and I could see the entrance from where I was parked. Liza didn't come out, but someone locked up the store and turned off the lights. Something is going on."

"Maybe she went out the back," the female deputy with Ross on her nameplate said.

"And just walked home without telling me?" Michael asked. "I don't think there's anyplace else open down here where she might go. We've tried her cell and home phones and gotten no answers. I even called

Mrs. Halvorsen to go and knock on Liza's door — nothing."

He took a deep breath. "I can't say what happened. Maybe Liza walked in on some junkie robbing the store. But, Sheriff, there's been one murder in town already —"

Clements held up a large hand to cut off that line of speculation. "We're not leaving yet. But I think we'll hold off on anything more until we hear from the car I dispatched along Liza's likely route home."

After a long, tense moment, Gary slowly relaxed. Liza decided a little distraction might help. "So you broke all those windows, and then you brought Chissel down to the beach?"

"We've got a handcart for moving deliveries. Mom and I sort of strapped him to that and moved him that way. I wanted just to throw him off the boardwalk, but the tide was out. Mom remembered that we've got an old shovel in the trunk of our car. She suggested — insisted — that we bury Chissel the way that you found him." He stumbled over those last words.

"I figured it was strange enough to confuse everyone. More like something you would see in a movie, with all those movie people around. Besides, it's only what that man *deserved.*" Nora's voice was adamant, emphatic.

And no sooner did she speak than the knob on the back door rattled.

Gary aimed the gun, making wild shushing gestures with his other hand. Liza almost made a move, but Nora grabbed her.

Then there was silence.

"Guess he didn't hear anything," Gary whispered.

Curt Walters returned from his scouting expedition down the back alley. "The door's locked," he reported. "But I heard something — a voice, I think."

"You think." Sheriff Clements shook his head. "Well, we haven't caught a sniff of Liza anywhere in town. Nora Schilling may be ready to skin me alive, bashing in her door after she just had to replace a window. But I don't see any other way."

The sound of shattering glass up front brought Gary to the prescription desk, aiming his pistol across the chest-high barrier.

"This is the Sheriff's Department." Bert Clements's voice seemed to echo through the store. "We know someone is in here."

"Get out! Get out!" Gary's voice rose. "I — I've got a gun, and a hostage!" He turned his weapon on Liza.

"Now calm down, son." Clements paused for a second, then said, "Is that Gary? Gary Schilling? Look, we can talk this out —"

"Just go away." Gary's voice was so low, Liza wasn't sure if he was referring to the sheriff or the whole situation.

"Gary," she said, "I know you were just trying to help your mom —"

"What else could I do," he demanded, "after coming out and finding him dead?"

"But — he wasn't dead."

"What?" Gary almost shoved the gun at her.

"Chissel wasn't dead," Liza said. "The sheriff read out the cause of death from the medical examiner's report. He drowned."

"But that's —" Gary began, but Liza continued.

"And someone slapped a tape gag over his mouth before that happened."

For a long moment, mother and son stared at one another.

"He deserved it," Nora hissed. "The bills and debts have been piling up — we've been drowning in slow motion ever since your father got sick! Chissel was part of that — why shouldn't he find out what it feels like?"

Even in the shadows, Liza could make out Gary's sick look. Fresh out of pharmacy school, his first big case — and not only did he fail to realize the patient was still alive, he unwittingly assisted his mother in killing the man.

Gary tore his eyes away from his mother and suddenly dashed round the prescription desk. He flung up the drop leaf so it crashed on the outer counter and started down the main aisle of the store. With the clumsy gun in both hands, he advanced toward the sheriff and his deputies.

"Gary!" Nora screamed.

But his shouting voice drowned out hers. "I killed Oliver Chissel when he threatened my mother, and I'll kill anyone who gets in my way."

The police showed as shadows against the front window. Gary turned so his gun aimed directly at the shortest shadow — Brenna Ross, Liza realized — and he began running.

"Gary — stop. Stop! *Freeze!*" In four words, Bert Clements went from friend of the family to stone-cold cop.

Gary took another step, then his gun went off. Liza could see the plume of flame. She also could see that it was aimed at the ceiling.

Her ears rang and she could barely hear Clements yell, "Hold your —"

The rest of his words were lost as three deputies let off shots. Liza grabbed hold as Nora tried to claw past her, bringing the woman out of the line of fire.

But Liza's head was still above the prescription desk as Gary Schilling staggered, spun, and went down.

23

Spurred by the gunfire, deputies at the back door broke in and hauled Liza and Nora out into the rear alley. Liza was just as glad not to go out through the front of the pharmacy, passing the still form of Gary Schilling on the floor. A deputy was already trying to resuscitate him as they left, but the prognosis didn't sound all that good.

When they arrived up front, Sheriff Clements was glad to see the apparent hostages rescued. He was less happy with his troops up there. "When I want you to shoot someone, I'll say 'Open fire,' " he growled. "When I start an order with 'Hold your,' what do you think I'm expecting you to hold?" Clements glared at the three shame-faced male deputies.

"The only one not making like the Fourth of July was Brenna — and she was the one the perp had started off aiming at!"

She missed Clements's next comments

because Michael came up and flung his arms around her. Liza found herself hugging him back just as tightly. She had a grim notion that Gary's last stand would play prominently in her nightmares for years to come.

"You're okay? They — he — didn't hurt you? I was so worried — go in or call the cops —" Michael babbled in her ear.

"I think you did the right thing," she told him. "You can't go around kicking the hell out of everybody."

Liza turned to hear racking sobs. Nora Schilling hung between a pair of deputies who struggled to hold up her limp weight.

Guess the full realization of what happened finally hit her, Liza thought.

The woman only came to life when an ambulance arrived from County Hospital. She tried to throw herself on the gurney as paramedics wheeled Gary away, his face already hidden under an oxygen mask. Suddenly the two deputies found themselves struggling with a madwoman straining after her son. "Gary! Gary! Oh God!"

Clements caught the attention of one of the men. "I suppose she ought to go to the hospital," he said gently. "But I don't think she should ride with her boy. Take her in a cruiser."

The deputy nodded. "Come on, ma'am, they have to work on him in there," he said as Nora again tried to lunge after the ambulance. "We'll take you to the hospital. We promise."

Between them, the deputies moved the broken woman to a patrol car.

Liza watched their exit with torn emotions. Clements looked fairly satisfied — even if Gary didn't make it out of the hospital, he'd confessed to a roomful of people and backed it up with a gunshot.

She wondered if the sheriff's jovial expression would change when he got to hear her statement.

"Well, I have to admit, you figured it out before I did," Clements admitted. "Very impressive, except for the part where the kid pulled a gun and took you hostage. You might want to consider a little more liaison with the professionals before you attempt an apprehension on your own."

He cast another glance at her. "Or should I worry about running against you in next year's primaries?"

Liza shook her head, her ears seeming to ring with the magic word Clements had just uttered. "I've got enough on my plate as it is, Sheriff," she said. "Do you want to get my statement while it's all still fresh in my mind?"

They went to the City Hall, and Clements *wasn't* happy with what Liza had to tell him. He'd expected only to put a nice bow on top of the confession he'd heard. Instead, all his ribbons were unraveling. Most important, if Gary didn't pull through, he'd only have Liza's hearsay evidence.

Still, Clements was fascinated with the case Liza outlined, although she was diplomatically vague about where she'd learned about the glass fragments found with Chissel's body. The sheriff shook his head. "So you went in there to brace Nora Schilling about the murder — and you had nothing! All she had to do was start yelling at you for making crazy accusations — or if she could hold it together, to stonewall you. And what would you do?"

"I figured I could go to you with information about the earlier swindle. There would have to be records, client lists or something, from Chissel's brokerage days. Really, all I expected to do was find out whether Nora knew Chissel before. But when she reacted the way she did, things just sort of snowballed."

Now that she'd gotten it all out, Liza found herself shaking — as the reality of

334

what had happened finally set in.

Clements stood and shook his head, looking down at her from his considerable height. "Well, I guess your part is done. You can go while we start all the boring things you see on crime scene shows — trying to find any pieces of those broken bottles in the window to test against the pieces on Chissel, poring through records, trying to match the tape to something in the pharmacy's stock."

He scowled. "Just our luck, the most important part of crime scene evidence floated out to sea. We might have been able to get a fingerprint off the adhesive on that piece of tape. And if the print turned out to be from Nora Schilling, we could connect her directly to the crime."

Liza gave him a smile. "As a cop once told me, that all sounds like a lot of what-if and maybe."

Clements sighed. "Maybe it does," he admitted. "Maybe it does."

Michael drove Liza home with all the car windows open. It was kind of chilly, but at least he wasn't sneezing his head off. When they arrived on Hackleberry Avenue, Mrs. Halvorsen was already in front of her house, waiting to intercept them.

"The Maiden's Bay gossip grapevine is

alive and well," Liza muttered as she got out of the car.

"Are you all right, Liza?" Mrs. H. asked anxiously. "With all that shooting and everything, you must be a bundle of nerves."

"And you won't be able to get anything at the pharmacy for them," Michael couldn't resist putting in.

"Come in, come in," Mrs. H. shooed them into her house and installed them in her living room. Liza just sighed and let herself sink into the sofa. Right now, getting up — or out — was more work than she wanted to think about.

"Perhaps a glass of sherry would help," their hostess said.

Before Liza could get her mouth open to object — she'd had Mrs. H.'s sherry before — the older woman went on, "Wait, I think we still have some of that rum we won at the Kiwanis raffle."

In fairly short order, Liza sat with a cup of the inevitable tea liberally laced with a very good rum.

It would be so easy just to close my eyes, Liza thought drowsily.

But when her lids fluttered shut, her memory insisted on replaying the image of Gary Schilling's fall to the floor.

That brought Liza back to the land of the

living with a jolt.

She explained the chain of logic that had led to her conversation with Nora Schilling, crediting Mrs. H. for her information on the Timmons connection. Michael listened in fascination as Liza tied the various elements into a case. Then he got extremely upset as she described the aftermath of Nora's wordless confession.

"You made me drive you over there, sneezing and wheezing, so you would pull a stunt like that?" Michael burst out.

"Yeah, and I even forgot to get you a bottle of nose spray." Liza gave him a feisty stare from the depths of the overstuffed upholstery.

"I don't care about that," Michael almost shouted. "I want to holler at you for putting yourself in danger the way you did." His voice got quieter. "Even if you tell me I don't have the right anymore."

"Certainly you have the right," Mrs. H. interjected. "You still love her, don't you?"

"I — I — yes," Michael stuttered.

Mrs. Halvorsen nodded. "Well, holler away then."

Michael opened his mouth, looked at Liza, and shut it again. "I seem to have lost the words."

"Really," Mrs. H. huffed. "And you an

author."

The would-be matchmaker subsided, glaring at them in annoyance. But the silence between Liza and Michael as she finished her tea wasn't exactly unfriendly.

Finally, she started struggling out of her overstuffed cocoon, sighing. "I have to get up. Ava will probably want to do a telephone interview with me about all this for the paper. And then there's one more mystery to solve."

"What are you talking about?" Michael said. "You figured out everything that happened up here."

"That still leaves what happened in Santa Barbara," Liza replied. "I think I've figured out a way to get Derrick's money for Jenny."

"You mentioned wanting to get in touch with your Uncle Jim," Michael began.

"Oh, the spy over in Japan?" Mrs. Halvorsen asked.

Liza shot her a look, wondering exactly how far Mrs. H.'s gossip hotline extended.

"Did he give you some sort of pointer about codes?" Michael asked.

"No," Liza admitted. "It was Sheriff Clements who gave me the clue — and you were right there when he did."

Michael took hold of Liza's hand and helped to haul her out of the couch's embrace. "This I've got to see."

Thanking Mrs. H., they headed over to Liza's place. Of course, Michael began sneezing as soon as he encountered Rusty.

Liza ran up the stairs to the bathroom and returned with the bottle of nasal spray. "Here." She offered it to him. "Maybe this will work. It's, uh, only slightly used."

Michael squinted at the little bottle and then shook it. "Eh," he said. "We've shared worse."

While he dosed himself, Liza sat at her computer, getting online. Soon Michael was looking over her shoulder. "What are you doing?"

At least he didn't sound so nasal, and he wasn't erupting every couple of seconds.

"I'm Googling for a decent history of the 1984 election — specifically, the run-up to the conventions."

"And the sheriff told you to do this?"

"No, but he reminded me of something that showed Derrick hadn't made a mistake when he wrote 'candidates' in his message." Liza glanced back at him from her screen. "Walter Mondale was the Democratic presidential candidate who lost the election. But there were a bunch of other Democratic presidential candidates who lost in the primaries."

"And Sheriff Clements did mention that word," Michael admitted.

Liza was already busy with her mouse, scrolling down the list of Web pages. "Here's one that looks promising."

She clicked on the link, and a document on the 1984 campaign came up. "Iowa caucuses, New Hampshire. Right — here's a list of some of the other people running in the primaries. Gary Hart, John Glenn, huh, Jesse Jackson . . ." She ran down the list of past political luminaries. "And — aha! — the governor of Florida."

"That wouldn't have been a Bush," Michael ventured.

"Nope, his name was Askew," Liza said. "And can you guess his first name?"

Michael frowned. "How could I do that?"

"Name Derrick's favorite sandwich."

"A Reuben?"

"That's the name!" Liza told him. "Reubin Askew."

She could feel the puff of irritated breath Michael directed down into her hair. "And this helps us how?"

Liza dug around for her notebook with Derrick's puzzle and held it up. "It means we're not going to get anywhere with straight sudoku logic. We've got to look at it askew, to find two sets of nine numbers that no sudoku player ever looks for."

Michael stared at the puzzle solution. "What?"

"When you do sudoku, you look to find the numbers that fill the spaces in all nine rows — and all nine columns. Derrick's clue is trying to get us to look at the puzzle in a different way, askew, at an angle —"

"The diagonals!" Michael burst out.

"Exactly!" Liza began writing down the numbers 451846139. "There we go, from upper left to lower right. As the most likely choice, I'm betting that this is the account number. Then we go from lower left to upper right and get the password — 793147872."

"I think you've got it."

Liza shrugged. "I'll pass it along to Jenny tomorrow. Josh Colberg must know which bank in the Caymans Derrick dealt with. Then Jenny can put the numbers to the test." She shrugged. "Besides, I've got other fish to fry."

"More expensive than three-quarters of a million smackers?" Michael asked.

"As much as my life is worth!" she replied. "I've got two jobs — and two masters, Ava and Michelle."

"Mistresses," Michael corrected.

"That makes them sound like either kept

women or the female leads in an X-rated feature film," Liza complained.

"Well, with Michelle, it may not be far off."

Liza laughed. "She will probably be getting out her whip. Chissel's murder being solved is news. And however the story turns out, we've got to spin, spin, spin — turning *Counterfeit* into *the* film to be seen when it opens!"

She couldn't help but notice the glint of disappointment in Michael's eyes as she picked up the phone.

"Well," he said, "as soon as you come up for air —"

Michael bent to plant a kiss on the top of her head, then abruptly reared back with a loud "Ah-*choo!*"

"Looks like you're the one who needs air." She ruffled her hair. "You never know where dog dander will collect, I guess."

"As long as it's the dog," Michael told her, "and not you."

"Perish the thought," Liza replied, with a sidewise smile. "Not when things are beginning to get interesting."

SUDO-CUES
TOO HARD?
TAKE IT EASY!

WRITTEN BY OREGON'S OWN LEADING
SUDOKU COLUMNIST, LIZA K

Do you sometimes wish there was a lemon law for sudoku? Or at least that some kind of truth in advertising applied to puzzles?

Rating the difficulty of sudoku stands as a thorny issue for prospective puzzle solvers. You've probably encountered it. Perhaps you're traveling, pick up a newspaper, and find a sudoku puzzle claiming to be a great challenge. Yet you blow right through — it's way too easy. Or maybe there's one listed as moderate, but it refuses all your best techniques!

We have to face the sad fact that while crossword puzzles developed a fairly standard system of rating difficulty, sudoku hasn't. Of course, crosswords have been around a lot longer. Perhaps by the end of this century, sudoku scholars will write condescending pieces on this whole contro- versy. Here and now, however, the rating question is enough to cause civil war in Sudoku Nation.

At least the competing schemes make for some colorful language. Our British cousins, especially, come up with interesting grades. Starting off with "Gentle," they quickly escalate to "Diabolical," "Fiendish," or "Horrible." Not to be outdone, other repre- sentatives of Sudoku Nation have come up with ratings like "Maniac," "Nightmare," "Insane," "Evil," and "Mind-bending."

Judging by the success of these titles, one thing seems clear — sudoku solvers must have a perverse, even masochistic, streak. When I first got this job, I thought I'd cash in on that with my G-ratings system: "Grungy," "Ghastly," "Grotesque," and "Godawful." For some reason my editor killed that idea, along with my next set of ratings: "Devious," "Tricky," "Are you Kid- ding?" and "I Want My Mommy!"

Hey, it's no worse than the suggestion from one of the programmers at Solv-a- doku for the highest difficulty level: "Cap- tain, It's Goin' to Blow!"

The taglines may be funny, but they're also imprecise. Difficulty remains all in the eye of the beholder. One solver's "Fiendish" may be another solver's "Moderate." So how can we get a rational handle on the problem?

In the beginning, people tended to equate difficulty with the number of clues in a puzzle. It seemed logical enough. The fewer clues in the sudoku, the more spaces to be filled — and the more work for the solver. Unfortunately, that logic isn't necessarily consistent.

Mark Danburg-Wyld, a fellow Oregonian and sudoku colleague with puzzles in several newspapers, presents the shortcomings of the clue-counting method on his website, www.sudokuplace.com, and he's graciously allowed me to use two of his puzzles.

As you can see, the pattern is the same for both puzzles, the number of clues the same, and the upper left-hand box is identical. But what happens when you start scanning the clues for answers? The shaded spaces show how many results a solver can get.

Do the math, and you could say that Puzzle Two seems about four times harder than Puzzle One. So much for all clues being equal. Go to Mark's site for a discussion of the way he maps subsequent moves to generate his own rating system.

People who develop sudoku-solving programs often brag about how few microseconds it takes for their creations to grind out a solution. But these programs usually use the brute-strength, trial-and-error mode allowed by the computer's speed. That's not the way human beings solve sudoku.

More recently, though, programmers have attempted to mimic human logic, coming up with computer versions of the various solving techniques. By assigning point scores to each technique and additional points for repetitions, they can actually come up with numerical ratings for solved sudoku. A simple exercise that requires only hidden singles and listing candidates might get around 50 points. Puzzles that demand higher-order techniques like naked pairs and Row and Box/Column and Box interactions might score around 100. A puzzle that needs an X-wing to solve it might come in around 500. Repeated applications of X-wing or swordfish techniques could push a score up past 1000.

A participant at the Sudoku Programmers Discussion Site proposed the following price list.

The terminology may be different, but you can figure it out (or look it up). After running a number of *London Times* puzzles on his solver, the participant reported an average score of 4600 for "Easy" puzzles, and average of 5200 for "Mild," 5600 for "Difficult," and 6500 for "Fiendish."

The sudoku section at the playr.co.uk site uses several numbers to rate its puzzles.

First, the site organizes eighteen techniques into five levels of difficulty from simplest to most esoteric. Then they count how many separate techniques from each level went into solving a puzzle. A "Hard" rating might come in a 1.3.2 — one first-level, three second-level, and two third-level techniques required. An "Extreme" puzzle might get a 2.5.2.2.1 rating.

Both systems are interesting — one counts successive uses of a technique, while the other offers a scorecard of the number of techniques used.

Interestingly, farther along in the string on the Sudoku Programmers Discussion Site, the same participant raised another yardstick of difficulty — the number of valid moves available for each step along in the puzzle. Maybe I should send him the URL for Mark's site.

Moving away from the computer world, a new movement has arisen in the past few years using human solvers to rate a puzzle's difficulty by the amount of time they take. It makes sense — after all, this is the way competitive sudoku is scored, and more and more competitions seem to be cropping up. There's even a book out offering puzzles with a time score to beat — something to

Method name	First	Subsequent	
SINGLE CANDIDATE	100	100	
SINGLE POSITION	110	110	
CANDIDATE LINE	350	200	
DOUBLE PAIR	500	250	
MULTILINE	700	400	
DJSS2	1000	750	(naked pairs)
USS2	1400	1000	(hidden pairs)
DJSS3	2000	1400	(naked triples)
USS3	2400	1600	(hidden triples)
X-WING	2500	1800	
SWORDFISH(3)	5000	2000	
FORCING CHAINS	4200	2100	
DJSS4	7000	5000	
USS4	8000	6000	
SWORDFISH(4)	8000	6000	

Price List

make even "Easy" puzzles more challenging.

Yet even with a time-based rating, questions arise, as one participant on the Sudoku Addicts Discussion Board pointed out. Mightn't a more accurate rating scale take into account the average time along with number of puzzles submitted — and the number of incorrect puzzles?

I have to confess, my favorite response among all the discussions of difficulty was the participant who admitted that he never looks at scores, number of stars, or descriptive ratings. He just does the puzzle.

If you can take your sudoku one at a time,

without getting snotty or worrying about bruised egos, at least you can enjoy the fun of the chase, whether you solve it or not. After all, for most of the folks in Sudoku Nation, puzzles aren't a job. Aren't we supposed to have fun?

PUZZLE SOLUTIONS

2	8	4	5	9	3	7	1	6
9	7	3	4	1	6	8	5	2
1	6	5	2	7	8	4	9	3
4	9	8	6	5	1	3	2	7
3	1	7	9	2	4	6	8	5
6	5	2	8	3	7	1	4	9
8	4	9	3	6	2	5	7	1
5	3	1	7	8	9	2	6	4
7	2	6	1	4	5	9	3	8

Puzzle from page 24

2	1	5	6	7	4	9	8	3
4	7	3	9	8	2	1	6	5
9	6	8	5	3	1	2	7	4
6	8	7	1	5	3	4	2	9
1	2	9	4	6	8	5	3	7
5	3	4	2	9	7	6	1	8
3	9	2	7	4	6	8	5	1
7	5	6	8	1	9	3	4	2
8	4	1	3	2	5	7	9	6

Puzzle from page 104

5	3	2	6	9	8	7	4	1
6	8	9	7	4	1	2	5	3
1	4	7	2	5	3	8	6	9
4	2	6	3	1	5	9	8	7
9	1	3	4	8	7	6	2	5
7	5	8	9	2	6	1	3	4
8	9	4	5	7	2	3	1	6
3	7	1	8	6	4	5	9	2
2	6	5	1	3	9	4	7	8

Puzzle from page 187

7	6	8	5	2	3	4	9	1
4	1	5	9	6	7	2	3	8
3	2	9	8	4	1	7	5	6
9	3	4	7	5	6	8	1	2
2	5	1	4	3	8	9	6	7
8	7	6	1	9	2	3	4	5
5	8	3	2	1	4	6	7	9
6	9	7	3	8	5	1	2	4
1	4	2	6	7	9	5	8	3

Puzzle from page 216

4	8	7	6	3	9	5	1	2
2	5	6	4	1	8	9	7	3
9	3	1	7	2	5	8	4	6
6	1	2	8	9	7	3	5	4
5	7	9	2	4	3	6	8	1
3	4	8	1	5	6	2	9	7
8	6	3	9	7	4	1	2	5
1	9	4	5	6	2	7	3	8
7	2	5	3	8	1	4	6	9

Puzzle from page 296

We hope you have enjoyed this Large Print book. Other Thorndike, Wheeler, and Chivers Press Large Print books are available at your library or directly from the publishers.

For information about current and upcoming titles, please call or write, without obligation, to:

Publisher
Thorndike Press
295 Kennedy Memorial Drive
Waterville, ME 04901
Tel. (800) 223-1244

or visit our Web site at:

http://gale.cengage.com/thorndike

OR

Chivers Large Print
published by BBC Audiobooks Ltd
St James House, The Square
Lower Bristol Road
Bath BA2 3SB
England
Tel. +44(0) 800 136919
email: bbcaudiobooks@bbc.co.uk
www.bbcaudiobooks.co.uk

All our Large Print titles are designed for easy reading, and all our books are made to last.